The Honorable Traitor

The Gareth and Gwen Medieval Mysteries:
The Bard's Daughter (prequel)
The Good Knight
The Uninvited Guest
The Fourth Horseman
The Fallen Princess
The Unlikely Spy
The Lost Brother
The Renegade Merchant
The Unexpected Ally
The Worthy Soldier
The Favored Son
The Viking Prince
The Irish Bride
The Prince's Man
The Faithless Fool
The Honorable Traitor

The Welsh Guard Mysteries
Crouchback
Chevalier
Paladin

A Gareth and Gwen Medieval Mystery

THE
HONORABLE
TRAITOR

by

SARAH WOODBURY

To my Taran

Cast of Characters

Owain Gwynedd—King of Gwynedd
Cristina—Queen of Gwynedd
Hywel—Prince of Gwynedd (Owain's son)
Gwen—Prince Hywel's spy, Gareth's wife
Gareth—Prince Hywel's steward, Gwen's husband
Llelo—Gareth and Gwen's son, investigator
Dai—Gareth and Gwen's son, Dragon member

Meilyr—Bard, Gwen's father
Gwalchmai—Bard, Gwen's brother
Tangwen—Gareth and Gwen's daughter
Taran—Gareth and Gwen's son

Gruffydd – Prince Rhun's former captain, Dragon member
Cadoc – Assassin, Dragon member
Steffan – Dragon member
Iago – Dragon member
Aron – Dragon member
Evan – Dragon member

Rhys—Abbot of St. Kentigern's monastery
Nest—Abbess of Holywell Abbey
Taran—Owain's steward
Marged—Nanny for Taran and Tangwen
Sioned—Cristina's maid
Helen—Taran's friend

Cadwaladr—Prince of Gwynedd (Owain's brother)
Ranulf—Earl of Chester
Madog—King of Powys
Susanna—Queen of Powys

1

January 1150

Chester Castle

Day One

Ranulf

Madog, the King of Powys, paced back and forth before the brightly blazing fire. "Why haven't we heard from him? He promised us a full description of Owain's situation."

"You know how rarely Cadwaladr does anything on anyone's schedule but his own." Ranulf, the Earl of Chester, set down his goblet. "Besides, he must not be caught. He has to be careful not to expose himself."

Ranulf and Madog were old friends—enemies too, but currently united once more over the predations of Owain Gwynedd. Their alliance with Cadwaladr, Owain's slippery younger brother, was tenuous at best, born more of circumstance than trust, and they both knew the man's loyalty lay with himself and no other.

Nobody, except perhaps Cadwaladr himself, was confused about why he was back in Gwynedd's court, once again in favor. Owain hadn't accepted his allegiance out of some misguided belief that Cadwaladr had truly changed his colors. He'd been forced to do so as a condition of Owain's pact with King David of Scotland, Prince Henry, and Earl Ranulf himself. That the treaty had never been ratified was beside the point at this late date. Owain's choice had been to give his brother a place in Gwynedd or to return him to England and watch him openly cavort with Gwynedd's enemies, Madog and Ranulf among them. For now, Owain was choosing to keep Cadwaladr close.

Which was all to the good as far as Ranulf was concerned. Perfect, in fact. He would have been far more concerned had Cadwaladr been ensconced in Madog's court, since Ranulf had been doing some lying of his own: namely, he had never revealed to Madog the full nature of that agreement made with Owain. While the main thrust was a peace treaty and overall alliance, which was the part Madog knew about, the document had also promised that, once Henry became King of England, he would recognize Owain as the preeminent ruler of Wales, its *princeps*, to use the Latin word from the treaty.

If Madog had known about that part, he would not be colluding with Ranulf now. Keeping Madog distracted with his hatred of Owain seemed the best policy for Ranulf's own protection, at least until more time had passed. Owain would remember the significance of the treaty forever, but Ranulf was quite sure King David and Prince Henry had forgotten it already.

"I assume you have given him the details of our intended course of action?" Ranulf asked this, even as he chastised himself for doing so. It was dangerous to show too much interest or make any assumptions in regard to either Madog or Cadwaladr.

"He will have it just as soon as our messenger can get word to him."

"There you go. Cadwaladr will send a reply at that time. You can't be impatient, Madog."

"He is not making it easy." Madog kicked a log back into the fire. "I just wish appearing to be loyal to his brother and actually being loyal didn't look exactly the same! He's hedging his bets, waiting until the last moment, to see how the wind is blowing, before he jumps."

"That is only to be expected. If you're so worried about his loyalties, you could do something about it. The ability to keep an eye on Cadwaladr was one of the reasons I suggested you attend the peace conference in the first place. If you do not appear within a day or two of Owain's own arrival, he is going to know something is amiss and grow suspicious."

"I will not treat with that—that—" Madog practically shouted his derision, unable to sufficiently express with words how deeply he detested his brother-in-law—the brother-in-law in this instance being Owain Gwynedd.

"Then you have to accept that Cadwaladr will help us or he won't, and if he doesn't, we are on our own in this. Are you still committed to the endeavor if that's the case?"

"You know I am." His look was fierce. "It isn't *your* lands Owain threatens."

"Careful, Madog. Owain did take Mold from me."

Madog barely refrained from snorting. "Which you took back last summer, against my counsel, I might add. We wouldn't *be* so hemmed in now if you had listened to me. We should have bided our time, waiting until we could take him down in one go."

"As we are about to do."

"With no help from Cadwaladr. The next time I see him, I'll run him through and rid us of his twisted plots forever."

"Those twisted plots haven't done you any harm as yet."

"Nor have they done me any good!" Furious now, Madog swept his hand across the table, tossing Ranulf's dinner plate onto the floor. Thankfully, it was mostly empty and made of tin.

Ranulf put up with such behavior because Madog had proved useful in the past. Ranulf was hoping he could be useful again, though as the conversation had gone on, he was beginning to have his doubts. Now he eyed his companion. "Our forces will soon be in place, whether Cadwaladr aids us or not. Owain will be expecting a peace delegation. Instead he will get a war."

"Is that glee I hear in your voice? More power for you, eh?" Breathing hard, Madog visibly got control of himself. It was good to see he was still capable of it. He grew more erratic with every passing year. And that glee Madog was referencing was his own, not Ranulf's.

"For you as well."

To reply, Madog lifted his cup to Ranulf in a kind of salute. "With Owain's death, his sons and Cadwaladr will fall to bickering.

The people of Gwynedd will never accept Cadwaladr as king, no matter what lies he tells himself about the matter." His eyes were bright now, and the red and orange flames of the fire gave a sinister cast to his smile as he put into words his deepest desire. "My wife is Owain's sister. I have claim to Gwynedd through her. If things go according to plan, in a few more days, the whole of the north will be mine for the taking."

2

Holywell Abbey

Day Two

Helen

Having left her horse among the fifty or so in the large field adjacent to Gwynedd's encampment, Helen skirted the village of Holywell and approached the abbey, located on the hill above the holy well dedicated to Saint Gwenffrewi.

Helen hadn't been here in decades, but as she neared the unguarded side entrance, it was as if she were that same uncertain and unloved daughter again, stashed at Holywell by a father who thought of her as a pawn in his game of chess, or perhaps a weapon in his arsenal, when he thought about her at all.

Avoiding the village and the main gate was a habit after so many years of living in the shadows, pretending to be other than she was. For better or for worse, she had trained herself well. Not far away was Gwynedd's pavilion, in which all the pomp and glory of Owain's court was on full display. She would find friends there. She'd parted from one of them just two days ago in Chester, telling him she had business of her own to attend to before she finished her journey. It hadn't even been a lie.

Jehan had balked at leaving her, as well he might, since they'd traveled all the way from France together. He was looking forward to being greeted with one of King Owain's generous hugs and subsequently feted at that same high table she could almost see from where she stood. That wasn't Helen's way, however, and she'd put him off, not quite ready to come home, even as she appeared to have done exactly that.

A shadow moved ahead of her, dividing into two a moment later.

Stilling, though breathing easily as she stood in the dark just off the path, she watched two men in monks' robes swing themselves over the abbey wall with the aid of the spreading branches of an old oak tree, its roots so large it deformed the base of the wall by which it stood.

Compline was upon them, the last holy office of the day, so this part of the monastery was empty of people. Every monastic here, both nuns and monks, since Holywell was a double monastery, would be on their knees in the church at this very moment. Except for these two, apparently.

Never one to dismiss what she didn't understand, Helen waited a beat or two until they disappeared on the other side of the wall and then she went through the unguarded gate herself. Truly, they could have used it, and if they had, she would probably have thought nothing of them. But they were thinking about remaining undetected, and thus the hardest thing for them to do was to act normally.

They were no trouble to follow either because they didn't go far, just to the guesthouse located in one corner of the abbey grounds, set apart from the other buildings because guesthouses were for visitors, not monks or nuns.

One of the monks followed what would have been Helen's advice and went straight to the front door. The other split from him to move around to the rear. The closest buildings here were the stables and the laundry, with the abbey gardens expanding into the distance behind those buildings. As Helen moved silently after the second monk, he took a ladder from the back of the stables and propped it under one of the second level windows. To say that was odd was to woefully understate the case.

And then, as he climbed that same ladder to the second floor, the shutter above him opened to reveal his companion, holding a lantern. Both men had pushed back their hoods by now, and light shone on their faces. Helen didn't recognize the one in the window, but the one on the ladder was an old acquaintance of hers, formerly at court, and a man she'd assumed died years ago.

What he was doing climbing through the window in an abbey guesthouse in Wales, Helen couldn't say.

At this moment, she wanted more than anything in the world to find out.

3

Day Two

Helen

Helen deliberated for a long moment. She *knew* Jacques, or at least, she had known him. Back in the day, he'd been a petty thief and occasional informant. Even though it had been at least a decade since she'd seen him, she would have recognized his narrow face and pointed beard anywhere. So if this was thievery, she wasn't going to put up with it, not if she could stop him. She blessed the impulse that had urged her to avoid the feast and reacquaint herself with the abbey instead.

Before she could second-guess herself, she pulled the ladder away from the wall. It was heavier than she'd expected, and she had to fight not to let it bang against the side of the guesthouse. She eventually wrestled it back down to the ground and left it lying on its side against the wall, rather than putting it back where Jacques had found it.

Having foiled the intruders' easy escape route, Helen now moved around to the front of the guesthouse and entered through the main door as Jacques' companion had done. Once inside, she found it to be as she remembered, and exactly like any abbey guesthouse she'd ever entered: of wooden construction, simple, with a common room and a few bedrooms on the ground floor, and a narrow stairway that led up to more rooms on the floor above.

As far as she could tell, except for herself and the two men, the building was entirely empty. As she'd concluded when she'd entered through the abbey gate, everyone else was either at Compline or at the feast.

For their part, the men were being very quiet, and she couldn't hear anything from them until she was directly outside the room they'd entered.

They'd closed the door, but she could hear them talking in French in low voices on the other side.

"Hurry up! Get the treaty, and let's get out of here! What's taking so long?"

"Give me a moment! There's a hundred documents in here." This second voice belonged to Jacques.

"Take them all. This was supposed to be easy."

"I can't take them all. There's too many. Besides, King Madog was adamant that King Owain can't know we were here."

"I still think once we find it we should burn this place to the ground. That would hide our tracks."

"That's why I am in charge instead of you." Jacques' tone was disparaging.

Helen thought his companion wasn't entirely wrong. Fire could hide many ills. But logic aside, the talk of fire made her blood run cold. Jacques had not been a violent man when she'd known him, but the casual way his companion talked about burning the guest-house to the ground, following hard on the mention of Madog, had her rethinking her original plan just to eavesdrop on what they were doing and then follow them to their lair. This wasn't simple thievery. This was war.

"Leaving a blank document to replace the one we take is stupid." This was the second man again. "They'll notice."

"They won't. They don't want to unroll every scroll. They'll count to see how many there are and when the number tallies, they'll assume all is well. If we do this right, they won't look in the trunk at all because they won't think to." Jacques' tone was calm and certain. "There! I have it! Let's go!"

Footsteps crossed the floor, followed by a curse and, "What happened to the ladder?"

It was time to move while they were still preoccupied with the surprise.

Helen pushed open the door, her belt knife at the ready. Jacques was standing with his back to her, one hand holding a rolled document at his side. His companion was bent over the sill of the window, undoubtedly looking for the ladder, which was now on its side against the bottom of the wall.

Helen took two quick steps into the room and snatched the paper from Jacques' hand before he even knew she was there. It was only once she had it that she realized she hadn't given a thought to what she would have done if he'd already hidden it in his jacket.

As it was, Jacques spun around, his mouth open first in surprise—and then in recognition. She slashed at him with her knife, a back-handed blow that wasn't intended to connect so much as discourage his forward movement.

It connected anyway, somewhere in the middle part of his body, and he let out a startled cry. She didn't take the time to see how badly she'd wounded him, opting instead to flee through the open door behind her.

Unfortunately, she was far older, and more importantly, far less agile, than either of the two men, particularly Jacques' companion. He leapt past Jacques to reach her before she'd gone two steps into the corridor, grabbed the arm that held the blade, and forced it from her hand. Even so, she managed to twist around enough to knee him in the groin.

The blow connected well, but at the same time wrenched her hip, costing her a few heartbeats' of time and her freedom. Having taken fewer breaths than she to recover from her blow, the intruder's knife swung at Helen's belly, slicing through her dress into her skin.

Perhaps he was still suffering from the blow she'd dealt him, because his aim was slightly off, so the blade didn't cut as deeply as he'd intended. Bleeding but undeterred, Helen scrambled away again, this time making for the adjacent room. She had to hide the scroll. It was too late to save herself. Throwing herself through the doorway, she shoved the door closed and pulled the latchstring.

Now cursing her impulse to meddle (instead of blessing it), she unrolled the document. If she was going to die, she wanted to at least know what she was dying for. Seeing what she'd taken, however, all regret fell away. As she secreted the document in the darkness of her hiding place, she renewed her faith in her instincts. Always, her loyalties were clear.

A moment later, Helen was standing unmoving in the center of the room, her hands at her sides, ready for when Jacques' companion splintered the frame of the door with the heel of his boot.

4

Holywell Abbey

Day Two

Gareth

Gareth told himself, not for the first time, that Queen Cristina was fundamentally unhappy, and an unhappy person was bound to do all sorts of irritating things as she spread her unhappiness around to others. It didn't mean her behavior had anything to do with him personally. He definitely shouldn't take whatever she said or did to heart, even when it was directed at him.

This was what he tried to tell himself most days anyway, and the admonition was brought to the fore yet again as the queen arrived in the pavilion with her nose in the air, haughtily ordering Taran to vacate his chair so she could sit beside Gareth. Taran was not only King Owain's steward but also the man for whom Gareth's youngest son was named.

This was their third evening at Holywell Abbey, to which they'd come to participate in a new round of peace talks with King Madog of Powys, who'd been delayed by adverse weather. Ever since

Earl Ranulf had taken back Mold Castle in the summer, and King Owain had not immediately retaliated, complaints had begun among Owain's vassals that he was growing old and soft. He had weathered those rumors, as any king must, with an eye always on the larger issues. Last May, he and Earl Ranulf had ostensibly been allied. The treaty had never been signed at Carlisle, however, so Ranulf had felt free to renew hostilities with Gwynedd, and Owain would tell anyone who spoke directly to his face of their concerns that his aim was to win the war. Single battles, single castles, didn't matter.

And that meant peace with Madog.

While King Madog hadn't outright refused to attend the peace talks, throughout the autumn he had delayed and stalled and vacillated. Then Madog himself had suggested they meet at Holywell Abbey which oversaw the healing well of Saint Gwenffrewi. This well had been a place of pilgrimage for centuries, not just for the Welsh. While the region was contested, King Owain agreed that the abbey itself was appropriately neutral ground. It might even be the only neutral ground in this entire region of Wales, particularly now that the old Norman motte and bailey castle that had perched above the holy well had been razed in earlier fighting.

Holywell was a double monastery, which meant it contained both men and women within the same community, all under the oversight of an abbess. And the abbess here was none other than Gareth's old friend and mentor, Nest. Nuns and monks had their own dormitories, of course, and many of their duties were separate, even as they worked together for the good of the abbey. This religious structure was ancient, dating back to the beginning of Christianity in

Wales, and this particular house was equally old. Queen Susanna herself had long had a personal interest in the site, and it was at her request that Nest, whose former small convent had adopted Gareth years earlier, had been asked to take charge as the abbess.

Once the monastics present for the feast had left for the holy office of Compline, Taran had been in a particularly cheerful mood, entertaining the entire table with stories of his antics with King Owain during their youth. The pair had been reckless, to say the least, risking life and limb at times as they raced horses, confronted wild boars, with or without a spear, and fled from angry husbands and fathers who objected to Owain cavorting with their wives and daughters.

In short, King Owain's behavior had been remarkably like Hywel's before he'd settled down. That wasn't exactly a surprise. Sons took the good and the bad from their fathers and made both their own. In truth, King Owain's infidelities had continued through-out longer-term liaisons and marriages. He never saw a reason to sleep alone, and, as king, was never short of women who would be happy to give him a son. Hywel, for his part, seemed to have decided that wasn't the proper course for him. Or rather, if he was having af-fairs, Gareth didn't know about them. At the very least, Prince Hywel had produced no children other than those he had with his wife, Ma-ri.

Cristina had arrived at the culmination of Taran's latest joke, which the steward finished as he stood, inciting laughter in everyone but Cristina (naturally) and a general dispersal to stretch, to find more drinks or companionship, or to use the latrine. Given the nature of the jest, it was no wonder the queen's tone was overtly sour.

Thus, few were left to overhear Cristina's next demand: that Prince Hywel return to the dais with Gwalchmai and Meilyr, Gwen's brother and father. This would be for a second time, since Hywel had already sung once that evening, inspiring tears in his audience. It was unfair, not to say embarrassing, to ask him to do it again. It just wasn't *done*. Mari might have protested on her husband's behalf, but she and Gwen had left already, both thinking the moment had finally come for their children to sleep.

Despite his stepmother's imperious ways, Hywel was gracious, as he always tried to be with his father's wife, masking his dismay with a smile and a wry look directed only at Gareth. With a more formal bow towards his stepmother than was usual for him, he walked away.

Side-by-side, though not willingly on Gareth's part, he and Cristina watched the prince saunter casually across the pavilion towards the dais. Gwalchmai and Meilyr had been slaking their thirst, having themselves taken a break from making music. When Hywel reached them, the three men consulted, and because Gareth was watching carefully, he noted the way Meilyr narrowed his eyes in the queen's direction. But then he turned back to Hywel to nod at whatever he'd just suggested.

Brilliant as always at reading the crowd, Hywel settled upon a tale about King Cadwaladr ap Cadwallon, Hywel's own ancestor and a King of Gwynedd centuries ago. The song had a strong beat and a rousing tune, one everyone knew. In a moment, most of the onlookers were on their feet, clapping, stamping, and singing along with the bards at the top of their lungs.

It was then, with a satisfied smile that had put fear in the hearts of men of greater worth than Gareth, that Cristina turned to him, leaned in close in a way that made him uncomfortable, and said right into his ear, "Your wife needs you back at the guesthouse. A woman was attacked in my room."

5

Day Two

Gwen

A half-hour earlier ...

The shriek emanating from the room above her head had Gwen practically throwing her body over the top of her son. Young Taran had just fallen asleep, and at nearly two and a half, he was so curious about everything that he resisted sleep whenever possible. Tonight, she'd held him in her arms at the feast as Gwalchmai sang, rocking him while standing in the grass in the dark beyond the lights that shone from the pavilion. Then she'd finished the job in their room at the guesthouse with a lengthy nursing session.

Despite the screams—and warranting some extra prayers of thanksgiving in church tomorrow for the miracle it was—Taran's eyes stayed closed. He didn't even stir.

Gwen eased away from him and rose to her feet. A moment later, she stepped into the corridor, where Marged, her children's nanny, was just coming from the common room.

Gwen gave Marged a rueful smile. "That sounded like Queen Cristina's voice."

"Indeed it did."

"I thought she was still in the pavilion?"

"She was not far behind us on the path as we left." Marged's look was knowing. "You should go, my lady. All the men are still at the feast. Even if the queen's source of discomfort is merely a mouse, you know she will require your assistance to recover from the indignity of it."

Their mutual disdain for the vagaries of the Queen of Gwynedd was undoubtedly unhealthy, but deserved nonetheless. With every year of her marriage to King Owain, Cristina had become more volatile and less forgiving of any circumstance that wasn't immediately favorable to her. Having given King Owain two sons, Dafydd and Rhodri, who'd be five and three this year, she had become more and more focused on their future. They were her husband's youngest sons, and she feared that with his death—whenever that might be— they would be left out of the inheritance.

Thus, Cristina dared not leave her boys with their nannies at Aber. Instead, they traveled wherever the king's court went. On the one hand, she didn't trust anyone else to raise the boys properly while she was gone. On the other, she wanted them always around Owain, as a constant reminder they were his and he should not only remember them, but favor them and take steps to ensure their future.

Somehow along the way, Cristina had decided she trusted Gwen, and even more, trusted Gareth, who remained safely at the feast, in his role as Prince Hywel's steward. She had even insisted that they, out of all the members of her husband's court, occupy the lower floor of the guesthouse. Gwen herself had been both astonished and disappointed by the queen's request because it meant she and Gareth wouldn't get to sleep in their new family wagon, their home away from home, while they were at Holywell. Built along similar lines to the vehicle in which her father and Saran traveled, this had been its maiden voyage, and Gwen had grown increasingly fond of it during their journey. She certainly appreciated not having to unpack all of her things into a tent every night.

In truth, since they'd left Aber, she'd been swallowing down her resentment at being continually at Cristina's beck and call. Only the need to attend to Tangwen and Taran had enabled Gwen to refuse any of Cristina's various demands. In this she had been supported not only by Gareth but by King Owain himself. And since Cristina's entire being was focused on pleasing her husband above all others, she'd ungraciously acquiesced.

Thus, Gwen's thoughts were bitter as she climbed the stair to the upper floor, admittedly at a quickening pace as her own name echoed down the stairwell towards her. "Gwen! I need you!"

When the king, queen, and their children had taken over the entire building for their exclusive use, Abbess Nest had *almost* rolled her eyes, the closest Gwen had ever seen a nun come to doing so. Cristina had demanded all six rooms, even though she had use for only five, since she didn't want to share her space with anyone else. Maybe, despite her new-found love for Gwen and her family, the queen would have insisted nobody use the rooms on the level below either, if not for the way Nest's face had turned to granite at any hint of extending her initial demands. Even Cristina could occasionally recognize when what she wanted exceeded that which was reasonable.

Upon arriving in the queen's doorway, Gwen took in the entire scene with a sweeping glance. The queen stood with her hand to her mouth while her maidservant, Sioned, was on her hands and knees on the floor a few feet into the room. Further on, the body of a similarly middle-aged but unknown woman was propped against the far wall, her legs splayed in front of her and blood from a vicious head wound trickling down the side of her face.

6

Day Two

Gwen

Skirting the queen, Gwen went immediately to the stranger. Her attire consisted of sturdy leather boots, not slippers, and dark-colored traveling clothes, not a nun's habit, which made her a visitor to the abbey rather than a resident. It was also impossible to miss the tight, thick weave of the wool cloth that made up her burgundy dress. It was cut in the latest Norman style with a square bodice and wide sleeves. The thick cloak wrapped around her body was of equally high quality and promised to keep out any kind of weather.

Gwen put the back of her hand very gently to the woman's lips, and let out a sigh of relief to find it warmed by the woman's breath. "She's injured but alive."

It had been the trickle of blood from the head wound that had given Gwen the first clue. Dead people didn't bleed. Closer inspection of the woman's face revealed her to be in her late forties or early fifties, with dark hair shot with gray, attractively so. To Gwen's mind, she herself would be blessed to be this lovely in thirty years' time.

Cristina, who remained leaning against the wall by the door, said, "Sweet Mary, I was worried."

Gwen then moved her hand to the woman's belly to feel the reassuring expansion and contraction that indicated life was, indeed, ongoing.

It was only then that Gwen took a moment to glance around at the room in which she found herself. In a word, it was *destroyed*. Someone had pushed the mattress partly off the bedframe, and there was a gap in the supports where one of the bed slats was missing. The bedding had been swept onto the floor, and clothing spilled out of the queen's trunks as if someone had ransacked them in a hurry. Given the way the door jamb was splintered, something Gwen had noted initially out of the corner of her eye when she'd arrived but hadn't fully registered, that same someone had used the sole of his boot to get through the door.

By now, Sioned was no longer on her hands and knees but sitting more upright. Gwen didn't know if she had genuinely fainted, or simply collapsed to the floor in her shock. Hitting the room's wooden floorboards would have hurt Gwen's knees, and she was in her twenties. Sioned was considerably older, having lived an entire life before coming to work for Cristina around the time of her marriage to King Owain.

"We need the healer." Cristina wasn't wrong, but she also didn't make a move to do anything about the professed need either.

Gwen knew something of healing herself and, now that she had assessed the stranger, she eased her flat onto her back on the floor. With the motion, the woman's breathing became easier, as if she hadn't been able to get a proper breath slumped as she'd been against the wall. She still didn't wake. Gwen's eyes were drawn to her head wound, which was swelling badly even as it continued to seep blood.

In addition, in the process of moving her, Gwen had shifted her cloak to reveal a tear in the woman's dress in the vicinity of her abdomen. Gwen carefully pulled the fabric apart to reveal another wound, this one six inches across. Most of its length was hardly more than a deep scratch, but as the cut neared her right side it went deeper, perhaps a finger-nail's length in depth.

Sometimes Gareth could determine the type of knife used in an attack by the nature of the wound it left behind. Unlike the woman's head wound, this was a clean cut, made by a sharp blade that appeared to have been turned aside before it could cut deep enough to kill.

Given the state of the room, Gwen wasn't entirely surprised when she looked next at the woman's hands and saw bits of skin and blood under her nails. She had lost the battle with her attacker, but she'd also marked him in the process. It would be something to look for when it came time to identify him.

The woman was lucky to be alive. Just looking at her injuries made Gwen feel slightly ill herself. Her hand to her own belly, she sat back on her heels, studying the length of the woman, watching her breathe and giving thanks they had not yet entered the realm of a murder investigation.

"Why was she in my room?" Cristina's tone was less distraught now than angry, indicating she was coming more to her usual self.

"I do not know, my lady, but we will endeavor to find out." She glanced over her shoulder at the queen.

Though Cristina had a set to her jaw Gwen had seen before, she was still weaving on her feet. She was also holding her belly in a similarly protective manner to Gwen, and with a moment of insight, Gwen put together the other differences in the queen's appearance she hadn't fully appreciated until this moment: her somewhat rounded cheeks; her slow starts in the morning; and the tightness of her dresses at the bodice and waist: she was pregnant again.

Gwen understood from personal experience the effect adverse sights and smells could have on the newly pregnant. She wasn't entirely well herself! And since the injured woman was unlikely to come to any further harm where she lay, it made sense to prioritize attending to Gwynedd's queen.

A shriek or two were one thing. Vomit would have to be cleaned up and guarantee the need to move the injured woman from the room immediately. Gwen was loath to do that before she knew how much more might be wrong with her, who she was, and the circumstances of the attack. So while Gwen was glad the queen was still holding herself together, it was even more urgently obvious that she wasn't going to be of any help to Gwen, and thus she needed to find a quiet place to leave her.

That was easier said than done, given the way Cristina had distributed her family and servants among the rooms at the guesthouse. Each of Cristina's young sons had a room of his own, an unheard of luxury but something upon which Cristina routinely insisted, saying they slept better when they were unlikely to be disturbed. *Everyone* slept better when they were unlikely to be disturbed but very, very few were able to achieve such solitude. Cristina's boys, like Gwen's children (hopefully), were asleep at this hour, and even if they weren't, their nannies wouldn't thank Gwen for bringing their near-to-vomiting mother and her semi-hysterical maid into their room to further upset them.

Other comfortable places Gwen could put Cristina and Sioned until more help arrived included either of her servants' rooms, located further along the corridor; the empty room, which was so small it could almost be called a cupboard; the common room downstairs ... or King Owain's own quarters. Latching on to the obvious solution, and instantly dismissing all other options as either unfit for a queen in distress or too public, Gwen assisted the queen and Sioned into the corridor and then headed straight for King Owain's door.

"Don't!" Cristina exclaimed aloud and dug in her heels, going so far as to lean backwards to stop Gwen's forward progress. "He doesn't like anyone to enter his room without his permiss—"

7

Day Two

Gwen

As it turned out, King Owain hadn't been wrong to be concerned about unauthorized people entering his room. The unauthorized persons in this case just weren't his queen and Gwen.

Gwen had already been pulling at the latch as the queen began to protest and thus had the door halfway open before she'd finished her sentence. Gwen had known invading her king's privacy was unacceptable under most circumstances, but she had been convinced this wasn't *most circumstances*. For all that the constant desire of everyone in Gwynedd's court was to serve the king, she was quite clear on the fact that, in this case, serving him best was finding a way to keep his queen out of sight. Unconscious and wounded women provided an exception to every rule, and his room in this moment was the best retreat.

Possibly, her thinking also implied a dangerous arrogance about her own worth.

To be honest, a small part of Gwen had been glad to see Cristina concerned about what her husband wanted even when he wasn't present. Gwen, on the other hand, and perhaps oddly, hadn't been at all concerned—until she opened the door.

The scene that confronted them was almost worse, at least in its implications, than the one next door in Queen Cristina's room. It was the blood, really. Not a notable amount, perhaps, as these things went, but enough that whoever had been injured had left drops and smears on the floor. Bloody discarded cloths on the bed indicated an attempt to bandage a wound, or maybe a half-hearted attempt to clean up the mess, and the deep red blood stood out in sharp contrast to the creamy white of the undyed wool blanket. Even more disconcerting was the bloody handprint on the equally white bed curtains, which moved in the breeze that came from the open window on the far side of the room.

Gwen went immediately to the window to look out. The king's room was located one floor above the ground, so it was not an easy jump, especially for a wounded man. Navigating a hook and rope in the dark would have been tricky too. Then Gwen saw the long ladder laid on its side against the bottom of the wall. Depending on the extent of his wounds, an injured man who was otherwise fit and strong could have handled a descent from the window by ladder.

Sioned took one look at the blood and went straight to the carafe of wine on the nightstand in order to pour herself a full cup, which she downed practically in one breath.

Gwen's only consolation, and hopefully King Owain's too once he learned of the intrusion, was that his gold had not been brought into the guesthouse, which was why the building hadn't been guarded. A trunk of documents had been carried inside to protect its contents from damp weather, but all the items with any value remained in the charge of his steward, Taran, who slept in the very well-guarded central tent in Gwynedd's encampment. That encampment was also where most everyone else was sleeping tonight. King Owain had a room in the guesthouse at all only because Cristina had insisted on it. She thought sleeping outside was bad for her husband's aging joints, and she despised trying to sleep with merely a thin piece of fabric between her and the elements.

Gwen knew this because it was a complaint they'd all heard every morning of their journey here, a journey that had required numerous nights sleeping in tents (though Gwen and Gareth had slept very happily in their wagon). Her complaints had begged the question, of course unasked: *why then did you come?*

Cristina had her reasons, as they all knew. She might be regretting them now.

The queen took in the room with a sweeping glance and, in contrast to her earlier incapacitation, reverted to her usual form by snapping her fingers at Sioned. In a way, it was a relief. "This is intolerable! Put that down and come with me."

While Sioned gaped at her, Cristina turned back to Gwen. "As for you, I will fetch your husband. Is it your understanding he is still in the pavilion?"

"He was there last I saw."

"Marged can fetch the healer from the infirmary and the abbess as well. The injured woman needs help far more than Sioned or

I do. I'd prefer to ask Saran, but I can't fetch both her and Gareth from the pavilion at the same time. Someone will notice, and we need to keep this quiet."

To fetch Saran, Gwen's stepmother, would have been Gwen's preference too, and the logical choice to help, since she'd worked with Gareth and Gwen on their investigations many times over the years.

"You feel it's that important to keep what has happened here a secret?" Gwen had her own reasons for doing so, but she didn't think they would be the same as Cristina's.

"Of course it's important! Haven't you been paying attention?" The queen really was back to her normal self.

"My apologies, my lady, but I don't understand."

Cristina's shoulders straightened. "We don't want Madog to hear that a woman was attacked in our quarters. It will cause him to doubt, and he could use it as an excuse not to come to the table and treat with us. I don't want him here at all, but if he's coming, he needs to be appeased and happy."

It was Gwen's opinion that nothing was going to appease Madog or make him happy—nor bring him to the table in a friendly state of mind. She didn't say that either. "Word will get out eventually, my lady. Madog could then claim we hid the truth from him so as not to lose the upper hand in the talks. He likely has spies here. We can't forget that."

"You mean like Cadwal—" The queen broke off, shaking her head for a moment, and then she continued as if she hadn't almost spoken frankly. "We will deal with such an eventuality when it is before us. He isn't here yet, is he? If you and Gareth do your job, you could have this all cleared up before he arrives." It almost sounded like a threat.

"Yes, my lady." Gwen saw no point in challenging her on it. In truth, in conversations with the Queen of Gwynedd, it wasn't unusual for Gwen to keep the vast majority of her thoughts firmly to herself. Besides, regardless of the queen's true motivations, her overall reasoning was sound. Gwen had been part of enough investigations by now to be aware that if the attacker knew his victim was still alive, he might come back to finish the job. It looked very much to Gwen like whoever had done this had left the woman for dead.

"That's not the real reason she wants to keep this a secret." Sioned spoke in a dull tone, which made her words all the more penetrating. She also hadn't put down her cup as Cristina had ordered, instead filling it to the brim for a second time. "She doesn't want anyone to know a woman was waiting for King Owain in the guesthouse."

Cristina rounded on her, ready with an acid comment, but as Sioned stared blankly back, the queen's shoulders slumped. "I could argue, but she's right. You know everything else. You might as well know that too."

"The king hasn't left the pavilion tonight, my lady," Gwen said gently. "We don't know for certain that the stranger came here to see him."

"Don't we? Why else would she *be* in the guesthouse?" Cristina flung out an arm to point at her through the wall.

Cristina's distress made it easier for Gwen to be matter-of-fact. "I can't say why she was here. It might be important to remember that she was found in your room, not the king's. But maybe you're right. Maybe she was here for him. So was the intruder. Which means we should be grateful to her instead of condemning. Her presence in the guesthouse tonight may have saved King Owain's life."

8

Day Two
Gwen

Cristina's skin paled. It hadn't been Gwen's intent to upset her again. She had merely wanted her to think about the situation differently. Whether or not the stranger had been waiting for Owain to return from the feast, the one who'd hurt her and to whom the blood belonged, had been here too. Gwen also wasn't sure Cristina was right about the woman being Owain's mistress. One of them had been searching for something. Both of them had ended up injured. Gwen did not have enough evidence to say who attacked first.

"Given the way people have been in and out of the guesthouse this evening, all of this must have happened very recently. I would think within the last hour. Did either of you notice anything unusual tonight?"

Cristina shrugged helplessly. "We are in a strange place. Everything is different. Every person is someone I've never met before."

But then her eyes narrowed. "Except for those we brought with us. In the encampment and pavilion, a stranger would stand out."

She still hadn't looked directly at Gwen, as if she didn't want to meet her eyes and see something she didn't like there—such as pity. It wasn't just her sons' inheritance that preoccupied Cristina. Concern about her own status was another reason the queen accompanied her husband on his perambulations about Gwynedd. Owain couldn't marry another woman while Cristina lived, but he could put her aside. Kings had done so in the past.

"I left the feast right after you did. My head was aching. You know how the stories become ever more offensive as the evening progresses. In addition, I couldn't bear to hear one more conversation about the possibility of peace. Madog wants all of the lands east of the Clwyd that he's lost to Owain. What he still holds he is going to keep at all costs, and he is never going to agree to a lasting truce. I don't understand why Owain can't see it—or Abbot Rhys, or this Abbess Nest, for that matter. My family has held lands in this region for generations. We know of what Madog is capable. We certainly cannot trust him."

Gwen had never before heard the queen discuss politics with such candor. She was holding onto what she had with both hands, and she feared her husband cared more about peace than he did about her. Owain would do what he wanted, as he always did, about every one of Cristina's issues: her marriage, her status, her sons' inheritance, and her family's lands. If Gwen hadn't known Cristina so well, she actually might have felt pity to see how powerless she must feel every day of her life. The queen whispered in her husband's ear to counter what everyone else was saying out loud and to give herself a fighting chance of controlling his actions.

Cristina also knew that, while Owain had been very much besotted with her when they'd married, half the reason he'd married her, instead of simply keeping her as his mistress, was because he wanted the lands their marriage would bring him. *These lands.* She could complain about this peace attempt all she wanted, but Owain had married *her* to keep the peace. He couldn't marry Madog, but he could talk to him.

Gwen nodded in the queen's direction, a movement she may or may not have seen, since she was still looking away. "So you left the feast shortly after I did and came straight here?"

"Yes. Marged was in the common area when we entered. I greeted her, climbed the stairs, and found the woman on the floor of my room."

"Did you see anyone else on the way here, anyone at all?"

"Only a pair of monks." Cristina made a dismissive motion with her hand, but then arrested the movement halfway through. She'd been unenthusiastic about the questioning from the start because she thought she knew nothing that would help, and thus any questions directed at her were a waste of time. Now her focus sharpened as she realized, in light of what they'd discovered in these rooms, she might know more than she thought.

Speaking slowly now, Cristina added, "They were headed away from the guesthouse as I was coming towards it."

"Did you see their faces? Was either limping?"

"I'm sorry, I didn't notice anything like that, but I'm not sure I would have. I was preoccupied with my own concerns." She shook her head. "Their hoods were up anyway, and with no real light near them, their faces were fully shaded. I don't even know if they wore beards." Then she frowned. "They had been talking as I approached, but ceased to speak before I got close enough to make out what they were saying. And then they were gone." Cristina had forgotten not to look at Gwen. "Do you think I saw the woman's attacker? It should have occurred to me that all good monks would have been in their dormitory or in the church!"

"Abbot Rhys had been at the feast. Those monks could have been walking that path for completely ordinary reasons. I am glad you remembered those details, however. Please know that if you— either of you—" Gwen shot a worried look at Sioned, who, unlike Cristina, showed few signs of recovering from her ordeal. Her eyes remained blank and a bit of wine ran from the corner of her mouth, "—think of anything else about this evening that strikes you as unusual or even just a little different, I am happy to hear about it at any time. As I think you know, even the smallest details can be important."

"I do know that." Cristina nodded once. "I will think on it."

"Thank you, my lady. For now, perhaps some air not found within the guesthouse would be good for both of you."

"I'll send Gareth, and I will be discreet." She paused before repeating, with an intense look, what she'd emphasized before, never mind the reasons: "I expect you to be so as well."

"Of course, my lady. As you wish." Inside, Gwen added, *for now*. It was definitely not something she needed to say out loud at this juncture.

Cristina had her hand under Sioned's arm, and she nodded as if she and Gwen were in complete accord. As far as the queen was concerned, they were. "I'll wait until your brother is singing. Maybe I'll encourage Hywel to join him. Everyone will be watching them, and nobody will care when the prince's steward leaves the pavilion."

On that uncharacteristically positive note, Cristina departed, leaving Gwen shaking her head. The most surprising thing that had happened tonight might not be finding the wounded woman or the state of Cristina and Owain's rooms, but the conciliatory attitude of Gwynedd's queen.

9

Day Two
Gareth

For a moment Gareth found himself incapable of reacting, so surprised at Queen Cristina's news and, despite himself, impressed at her deviousness. She had behaved exactly as everyone might have expected her to behave, while at the same time making them wish she wouldn't. With a wave of her hand, she'd instigated the current mayhem in the pavilion for the simple need of getting him away without anyone noticing or caring. The effort involved revealed the extent to which Cristina was aware of herself and how people perceived her. Before this moment, he would not have credited her with that degree of insight.

Once he recovered and mastered his expression, Gareth let out a slow breath. "From what you just said, you think the woman is alive?"

"Gwen says so. Breathing but unconscious. I sent your nanny to find the abbey's healer and Abbess Nest. Otherwise, I am determined not to let what has happened become public knowledge until I have no other choice. It is imperative no alarm be raised, not to-night."

He might have asked why, but he didn't need to. It was a matter of politics and a desire to maintain a façade of wellbeing, even if things were not at all well. And probably, for now, a way to protect the victim until they knew who she was and how she'd come to be in the guesthouse.

"I understand, my lady. I will be discreet." His eyes went to where the king sat at the high table. "However, we must take steps right now to protect the king."

"I will see that his guard is on heightened alert. They don't need to know why."

As a former guard himself, Gareth thought knowing why was always better than not knowing, so actual threats could be distinguished from imagined ones, but he let the matter go for now until he himself could assess the situation. "Am I also to understand you don't recognize the woman?"

"I don't. Not—" She shook her head. "Not to look at. If she could speak, maybe. I feel something about her is familiar. I just don't know what that might be." Now she grimaced. Her expressiveness tonight was an indication of how flustered she was on the inside, more than her voice conveyed. "Maybe she's an old flame of Owain's."

The comment startled Gareth, but the matter-of-fact way she spoke had him taking her words at face value. And appreciating them. "Thank you for telling me. I will go immediately."

The queen clenched his arm. "Slowly. Don't ruin all my good work."

Not for the first time, Gareth had to admire Cristina's fortitude, even as she terrified him. Like Prince Cadwaladr, who was also present this evening, holding court like he always did amongst his followers on the other side of the pavilion, the only thing predictable about Cristina was her unpredictability.

To keep up the pretense that nothing was amiss, Gareth drained the rest of the mead in his cup, in something of a show. Again, this was for appearances only. The cup was already empty. They both had been on their feet, so as not to distinguish themselves from the rest of the crowd while they were talking. With Gareth turning away, Cristina began to clap with enthusiasm. She was in good company with the rest of the inhabitants of the table, who'd come trickling back to listen to the music. These included Prince Hywel's Dragons, with Gareth's own son, Dai, posted right in the middle of them. Although initially he'd been keeping time to the music as heartily as everyone else, now he sent a sharp look in his father's direction.

Gareth flicked out his fingers in reply, telling his son to stay where he was, that nothing was afoot—or at least nothing Gareth wanted help with right away. From the thoughtful look on Dai's face as his glance moved to Cristina, Gareth was quite sure he was not fooled. He stayed where he was, however, doing as his father bid. By now he was well-used to taking orders and *mostly* obeying them.

Even with the raucousness of the crowd, Gareth could feel other eyes on him too and didn't dare look in the direction of the high table. A certain intensity was definitely coming from that vicinity. Even before Cristina had entered the pavilion, he'd sensed intrigue in the air tonight, if only because there were so many spies present. Not only had Abbot Rhys been sitting at the high table with King Owain, but so had Ralph, Rhys's former companion in the service of Empress Maud. Ralph was the father of Hywel's wife, Mari, and he was here because he had just this month retired from the empress's service.

Or so he said. Gareth thought it was too early to be sure whether or not he could believe him. Ralph had spent many years spying for Maud in the court of King Stephen. He said he had returned to Wales to spend his last years with his daughter and grandchildren. Which sounded reasonable enough.

Except that Ralph sat next to another Welshman, who called himself Iwan and who'd joined their company the day before. Gray-haired, with heavy jowls, he'd been weary from the road, covered in dust, and happy to slake his thirst with friends. But something about the way he'd said his own name in introduction had raised Gareth's hackles. He was cast in the same mold as Ralph and Abbot Rhys, with eyes that saw everything, even as their faces held the blandest, most innocuous expression possible.

Iwan had been given a seat at the high table because King Owain himself had embraced him, explaining to all within hearing how glad he was to see him after so many years. An explanation of where he had spent all those years wasn't offered, but it was clear Iwan knew Ralph even better than he knew King Owain. Prince Hywel's eyes had also turned thoughtful at the introduction, and he'd told Gareth under his breath that he had never met Iwan before. Taran's stories were all very well and good, but they didn't actually relay anything important, and it was disconcerting how little any of them knew about their king's early years. In truth, except for these few friends, and maybe Cadwaladr, nobody else in the pavilion had been alive at the time.

None of these men moved to follow Gareth, and he hoped he'd affected an adequately casual retreat. At the very least, he was putting off questions until he had anything approaching an answer.

But then, as Gareth strolled away from the table and then the pavilion itself, trying to make it look as if he was headed towards the latrines, his eldest son, Llelo, detached himself from where he'd been supporting a tent pole with his shoulder. Gareth didn't acknowledge that he'd seen him and continued across the darkness of the grass, heading away from the field to the abbey guesthouse.

Having drifted after his father initially, Llelo caught up with Gareth halfway along the path. "Something's happened. I don't know how you convinced Dai nothing was amiss, but I know better. I'm quite sure he did too, but he knows his duty and didn't follow you. I know my duty too, so you might as well tell me what's going on."

This was all said in a rush, with a defensive tone, as if Llelo expected Gareth to put him off. For his part, Gareth saw no point—and had no interest—in trying. Llelo was Gareth's apprentice and a knight in his own right. He deserved to come with him, regardless of what the queen might say about it. "There's been an attack in the guesthouse. The queen brought the news. Your mother is already there." He glanced at his son, a hint of a smile around his lips, despite the graveness of their errand. "I might be chastened that I was discovered so easily, but I prefer to be impressed. What in particular gave me away?"

To further the deception Queen Cristina had been adamant about perpetuating, Gareth had initially kept his pace to a sedate walk, just until he was out of sight of those in the pavilion. Now he lengthened his stride, and Llelo matched him. They weren't quite running, but both had long legs, which ate up the yards to the abbey gate.

"By the time you stood up, I was already suspicious."

"Of me?"

"Of the queen."

Gareth let out a laugh. To say he was proud of the man Llelo had become truly didn't convey how he felt. "Why? She irritated everyone, which is what she usually does."

Llelo ducked his head. "She came in with a flourish, maybe a bit more obviously than her usual fashion, but not uncharacteristically so. She was dismissive of Taran and of our prince."

"Which is typical."

"Well yes." Llelo quirked a smile. "What wasn't typical was the way she treated Sioned. Normally, when the queen reduces someone to tears, she behaves exactly as she did when she arrived at the table, as if that person is a beetle she would love nothing more than to squash beneath her shoe. Sometimes she already has. At those times, she acts as if it's the beetle's fault for having the indecency to leave a smear of slime on her sole that she has to wipe off on the grass. That wasn't the unusual part. It was while she and Sioned were still in the shadows at the edge of the pavilion, before anyone else was looking. Queen Cristina sat Sioned down on a bench at an empty table, set a cup and carafe of mead in front of her, and said, 'Drink'."

"In other words, she was too solicitous." Gareth shook his head appreciatively.

"I wouldn't say anyone else noticed. Honestly, she would have been better off letting Sioned weep in peace. But then, she was probably worried that Sioned would entirely fall apart and start sobbing in the middle of a song. In truth, I can't fault the queen's performance. It was only seeing her with Sioned, coupled with your departure, that set me following."

"You are observant."

"I do try."

"I know you do." They'd had this conversation before. Last May, Llelo had been knighted by the hand of Prince Henry himself, and thus was really no longer even Gareth's apprentice. But he still wanted his father's approval, and in recent months Gareth had become very careful about how he instructed him, if he instructed him at all. It felt as if his son had gone from child to man in a blink of an eye, and unlike Llelo tonight, Gareth was struggling to keep pace.

From what he understood, the pattern wasn't unusual with adult children. Gareth had only to look at the ups and downs of King Owain's relationship with Hywel to know he wasn't alone in his uncertainty as to how to be a father to a grown man. Gareth's parents had died when he was five years old, so he had little experience with fathers at all before being confronted with Llelo and Dai, who had been twelve and ten respectively when Gareth and Gwen had adopted them.

That upbringing meant that, after the age of five, Gareth hadn't been loved with the same ferocity he now felt for his own children. At times, he worried about them more than Gwen did, though he did his best to hide it.

Gareth and Llelo accomplished the rest of their walk in haste, entering the abbey through an unguarded side gate. Normally, this entrance would be locked at this hour, but it had been left open to allow free passage between the encampment and the abbey buildings. It was too bad, really, that no watch had been set anywhere but on the main gate that faced the town.

A moment later, they crossed the guesthouse threshold to find everything quiet. Without knowing what had brought them there, Gareth would have thought nothing was wrong. But then Marged rose from a low stool where she'd been sitting in front of the fire, warming her hands. The weather was uncharacteristically warm for January, but that didn't mean it was exactly *warm*. "Gwen and Abbess Nest are upstairs with the abbey healers."

"Are the children still asleep?"

"Even Young Taran. Nobody else knows what's happened."

Gareth nodded his thanks and took the steps two at a time with Llelo hard on his heels, thinking all the while that if his youngest son, who was the lightest sleeper of any of Gareth and Gwen's children, remained blissfully unaware of what was happening in the rooms above his head, Cristina had nothing to worry about.

10

Day Two

Llelo

As Cristina had promised, Llelo and his father arrived to find the stranger in the care of Abbess Nest and the two healers, Brother Adam and Sister Efa. That allowed Llelo's mother to meet him and his father in the corridor of the guesthouse and lay out in a few succinct sentences everything she'd learned so far. She'd even questioned the nannies, now that the queen's sons were asleep. Neither had heard or seen anything, not even noticing the broken doorframe before they'd retired with their charges.

Then again, their rooms were nearer to the stairs, and they'd been preoccupied with fussing children. They'd also arrived at the guesthouse only moments before Gwen herself, who hadn't noticed anything either. It put a sick pit in Llelo's stomach to think the attacker might still have been in the building while Llelo's mother was putting his little brother and sister to sleep.

Gwen herself attested that, if he really still had been in the guesthouse, he hadn't been making any significant noise, at least not enough to distinguish his movements from the complaints from Cristina's sons. It was her thought that the intruder might have been going out the back as she and the children had been coming in the front.

Or, if the monks Cristina had seen were relevant, there had been two intruders, not only one. "I know you'll want to examine the woman yourself, and not to distract you from her requirements, but there's something else you need to see first."

Llelo instantly became wary, less at what his mother specifically had said than at her sardonic tone. "Don't tell us there's another body!"

"I would have said if there was. It isn't a body." Gwen led them from the doorway of Cristina's room straight into King Owain's. "See for yourself."

Llelo was a step behind his father and came to a full stop on the threshold.

Unusually for him, his father swore. Llelo, on the other hand, found himself laughing, though he clapped his hand over his mouth so the sound wouldn't travel into the next room. A woman was injured, perhaps to death. It wouldn't do to laugh. He honestly didn't know why he had. Nothing here was funny.

Gwen seemed to understand, because she put a hand on his arm. "It is a little much, isn't it?"

Taking a few more steps into the room, Gareth lifted the lid of a nearby trunk. It contained ledgers and scrolls, all of which appeared to be in relatively good order—at least in every way Llelo could tell. The ledgers were stacked neatly, the scrolls aligned. If someone wanted to know about Gwynedd's finances, they could have spent hours poring over the documents and he wouldn't have been able to tell.

Llelo went to the window to look out. "Are we thinking the attacker went out this way?"

"That's what the blood trail says," Gwen said. "I didn't see any drops in the corridor."

Llelo looked dubious. "It's a long way to jump while bleeding."

"Better with the ladder," Gwen said. "They could have put it down after they used it."

"Why would they do that?" Llelo turned to look back at his parents, laughter again on his lips as he gestured to the blood in the room. "Because they hoped to hide their tracks?"

Gareth put up a hand. "We don't need to worry yet about the reason for any of this. We have our work before us, which we must begin at once. I need you to stay here, Gwen, in case the woman wakes. Llelo, your task is to find any sign of the attacker down there on the ground. He's bleeding heavily. Or was. Maybe he didn't get far."

"That leaves—" Gwen broke off as footsteps sounded within the corridor.

"That leaves me to determine what has been taken, if anything has been taken." They all turned at Taran's voice. Once through the doorway, his tone turned mildly exasperated at the surprise he must have seen in their faces. "You weren't talking quietly. I overheard the last portion of your conversation and must give the queen high praise for her mumming tonight. First, she practically shoves me out of the way so she can talk to you, Gareth, and then she sidles up to me after you leave to tell me I need to follow."

Though Taran was the same age as the king, Llelo thought he had been showing his age in the last year, with more gray in his hair and a bit of curve to his back. Just in the last few days, however, he'd seemed younger and more animated, like when he was telling stories at the table tonight. At the moment, he was standing erect and looking at them with an amused expression. "Wisely, the queen came to me to look into the matter before we had to disturb the king with it. He has drunk a great deal tonight, as you perhaps noted, and she is going to put him to bed in a tent, where she will stay as well. The servants are already rearranging things," he made a gesture with one hand, "though not to the point, of course, of fetching any items from the guesthouse."

"I'm sure that's for the best." Gareth urged Taran inside Owain's room. "See what you make of it."

The amusement disappeared as Taran surveyed the room, his eyes taking in the blood on the bed and the floor, and then going to where Llelo still stood by the open window. His eyes lingered there a moment while Gwen asked, "Do you have any thought as to why anyone would have been bleeding in the king's room?"

"We could ask Madog."

"He's easy to blame," Gwen agreed. "I want to too."

"If he comes," Gareth added.

Taran snorted. "Otherwise, your guess is as good as mine. Our king has enemies, and we are deep into territory Gwynedd hasn't controlled consistently since the time of Owain's father. Some here resented his reach then. They might prefer the looser—but more erratic—yoke of King Madog."

"What they will get is the far more restricting one of Earl Ranulf of Chester," Gareth said.

"We agree on that."

"Since Sioned seems to be too incapacitated to help, perhaps the king's manservant might be of assistance?" Llelo said.

"I imagine he would be if I knew where he was," Taran said.

Gwen frowned. "Marc was in the pavilion earlier. I saw him."

"I saw him too, perhaps at the same time you did," Taran said. "I thought it worth a moment to look for him just now before I came myself. He is in the king's confidence, as much as anyone is. But he was nowhere to be found."

Llelo looked at his father. "Is that suspicious?"

Taran scoffed at the idea. "Marc has been with the king for a decade, following the death of his own father, who served in the same position before him. He would never harm the king. His pedigree wouldn't allow it. He certainly wouldn't violate any domain he oversaw. He's young, but he has the heart of a man forty years older. You know how he gets when a single one of the king's hairs is out of place, not to mention if his cloak is crooked around his shoulders!" He paused. "Will you let me see who lies in the next room? Cristina refused to say anything beyond the fact that she doesn't know her."

Gwen wet her lips. "She feared she was one of the king's women."

Taran shook his head. "He wouldn't. Not here." Then his eyes narrowed. "I made him promise *not here*. We have no idea whom we can trust."

"He agreed to that?" Gareth asked.

"At the time." Taran let out a low laugh. "He's drunk enough tonight that it isn't an issue. I must say, I really thought I could believe him this time."

Llelo wouldn't have said Taran's perceptions about what the king was thinking or doing were wrong very often. But there didn't seem to be any point in inquiring about it further, especially as they would find out soon enough if Taran knew the injured woman.

"Perhaps you've encountered her somewhere, at some point, even if not in Owain's company," Gwen said. "She is dressed as a noblewoman, but everything about her is unfamiliar to me."

"I've met more people than any of you, if only because I'm older. Let's see what is what, shall we?"

Llelo had never thought Taran's face particularly emotive. As the steward to the King of Gwynedd, he had long experience hiding what he was really thinking. He hadn't bothered to do so with them up until now, but as Gareth led them through the damaged doorframe into Cristina's room and showed him the still form of the woman lying on the bed, Taran's expression reverted to ... nothing. Blank eyes, blank face.

Then, pulling in a breath, he walked to the foot of the bed. While they'd been inside King Owain's chamber, Brother Adam had left, leaving only Abbess Nest and Sister Efa, the other healer, who was sitting in a chair near the head of the bed.

Nest had been encouraging the fire to a greater blaze, warming the room for her patient, but as Taran gazed down at the woman, she put down the poker and said, not as a question, "You know her."

"I do." He made a noise that might have been a sob and walked around to the side of the bed in order to take the woman's hand. By now, it was obvious not only that he knew her, but that he was distraught at her condition.

Finally, Taran leaned over and kissed the woman's forehead. Straightening, he took in the faces of the others in the room. "Her name is Helen. She is the love of my life and always has been."

11

Day Two

Dai

Dai had thought Cristina's interaction with his father was odd, but he became certain something was genuinely amiss when Gareth stood, casually looked around in an attempt to affect total unconcern, and left the pavilion in the middle of the singing. Then Llelo, who'd been lingering on the edge of the crowd, followed.

The first look Dai had sent his father had been questioning. But Gareth had made a motion with his fingers, which Dai interpreted to mean either nothing was the matter or, at a minimum, whatever was the matter wasn't for Dai to worry about.

Yet.

It was unfortunate the Dragons didn't have a hand-signal to properly convey the words: *The queen has brought news that may or may not be bad, so I'm going to look into it before I alarm anyone else.* Clearly, it was time they did. Given the proclivities of Queen Cristina, undoubtedly they would use it.

Neither Gareth nor Llelo looked back once they'd left the pavilion, and Dai was mature enough not to be offended that they'd left him behind. He wasn't a child anymore, tagging along after his older brother and father, begging to be included. He was a man in his own right, soon to be sixteen years old, and a member of the Dragons. His father would tell him about whatever this was when it became relevant to him.

Anyway, tonight his job was not to respond to Queen Cristina's demands, unless asked directly of him, but to keep his eyes at all times on the king's brother, Cadwaladr, a task everyone who served Prince Hywel had long ago agreed was necessary. Ever since the treacherous prince had arrived at Aber from Anglesey, ready to undertake this journey to Holywell, they'd been taking turns watching him. They hoped that by changing up whose duty it was they would be better able to disguise the fact that they were watching him at all.

So far, Cadwaladr's behavior had been impeccable, if not unrelievedly boring. And not just tonight but for the last fortnight. Unbelievably, he hadn't done anything unexpected or met anyone out of the ordinary. His behavior was so bland, in fact, that it had made them more suspicious of him than ever. Nobody could be that good—especially not Cadwaladr—all the time. It would be more normal to behave irregularly or oddly at least once, whether riding ahead one day or taking a wander in the woods or merely speaking to one of the residents of any of the villages through which they'd passed. He hadn't even stayed in any latrine overlong.

Naturally, Cadwaladr had brought his own retinue on this journey, too many for the Dragons to keep track of, much less keep an eye on all of them all the time. Nor could they overhear what he said to his bed or dinner companions. If Cadwaladr was planning something nefarious with someone the Dragons trusted, or with one of his own servants, they would not know it. Even as talented and trained as they were, the Dragons were only seven. They couldn't be everywhere at once. And since one of the overriding principles of this current operation was not calling attention to themselves, there was a definite limit on how intrusive they could be into Cadwaladr's life.

That didn't mean, however, that they weren't going to try their utmost. Because his behavior wasn't normal or sensible, all of them had been feeling something was about to come to a head, whatever that something might be.

So when Cadwaladr rose to his feet shortly after Gareth's and Llelo's departure, and hard on the heels of Taran's, almost as if he had been waiting for them to leave the pavilion, Dai thought maybe the time had come. Trying not to convey how his heart had started racing, he rose to his feet too and followed Cadwaladr from the pavilion. Up until now, Cadwaladr hadn't left his table since the meal began, not even to use the latrine. Dai knew that because he'd been watching.

The feast had been underway for some time, so nobody was giving a second thought to any man's mumbled excuse about getting up from his seat. Part of Dai would have been relieved (ha) to see Cadwaladr avail himself of a bush or tree in the darkness, or make the trek to the latrines built on the edge of their encampment (downwind from the pavilion). And yet, when he didn't, Dai couldn't be surprised. This might ostensibly be a peace conference, but Cadwaladr's interest in peace was, and always had been, negligible. In fact, over the years he had been more often allied with Madog of Powys, for whose arrival they were waiting, than with his own brother.

Dai felt a surge of pride in the Dragons that they hadn't been lulled into a false sense of security. Still, Cadwaladr had chosen the perfect moment to walk away, right in the middle of the singing. Meilyr, Gwalchmai, and Hywel were three of the premier bards of Gwynedd, if not all Wales. When they opened their mouths, nobody was thinking about anything but the music they produced.

The back-handed compliment to Cadwaladr, even unvoiced, made Dai scoff under his breath. Cadwaladr had done his best to ingratiate himself into Gwynedd's court, but nobody should or would ever forget that it was by his actions that Prince Rhun had died. It wasn't any wonder that Hywel, Rhun's brother and closest friend, was always so out of temper when Cadwaladr stood at King Owain's side.

Like his father, Dai had endeavored to disguise his own departure from the table as nothing more than a casual need to stretch his legs. Like his father too, he'd failed in that attempt, as indicated by the sharp glance sent in his direction by Gruffydd, the commander of the Dragons. Gruffydd followed the look by saluting Dai with his cup of mead, and then slaked his thirst. Dai supposed it was only to be expected. Gruffydd was captain of the most elite force of fighting men in Wales. Prince Hywel retained his grip on his lands and his station because the men who reported to him missed very little of what went on within his domains.

The king's pavilion, along with the rest of the tents belonging to his retinue, had been set up in the fields to the northeast of Holywell Abbey. Gareth and Llelo had taken the path from the field directly back to the abbey guesthouse, located just inside the easterly gate. If Cadwaladr had ever really been intending to use the latrine, he would have followed that path or made his way to the encampment's latrines. Instead, he'd turned northwest, staying near the wall of the abbey and heading towards the Holywell stream.

Dai had been attempting to keep an eye on Cadwaladr's back and the ground at the same time, endeavoring not to stumble on unseen roots or dips. He hadn't dared bring a torch, which would have made obvious the fact that he was following. For now, he was navigating by the lights from the pavilion and abbey that were reflecting off the clouds above them in the night sky. Given that Cadwaladr was doing the same thing, Dai was feeling more confident that he was up to something. As they moved farther from the pavilion with every step, Dai's heart beat even faster, wondering if everything would change tonight.

If only they could be so lucky.

But because he was so focused, he missed seeing Abbot Rhys come out of the darkness until he was essentially upon him. "It's a lovely night for a ramble, isn't it?" The music behind them, coupled with the wind in the trees, was loud enough that they likely wouldn't have had to speak quietly to keep Cadwaladr from hearing, but Rhys had done so anyway.

Dai walked a few paces farther along the path they were following, trying to figure out how to reply. He decided innocence might do for a start. "I thought you had already retired for the night. Is something amiss?"

"You tell me."

Dai cleared his throat. "Er ..." He didn't know if it was acceptable to reveal his mission, even to as staunch an ally as the abbot. He was one of the mediators at the conference, after all. It might not be fitting for him to have information about one of the participants that he might later have to pretend not to know.

Abbot Rhys gave him another opening. "You looked like you could use some company."

"Did I?" Dai was still struggling with what to say. It wasn't a usual predicament for him. "I am off to the latrine."

"As am I. How convenient for both of us that we could go together. And look, Prince Cadwaladr had the same idea. I wonder how it is that we are all heading in the wrong direction."

This was getting ridiculous. Abbot Rhys was teasing him ... *wasn't he?*

They paced along the path another ten yards before the abbot proved it, dropping his voice even lower. "Never worry, Dai. I have the utmost respect for your abilities, but like you, I saw Llelo leave with your father and then Taran depart not long after. When you left too, but in a different direction, on the heels of Cadwaladr, it occurred to me that Gareth had an extra pair of eyes in Llelo, and you might be in need of another set as well."

Dai could no longer pretend he didn't know what Abbot Rhys was talking about. The man had been a spy himself, one of Empress Maud's famed *Four Horsemen*. Dai had long known that little got past Rhys, especially when it came to intrigue. In addition, Dai had known Rhys for almost as long as Dai had been Gareth's son. If he couldn't trust Abbot Rhys, he couldn't trust anyone. "Thank you, Father. I don't know if you're right that something is afoot tonight. But I won't say no to the company. At worst, as you said, we'll have a nice stroll together in the dark, in order to ready our stomachs for some more mead."

That prompted a slight smile from Rhys. "Of which, if I am not mistaken, you've partaken very little tonight."

Dai canted his head in acknowledgment. He had tried that route, at various times drinking to excess to blot out thoughts he didn't want to remember, or, more commonly, emotions he didn't want to feel. He had seen battle and death. Both his birth parents were dead.

At the time, he himself hadn't realized what he was doing. It had been his mother who'd made a somewhat pointed observation about his mead consumption levels. He'd paced around the hall afterwards, for the first time since he'd been adopted wishing she wasn't his mother. But afterwards, as he sought refuge in mead yet again, he'd seen the truth for what it was: drink was good for giving him relief from memory for a short while. But the ache in his heart returned with more force in the morning, almost as if the mead was making him feel worse. It was best these days to take it in sips. Since this realization, he had noticed as well that his standing with the Dragons, and particularly Gruffydd, had improved.

"I don't know what happened to make my father and Llelo leave the feast. If I had to guess, it was something none of us are going to like."

"Such was my impression too. Undoubtedly, if it is important, we will learn of it soon enough. Meanwhile, how lovely to distract ourselves by walking a path less traveled." This was a classic Abbot Rhys flourish. His advice was generally straightforward and to the point, especially to a young man who needed to be pulled up short and wasn't good at interpreting parables. In truth, his mother should have asked Rhys to tell Dai of the pitfalls of drinking too much. He might have listened sooner.

"It may be this will come to nothing."

"But if it comes to something, better to have a companion at your side to do your bidding."

"You being that companion?"

Up ahead, Cadwaladr stopped to adjust some article of clothing, a transparent attempt to see if anyone was behind him. Fortunately, almost as if he'd *felt* the change in Cadwaladr, Rhys had moved to hide an instant earlier and dragged Dai with him into the shadows of the trees along the path. They held completely still, not even daring to breathe. Cadwaladr looked around for another moment and then started walking again.

The path now curved to follow the bank of the Holywell stream. As far as Dai knew, there was only farmland and a few stands of trees in this direction. That might make it difficult to hide, but then, it also made it easier to see without a torch.

Dai and Rhys gave Cadwaladr a few more paces, allowing themselves to fall further behind, and then began walking again themselves.

"You think it beneath me?" Rhys picked up their conversation where it had left off.

Dai shook his head, less as a means of saying *no* than to clear it. "You answered my question with a question."

"Ah, yes. I should have known that Gareth's son would see right through me."

Dai didn't know that this was so, but he didn't argue with the abbot, instead waiting for the clarification he hoped was coming. It seemed now that Rhys had an ulterior motive for walking with him, and assumed Dai was man enough to know what it was. Truly, this was the first time in Dai's experience that Abbot Rhys had treated him like a man.

Finally Rhys emitted a little laugh. "You've learned the art of silence too, eh?" He nodded, not expecting an answer. "I was looking for a chance to leave the pavilion. I am not finding the company of my old companions as felicitous as I might have hoped."

Dai was coming to understand that Rhys spoke elaborately sometimes as a way to soften the force of his words. Dai was nonetheless surprised that Rhys would admit unhappiness, especially to him. He was quite sure Rhys had never before told him how he felt about anything. "Do you suspect one of them of something untoward?"

"Not exactly." Rhys gestured ahead of them to where Cadwaladr still paced, now nearly fifty yards ahead. Dai feared losing him, but Abbot Rhys didn't pick up the pace. Since he had more experience following a suspect, and had already saved them once, Dai allowed him to lead. And since they were well beyond any possibility that Cadwaladr was visiting the latrine, it would be harder to justify their presence if he looked over his shoulder and saw them. "Not like him."

Cadwaladr kept moving as if he knew where he was going, what he was doing, and didn't, in fact, care who saw him. He didn't check behind him again, and he kept heading northeast, through a crossroads, until finally he turned down a real road that led towards the stream itself. They had come down the hill from the encampment far enough that they were nearly opposite Gwenffrewi's well, which was located on the opposite bank of the Holywell stream and not reachable from here without going back up the hill to the bridge and down the other side.

Abbot Rhys slowed further. "He's heading to the mill."

"You're sure?"

They had come a good half-mile from the abbey by now. It was so dark Dai couldn't see Rhys's expression. He imagined, however, that it was sardonic because he said, "This particular path doesn't go anywhere else."

Dai made a gesture he intended to be apologetic. "I just don't want to lose him."

"Nor will you."

Which proved to be the case as the path opened out into a yard, cleared of brush and trees, where two carts were parked side-by-side. The sound of the water was quite loud this close to the stream, especially with the waterwheel quiet at this time of night. Dai touched Rhys's elbow and signed that they should hide themselves in the thick trees and undergrowth just off the path. Beneath the over-hanging branches, it was so dark Dai couldn't see his hand in front of his face.

But then, as if knowing their task was an important one, the moon came out from behind a cloud and lit up the night as Cadwaladr approached the entrance to the mill.

"He's meeting someone." Dai's voice was low and full of satis-faction.

"I remain impartial in all things," Rhys said, equally low and practically in Dai's ear, "but even I think it would be a good idea to know who."

"Perhaps it's a woman." Dai was trying not to get his hopes up. What he really wanted was to catch Cadwaladr in an overt act of treason.

"Women can be spies too."

They watched Cadwaladr enter the mill. As soon as he was out of sight, Abbot Rhys tugged Dai's sleeve to get him to move another ten paces deeper into the little wood, though remaining on the mar-gins of the mill's yard. It was more important than ever that Cadwal-adr not see them.

Dai followed, frowning. "Is it usual for the mill not to be locked?"

"No." The answer came immediately, in a grim tone that did not bode well for the monk who ran the mill. This wasn't Rhys's do-main, but Abbess Nest would want to know if the workers within her charge had neglected their duties. The mill contained grain, which was a commodity at times more valuable than silver. With the possibility of pilgrims about, even in January, and a fairly remote location, Dai would have thought it should be locked at night when nobody was there.

Reaching an old oak, one still with a few scraggly leaves that had not fallen to the ground, Abbot Rhys leaned against it and tipped back his head. "We may be here a while."

"One of us should check the rear of the mill."

Because of the moon, even under the trees, it was light enough for Dai to see the abbot rubbing his chin in thought. "Then we would have no way to communicate. It would all but defeat the purpose of me coming with you."

Dai wasn't ready to abandon the idea and thought it might be worthwhile for one of them at least to do a circuit of the mill, just to get their bearings. "We never have enough people. We always have to improvise."

Gwalchmai had explained once to Dai in his usual detail the different approaches to music a man could take, depending on what was expected and the extent of his talent. Any musician became better with practice, and a good one endeavored to work on each song until he knew it so well he could play and sing it in his sleep. That allowed him to perform whenever and whatever his lord demanded.

Bards like Meilyr and Gwalchmai wrote new music every day—some good, some bad, Gwalchmai always hastened to say—and were always expanding their repertoire. Producing a new song as directed by judges at an *eisteddfod*, a musical contest, was one of the especially wonderful, and occasionally painful, competitions in which bards participated. Neither man had attended any since the last such gathering a few years ago in Ceredigion, before Rhun's death, but Meilyr had won many in his time, which was how he'd become the premier bard in all of Wales. Dai knew for a fact that Meilyr thought it was time Gwalchmai made his own mark in that fashion.

And that meant Meilyr was teaching Gwalchmai not only to sing, but his *craft*. This was a very different thing. A musician with a grounding like Gwalchmai's had such a grasp of his profession that he could make up a new song on the spot, on command, and have it be as good or better than any of the songs he'd prepared in advance. In other words, he could *improvise*.

What's more, Dai had come to realize that *improvising* was something his parents did all the time in their investigations. In fact, it was clear to him they were teaching Llelo his craft in exactly the same manner Meilyr was teaching Gwalchmai. And, really, it was also the same way Gruffydd was teaching Dai. Any moderately intelligent knight could put his nose to the ground and follow where clues led. But one who could improvise could lift his head every now and again and see what was on the horizon. That was why his father was so trusted. Dai had never known him to fail.

Before Rhys even replied to Dai's suggestion, Cadwaladr was back, having hardly spent enough time in the mill to turn around. He took big strides across the yard to the path along which they'd just come. Dai was very glad Abbot Rhys had drawn him deeper into the trees, because otherwise Cadwaladr would have spotted them for sure. It was also just as well that Rhys had discouraged them from separating. Dai could have been on the other side of the mill by now, and then Abbot Rhys would have been stuck deciding whether to wait for Dai or to follow Cadwaladr.

For the prince's part, his hands were as empty as before, and Dai could discern nothing unusual in his demeanor. It looked as if he'd walked all the way to the mill only to turn around immediately and leave again.

Barely breathing and trying to become one with the shadows under the trees so Cadwaladr wouldn't notice them, they allowed him to pass by, returning to the pavilion exactly the way he'd come.

Once he'd gone, Abbot Rhys said, still speaking under his breath, "So, not a woman, or not one who kept him long."

If Rhys had been one of the Dragons, he might have accompanied this statement with a lewd comment. As it was, his tone was without affect. While the abbot had lived in the world far longer than he'd been a monk and had a community of monks under his care, he no longer felt the need to conform to the habits of normal men.

Dai wasn't one to tell the abbot what to do, so he phrased his next thought with respect rather than as an order. "If you could follow him, I'll check the mill."

Rhys simply nodded, patted Dai on the shoulder, and headed back down the trail to the pavilion, leaving Dai alone in the dark.

12

Day Two
Gwen

Gwen had wondered for many years about Taran's bachelor status. She'd always known there had to have been *some-one* in his life. As a young girl, during the years her father had been the household bard for King Owain's father, there'd been rumors of a liaison, but for whatever reason, nobody knew anything about it. In those days, Owain and Taran had been young warriors and had spent far less time at Aber or Aberffraw than they did now. It had been Gwen who'd stayed in one place, since she was tied to her father's duty. As the king had aged, he no longer even traveled from one *llys* to another, delegating the administration of his people to his steward or one of his sons.

And even then, Gwen had been far more occupied with her own heart to pay more than passing attention to what was going on with anyone else, much less an *old* man like Taran. Once her father had fallen out with Owain after Gruffydd's death, her family had spent years wandering Wales before finally returning seven years ago.

In his fifties now, the same age as Owain, Taran would still make someone a suitable husband. All Gwen had to do was look at King Owain—or her own father—to know what was possible. But since those early days, she'd never even heard a rumor of an attachment. She'd always assumed something had happened to that first woman, after which he'd simply put love aside in favor of duty. But the way he was bent over now, his shoulders hunched as if he, instead of the woman lying on the bed, had been stabbed in the belly, revealed the depth of his love and pain.

"Will she live?" Taran spoke as if the words were being drawn from him against his will.

Abbess Nest couldn't help but see how he was hurting, so when she spoke, her voice was gentle. "We believe so. We cannot promise, as you must know. So much depends on the severity of the blow to her head. Nor can I say what she will remember of the events leading up to this evening. All I can tell you is that we will watch over her, and care for her, and do whatever we can to help her heal."

"Are you saying, even were she to wake, she might not know me?" Taran asked.

Nest put a hand on his shoulder, her manner as gentle as her voice had been. "We have seen it. It is a rare occurrence, but I don't want to give you false hope."

"I don't want that either." Taran took in a ragged breath, and though his words were for Gwen, his eyes never left Helen's face. "Queen Cristina didn't recognize her?"

"No." And then Gwen amended, "She made it clear to me she didn't. Her astonishment and horror seemed genuine as well. Then again, she'd just been presented with an unconscious woman on her floor, not to mention a half-destroyed room."

While Gwen had been waiting for the healers to come, she'd reset the mattress on the bedframe, adjusting the slats to make up for the one she still thought was missing. She'd tidied the queen's clothes too, though she could do nothing about the splintered doorframe.

Taran's expression was thoughtful, and Gwen was glad to see his mind beginning to work again. This puzzle could distract him momentarily from his grief. "It may be we were more successful than we thought at keeping our connection a secret."

"I'm sorry to have to ask this, Taran, but we need to know when you last saw her." Gwen didn't want to start in with the questions already but knew she had to. The man who'd hurt Helen was well away. Every moment they delayed going after him was a moment lost. But if Taran knew something that would help them track him down, better to delay a few moments than to send Gareth or Llelo off in the wrong direction.

"It was two months ago, on the Feast of Deiniol." Taran let out another tremulous breath. "She stayed with me all night, and then she left."

"Why have we never met her? Why keep your relationship with her a secret in the first place?"

Taran's mouth twitched into a smile, one that was even briefly rueful, before his expression saddened again. "Helen is half-sister to none other than Earl Ranulf of Chester himself."

The whole time he'd been speaking, Taran had refused to look at any of them, so only Gwen saw the way this news rocked her husband and son, men who prided themselves on how rarely they were surprised by any news. They should have known better. Just when she thought she had a handle on the way things were, something rose up and slapped her upside the head. In truth, they all should know by now not to assume anything nor accept coincidences on their outward merits.

Gwen herself needed a moment to absorb that news, so it was Llelo who ventured, "You mean—"

"She was born to a Welsh woman and only occasionally acknowledged."

Gwen knew what that meant. Helen's father, who was also the father of the current Ranulf, Earl of Chester, had probably paid for Helen's upkeep as a child, but illegitimacy was far more complicated in the Norman world than in the Welsh. In Wales, illegitimate children acknowledged by their father could inherit equally with their legitimate siblings, hence the standing of Prince Hywel (and before him, his brother Rhun) as heir to the throne of Gwynedd. Among Normans, bastard children were seen as a stain on their parents' legacy. Even so, many powerful men had numerous illegitimate children.

But while having children out of wedlock was condemned from the pulpit, it was hardly unusual. What's more, if two illegitimate people married, their own children were lawful and accepted by the Church.

This connection between Helen and Taran was another reminder, if Gwen needed one, that the world often turned out to be smaller than expected. Gwen had a hundred more questions but respected Taran enough to ask only those most pertinent to the investigation. "So you hadn't seen her today?"

"No. I didn't even know she was back already."

"Was she supposed to be coming here?" Gareth said softly from his position near the door.

"She said she would meet me here if she could, though with the rivers running high, I truly didn't expect her so soon."

Gwen had been studying the shape of Taran, thinking through everything that these last few moments had taught her about him, coupled with the sight of the love of his life wounded on the bed. "Where has she been all this time?"

"Away."

Gwen didn't allow a sigh of exasperation to escape her lips at his reply, but simply waited for him to truly answer the question.

Taran then sighed and, for the first time since he revealed he knew the woman, looked over at Gwen. She tried to keep her expression as neutral as possible. He wouldn't want to be pitied. "Two months ago, I asked her to marry me."

Gwen would have understood if the admission had broken him completely. He still kept one arm around his middle, holding on, but suddenly his back was straight, and his eyes were clear.

"She said yes."

13

Day Two

Dai

As Abbot Rhys departed, Dai momentarily clenched his hands into fists. Even having made the decision that Rhys should be the one to follow Cadwaladr, he was torn between duty and duty. Watching Cadwaladr was *Dai's* responsibility, not Rhys's, but Dai was selfish enough to want to be the one to explore the mill. That Cadwaladr had entered by himself, even staying inside for as short a time as he had, meant Dai and Rhys had been unable to witness what he'd done while he was inside. What meeting could have been so short? If Dai entered the mill right now, would he catch the person with whom Cadwaladr had met?

It was a tantalizing thought but Dai dispelled it with a quick shake of his head. His charge was not to apprehend one of Cadwaladr's co-conspirators. He was to watch without letting Cadwaladr know he was being watched. That said, Dai was more worried than he could express about what information Cadwaladr had just conveyed or acquired, which was why Dai and Abbot Rhys had needed to separate. For now, the prince had to be left in Rhys's, admittedly very capable, hands.

Fortunately, Rhys was already gone, so Dai couldn't expend any of his anxiety on him nor rethink the decision. After another breath, he swallowed down his doubts, allowed another few heartbeats to pass, and stepped out from his hiding place to the edge of the yard. Even then, he stayed still for a further count of ten, wanting to be sure nobody else was exiting through the front door of the mill. The last thing Dai needed was to be attacked in the yard by a fleeing conspirator. When there was still no sign of anyone coming, he set out across the yard at a fast walk towards the entrance to the mill.

Occasionally a mill was driven by the power of the wind, but most mills in Dai's experience were driven by water, which was in abundance in Wales. A stream or river could be found in the vicinity of virtually every settlement throughout the entire country. Not all were appropriate for diverting to create a mill race, and Dai didn't pretend to know all the parameters for building a mill. He did know that mills dotted the landscape. Every monastery he'd ever been in, and also villages, particularly those adjacent to the king's *llys,* had one. Grain could be ground by hand, but it was labor intensive, and thus any community of any size had at least one mill for grinding grains. If the town or monastery was particularly wealthy or large, it might also have other mills, perhaps for milling wood, fulling cloth, or working iron.

This mill was powered by the flow of the Holywell stream, which ran relatively steeply from southwest to northeast at this location and emptied into the Dee Estuary. In many mills, at least one millworker would sleep in the loft overnight to guard the tools and the grain. This would be particularly important in an abbey such as this one, through which pilgrims to the holy well constantly passed. But if anyone was asleep here, he hadn't shown himself. Cadwaladr could even have come here to meet the mill's guard.

The entrance to the mill was accessed by stairs that led up to the middle floor of the three-story building. The door opened on silent hinges, testament to the smooth running of anything within the abbey's domain. Nest had been asked to become the abbess of this group of monks and nuns to put them in order, which she had done, the absence of a locked door at the mill notwithstanding. Dai himself had never had a real conversation with her. She was friendly but reserved, perhaps not unlike Abbot Rhys had been to Dai's family initially. Maybe one had to be like that in order to successfully run an abbey.

Here on the middle floor was the giant millstone, used for grinding the grain. Above Dai's head was the hopper, which descended through the ceiling from the grain storage located on the top floor. Grain was stored there under the eaves because it was the driest and warmest place in the mill. Once ground, the flour was sent down another chute that descended through this floor to the one below. There, it was collected in bags. That bottom floor was accessible by stairs and had its own exit out the back.

Before Gareth and Gwen had adopted Dai, he had been apprenticed to his birth father, who'd been a wool trader. Thus, Dai had never worked in a mill nor known much about their functioning, even mills that fulled cloth. But he had participated in many investigations with his parents, not to mention experienced nearly sixteen years of life. At the very least, he could tell the mill was not currently running, nor would it be at this hour of the night. And, by the quality of the silence, it was, in fact, empty.

For a moment, he stood in the doorway, listening harder, just to be sure. If the guard was a heavy sleeper, he might not wake just because the door opened. The hinges hadn't squeaked—which in retrospect might not be a mark in the mill's favor if it meant intruders could come and go as they pleased.

One of the difficulties in grinding grain was the ever present risk of fire. Even Dai knew you should never smother a fire with flour, which had a tendency to explode with the power of pitch wood. Thus, few mills worked after dark because of the danger of any kind of flame. Most had large windows to let in light, as this one did, though these were blocked by shutters at night.

Even so, a lantern hung on the wall near the door, and Dai took it down without lighting it. For the moment, the moon shone brightly enough through the open doorway to leave a square of light on the floor, and once he opened two of the nearby window shutters on the adjacent wall, he had the ability to see. Even a few hours ago, it had been raining, and Dai would have barely been able to see his hand in front of his face.

Cadwaladr hadn't opened the shutters, which indicated he'd known where he was going and had merely navigated by the moonlight coming through the door behind him. On the whole, Dai wouldn't have thought Cadwaladr, with his far older eyes, would have been able to see any better than Dai himself. As it was, with the shutters open, the moonlight illumined the millstone apparatus in the middle of the floor, which had been swept clean at the end of the day. That everything was so orderly only made the fresh chunks of grass and mud left behind by Cadwaladr's walk across the floor more obvious.

Dai had the same detritus on his own boots, and before he'd even entered, he'd availed himself of the boot scraper located just outside the door. He hadn't wanted to mar the scene more than was unavoidable by his very presence. With no real light to see by, perhaps Cadwaladr hadn't realized he was leaving behind such obvious evidence of his passing.

Cadwaladr's prints led to a bag of grain, as yet unground, but open at the top. A small pile of seed from it had cascaded onto the floor. While finding grain on the floor might be expected in a mill, the spill was out of place, given the neatness of the rest of the room.

Careful to avoid the trail Cadwaladr had left, Dai went to the sack and, before he could think too hard about what he was doing, plunged his own hand into it. More grain spilled onto the floor, adding to the little pile. He rummaged with his fingers within the sack, questing for what Cadwaladr may have left or the remains of what he'd taken, if anything. Even if he hadn't left such obvious evidence of his activities behind, the prince hadn't been in the mill long enough to do more than walk across the floor, collect or leave whatever had brought him to the mill, and exit again.

But Dai's hand touched nothing but grain. Disappointed, he sat back on his heels, thinking hard about why Cadwaladr might have come here and wishing he'd had the wherewithal to get ahead of him rather than just merely follow. Then again, he reminded himself that his charge had been only to follow, and Gruffydd or his father—or Prince Hywel, for that matter—wouldn't have thanked him for doing anything to give away the fact that they were watching. Every one of the Dragons would have liked to be the one who finally brought down the prince in a triumphant manner. That wasn't going to happen today. When it did, it had to really count.

In truth, Hywel had insisted repeatedly that none of them force his father's hand. As difficult as it might be to accept, worse than having to see Cadwaladr every day would be for King Owain to be coerced into exiling his own brother. He needed to come to that decision himself. In the meantime, it was the job of his men to protect him.

But if Cadwaladr had come to the mill to collect something and left with it, Dai saw no sign of what that item might have been. He was even having a moment's fear that Cadwaladr had deliberately led him to the mill as a trick, to distract him from real treachery occurring elsewhere. It was a chilling thought, but at the same time not something Dai could do anything about now.

Whatever else the mill might be, it wasn't a trap for Dai.

14

Day Two
Llelo

As Llelo descended the guesthouse stairs, lantern in hand, under orders from his father to follow the footprints and find the weapon used on Helen if he could, he thought back to that first time he'd been sent on his own to investigate. It had been at Dinefwr Castle, during an investigation that had produced a host of paths to follow, just like this one, with not enough people to follow them—again, just like this one. Llelo had known he was being utilized out of desperation. His father hadn't pretended otherwise. At the time, Llelo had been too proud and scared of what he was being asked to do, and uncertain of his own worth, to feel resentful.

That day, having been sent to find and question a woman who lived some distance from the castle, Llelo had discovered an important clue—perhaps *the* important clue—that had cracked open the whole investigation. Tonight, he had no expectation of doing the same. Unless Helen's attacker had expired on the path, he was going to be difficult to follow, and the hour of the night meant Llelo would have nobody to question within the abbey. None but the main gate into the abbey had even been guarded! In addition, monastics went to bed early. Likely, that was what the intruder had counted on.

His father, meanwhile, was hurrying to put the Dragons on alert, along with the personal guard, or *teulu*, of Prince Hywel and King Owain. Helen wasn't a total stranger or just any traveler. She was a friend, lover, and soon-to-be wife of the steward of Gwynedd. Leaving her for dead was a much bigger crime than Queen Cristina had thought when she'd gone to find Gareth an hour ago.

"What are you doing?"

Llelo snapped upright at Iago's voice, and then relaxed again as two of the Dragons his own father had gone to look for stepped out of the darkness. They'd come up the path from the encampment, which by now was well-trodden. "Er ... what are you two doing here?"

Iago scoffed at the way Llelo had turned his own question back on them. "We just spoke to your father, and he sent us to guard the guesthouse. Something is amiss, he said. Wouldn't tell us much, if anything. Only to be on alert. The only person we've seen is you, and I must say, you are behaving very suspiciously."

Llelo knew the Dragon was teasing, as he often did, but he also knew he *had* been behaving oddly. A moment earlier, he'd practically been on his hands and knees with his nose to the flagstones of the path, looking for footprints and, quite frankly, blood. The intruder had been bleeding heavily at one point. Llelo was hoping he still was.

It would serve him right.

Since Gareth wasn't here to gainsay Llelo, and he had enlisted the two Dragons himself, Llelo decided he could reveal something of what was going on, if not Helen's identity quite yet. "There's been an intruder in the guesthouse. I'm looking for a sign of which way he went."

That got the men's attention, as well it might, and they immediately became much more serious. "Where?"

"He was all the way upstairs. I started looking for him here, at the front, but there are signs he might have escaped out the back. I'm heading there now."

Steffan and Iago launched into a private war with each other, using some sort of quick hand game that Iago lost—or at least Llelo interpreted him to have lost, since he had to be the one to stay behind and stand guard at the entrance to the guesthouse, while Steffan fell into step beside Llelo. With that, both of them bent over and focused on the ground.

"What about the far side?" Steffan asked.

"I already looked. Nothing there. But here ... I see footprints."

"Many people must have come and gone tonight." Steffan had let Iago do the talking when they'd first arrived, but he was perfectly capable of speaking when he chose. "No telling when these were made."

"It rained right up until the feast," Llelo said.

It rained most days in January, if not every day. That made it a poor time for traveling, since roads turned to mud and river crossings washed out. The weather also made it a poor time to move armies, which was why King Owain had decided he was happy with setting the conference for this time of year, turning Madog's stalling into a virtue. They'd actually had good weather for the majority of their journey from Aber, which had made the time pass relatively pleasantly. Since they'd arrived at Holywell, however, it had rained every day, stopping today just in time for the evening meal to be served.

The rain had also given King Madog a good excuse for being late to the conference. A messenger had met them when they'd arrived at the abbey, apologizing for the delay. Given the rain, nobody could be surprised that one of the fords between Dinas Bran and Holywell was too high to cross. Madog was having to take the long way around, perhaps all the way to the bridge at Chester. Llelo thought he should have left to do that already. It was January, moving soon into February. The rain wasn't going to stop any time soon.

But because of the rain, any earlier prints would have been less clear, meaning any recent ones might be easy—or easier, anyway—to discern.

Steffan bent over more. "These are fresh."

Llelo thought so too. "One set is small, like a woman might make. Those others are larger."

They came around the back of the guesthouse where the ladder, perhaps the length of two men, was lying against the wall under King Owain's window. Many footprints had stamped the ground, which was soft and grassy, to the point of being more like grassy mud.

"Someone was here." Steffan stood with his hands on his hips, looking from the ground to the windows on the higher floor and back again.

"The ladder was used." Llelo pointed to two indents sunk deep into the earth where the bottom poles of the ladder could have rested.

The other prints were confusing, blending one with the other as people moved about, but Llelo thought he could make out the woman's prints along with at least two other sets, both larger. Even had Queen Cristina not reported seeing the two monks, Llelo thought it likely two men had been in King Owain's room. Really, he should have brought one of Helen's boots to match to the prints out here. He would do that as soon as he marshaled the courage to disturb Taran with the request, something he was entirely loath to do.

He had never been afraid of Taran. The steward had always treated Llelo well and had never implied, either in word or deed, that he was somehow lesser because he wasn't Gareth's natural-born son. This was despite the fact that Llelo hadn't always behaved in a manner appropriate to his father's station. He'd been twelve when he and Dai had been brought into Gareth's household, uneducated and ignorant of manners. Llelo had held his knife wrong and eaten too quickly at meals; worn muddy boots into the hall, tracking debris across the queen's newly laid rush mats; and had spoken at times in a manner unbecoming the son of a knight. Most importantly for his future as a knight, investigator, and steward to a prince, he hadn't been able to read.

That Taran had always been so kind made Llelo want to make things better for him if he possibly could. Maybe, in the end, that was something the two of them had in common, since Taran had spent his life making things better for King Owain and his court. Like Llelo, he wasn't happy unless he was *doing* something for someone else.

Tonight, all Taran could do was watch and pray. His helplessness had been reflected in his face. Llelo was thankful that he, in this instance, could do *more*.

Steffan put himself up against the wall, one arm stretched to its full length above his head. "That isn't too bad a jump. Hardly any problem if you hang from the sill first."

"It would be if you were bleeding."

Steffan turned to look at Llelo, eyes bright with interest. "Someone was bleeding?"

Llelo didn't bother to chastise himself for giving more away. Steffan *was* here to help, after all. "It seems so. Potentially a great deal."

Steffan scuffed the ground with the toe of his boot. "Blood won't be easy to see anywhere but on the flagstones, and even then only with a lantern." He indicated the path running between the abbey buildings and the gardens beyond. "Two sets of largish prints go that way."

Llelo kept his lantern low to the ground as he set off in the direction Steffan had indicated. "Then so should we."

15

Day Two
Dai

Cadwaladr had come to the mill to collect something. That meant someone else had left that something, and likely been the one to leave the door to the mill unlocked. That person might still be in the vicinity, watching Dai, even now. Earlier, when he'd been hiding with Abbot Rhys, Dai had meant to go around to the back of the mill, but had not had time to do so since Cadwaladr had entered and left so quickly.

The thought brought Dai to his feet and had him immediately moving up the stairs to the upper floor, just to make certain it was as empty as he felt it to be. When he saw nobody asleep on the cot against the far wall, he returned to the level with the millstone and, having given himself a good look at the steps down, closed the shutters and the door, plunging the mill again into real darkness. Then he moved by feel down to the next level. Like the rest of the floor except where Cadwaladr had walked, these steps had been swept clean too.

And soon he could see again because someone had left the back door off its latch, and it banged against the frame in a breeze.

Once more, Dai's heart started beating a little faster. The mill really had been left wide open. While he could believe the miller had forgotten to lock one door behind him, to leave both unlocked was either a shocking negligence of duty or had to be deliberate.

Dai went through the door—and was immediately disappointed to see nobody racing away across the fields in front of him. He should have known more sleuthing would be in order. To that end, he finally lit the lantern with a few strikes from the fire starter he kept in his purse. Now that he was outside, he felt it might be permissible to use it. He really did need to see better and had real hope he would find something worth seeing. It was one thing to sweep a floor clean of footprints. It was quite another to disguise one's passage through grass and muddy ground.

With the lantern held low, Dai found the first footprints right where he expected, both coming and going from the back door. Then he made out a second set, at which point his excitement started to wane a little. By the time he found the third set, he'd mentally returned to solid ground. *Of course* footprints would lead to and from the back door. The mill had many visitors and workers throughout the day. Whoever had left these particular prints could not now be determined.

He was about to give up when a final set of prints that were clear to see both coming and going caught his eye. Those headed towards the mill didn't end at the actual entryway, but slightly to the left of the door, as if someone had stood for a moment with their nose practically against the wall. The prints seemed more defined than the others too, as if they might have been made after the rain had stopped. That would also have been after all the workers had left the mill for the evening meal.

By now, more clouds were filling the sky, and the moon was gone again. Since he didn't expect the prints to survive the coming downpour, Dai didn't feel too bad about placing his own boots next to them, partly to judge the size and partly because he was trying to figure out why they were set the way they were. The prints were larger than his boots, indicating they belonged to a grown man.

And then, with a laugh, he understood how the intruder had entered the mill without leaving any trace of himself behind: he'd removed his boots and left them beside the door in order to walk about in his stocking feet. When he'd left, he'd quickly shoved his feet back into his shoes, impressing his prints deep into the mud.

Since these appeared to be the prints Dai needed to follow, and with nothing more to see for now inside the mill, Dai closed the back door and set out across the grass. He still held the lantern, telling himself the miller would just have to forgive him for taking it, and he would return it in the morning. Dai was no expert tracker and would be blind without it.

By now, he was also less worried about being seen from afar. Cadwaladr was long gone and so was this person.

Or so Dai thought at first.

As he followed the prints, however, he realized they were circling back towards the encampment. At times, especially when the prints went underneath trees, he was sure he'd lost them, but even here he found a narrow path, and he stayed on it until he could see the lights of the encampment in the distance, slightly below him at this point since he'd crested the last rise.

Instinctively, he snuffed out the lantern. It was one thing to be able to see Gwynedd's pavilion in the distance. It was quite another for anyone there to see *him*. The light of a lantern on this hill would make him not only a target, but a beacon, shining out in the darkness of the night and letting everyone know someone was coming towards them from the northeast. One of the people looking might be the one he'd been following, who was either already back at the feast or in the abbey.

It was frustrating to have come so far for so little. Then again, he knew where to look now for whoever had been at the mill. This person wasn't a complete stranger. Dai reached the field adjacent to the encampment, and was just opening the gate, his mind full of what questions to ask next and of whom to ask them, when he heard a woman scream.

16

Day Two
Rhys

Rhys had watched Cadwaladr return to the pavilion, having trailed the prince at some distance while always keeping him in sight to ensure he neither spoke with anyone nor detoured to anyplace but the actual latrine. It would be ironic indeed if the entire trip to the mill was a ruse to disguise a real meeting there. Rhys had been a spy himself too long not to consider it.

After Cadwaladr returned to the pavilion, Rhys kept temporarily to the margins of the festivities, near one of the posts, watching a dozen people enter and leave in the space of a quarter of an hour. It was a degree of activity Rhys hadn't noticed when he was sitting at the high table with the other guests of honor. In a way, he was ashamed of himself for not being more observant.

What kept him on the margins was an uncertainty about his next course of action. His first impulse was to make his way to where the Dragons still occupied a table not far from the dais. Prince Hywel was there, laughing with his companions, though none of Dai's family, nor Dai himself, of course, had returned. Iago and Steffan were missing too.

The remaining Dragons would have noticed by now that Cadwaladr was back and wonder what had become of their fellow Dragon. Since Rhys knew from Dai that the Dragons had set themselves the task of watching Cadwaladr, with Dai's continued absence, someone else would have to do the job. They would have to take it up with Dai when he returned as to why that was.

The festivities were winding down by now. Gwalchmai and Meilyr had stopped singing, though neither had yet left the pavilion. Meilyr sat on a bench beside his wife, Saran, strumming his lyre almost desultorily.

Of Owain's companions at the high table, only Iwan and Ralph remained. They were sitting close, talking seriously, their heads together. He didn't think they had noticed him yet, though likely it wouldn't be long before they did. Their eyes missed little, so if they saw Rhys making his way directly towards the Dragons' table, they might wonder what had brought him back so long after he'd left them with excuses about going to bed. In this moment, he couldn't be too cautious. As enjoyable as tonight had been, he was reminded of why he'd put away the things of this world to begin with.

Cadwaladr himself had rejoined some of his acolytes on the south end of the pavilion. Rhys agreed wholeheartedly, even if his office would not allow him officially to do so, that the demons which had driven Cadwaladr to arrange for the ambush and murder of both the King of Deheubarth and Gareth (although the latter ambush missed its target and found Prince Rhun instead), would not have changed. It would be foolish to think Cadwaladr could change, regardless of his outward penitence. He'd bent the knee and begged forgiveness of his brother in order to get his lands back and so he could once again stand at Owain's side as a prince of Gwynedd.

He wanted Owain's favor, but that wasn't because he wanted to serve him. He was only interested in serving himself. If that meant humbling himself before his brother a time or two, then he would do it. That Cadwaladr had been quiet since his return a year ago merely meant he hadn't yet reached the point where he had a workable plan to betray them all.

As Rhys watched, Cadwaladr, with a smile and a laugh, accepted a cup from a young woman servant—and then both froze as if struck by lightning as a blood-curdling scream rose up from behind Rhys, coming from the field to the northeast of the king's encampment.

Was it wrong of Rhys to think *that's more like it?*

Even a single evening with Dai had clearly been too much time already. He was starting to think like him.

But since Rhys had been dithering on the edge of the pavilion, he was able to respond first, grabbing one of the torches that had been stabbed into the ground to light the perimeter and setting off at a fast walk in the direction from which the sound had come. Other men reacted too, as they could not help but do. Gareth's good friend, the Dragon Evan, also carrying a torch, caught up to Rhys within a few strides. They went over a stile one after another—a little awkwardly for Rhys with his long robe held high in his free hand. At least he was wearing boots instead of the sandals that were required of some denominations founded in warmer climes even when those denominations moved northwards.

The screams stopped as Rhys returned to level ground. By then, Evan, who was younger and faster, had reached the woman responsible for the sound, to find her already in the arms of another man. As that man swung around to look at who had come, Rhys swallowed down a surprised laugh to see that it was Dai.

Dai's tone was rueful. "Hello, Abbot Rhys. Nice to see you again."

And then his expression turned a little bit fierce as Cadwaladr's resonant voice sounded behind them. "What has happened?"

Nearly the entire complement of guests who'd remained in the pavilion, upwards of thirty people, had followed them into the field.

Evan instantly reversed course, holding out one hand to the prince. "We don't know anything yet, my lord. Please, stay back."

"Why?" The word boomed out of Cadwaladr. He never liked being told what to do, particularly by anyone associated with Hywel or Gareth, and Evan was both.

To his credit, Evan spoke next in a lower tone, implying his words were intended for Cadwaladr's ears alone, though Rhys could still hear him well enough. "My lord, these people will obey you. If you tell them to keep their distance, they will. As I'm sure you're aware, if they come closer, they'll get their boots everywhere and confuse the scene."

Even coming from Evan, respect had an immediate effect, and Cadwaladr took over, gesticulating to the crowd, his voice as loud and commanding as before.

Rhys turned back to Dai and said in a low tone. "What *has* happened?"

"I honestly don't know. I just got here too." Dai was still holding the woman, whose face was to his chest as she let out great heaving sobs. "I thought stopping her from screaming should come first."

At that, the woman lifted her head. "Thank you for coming!" It was Cerys, the too young wife of one of the lesser barons who'd been sitting with Cadwaladr. Cerys's husband hadn't come with the prince into the field, which, from the way Cerys clung to Dai, was just as well. "The body of a man is lying just there!"

"A dead man?"

She flung out a hand to point deeper into the field. "How could he be alive? He isn't moving!" Her voice threatened to return to hysteria.

Rhys moved towards where she indicated, chastising himself for his moment of celebration that *something* had happened. A dead man was not the ending to the day they'd wanted or needed. Though, given everything else, perhaps they should have expected it.

"I'm so sorry you had to be the one to find him, Cerys. Would you like to return to the pavilion?" Dai was still holding her and hadn't moved. "You don't need to be here."

Cerys clutched at Dai's sleeve. "No. I'll stay with you." Though she'd certainly been weeping with abandon up until now, all of sudden a bit of steel entered her voice. She really didn't want to go back to her husband, no matter the shock she'd just experienced. She was a married woman, but a very unhappy one. Her tears tonight were nothing new, just for once about something other than her loveless marriage to an older man.

Rhys reached the body and waved at Dai to keep Cerys standing ten feet back. Dai obeyed, having also learned good sense from his parents about not disturbing crime scenes.

Stabbing his torch into the soft earth of the field, Rhys bent over the man, who was lying face down in the grass. He could have been sleeping but for the wound on the side of his head, matting his hair with blood. A sense of doom came over Rhys as he felt for a heartbeat at the man's neck. No offense to Dai, but he wished Gareth were with him. His continued absence had given both him and Dai the sense that something momentous was going on elsewhere, but a dead man in the field next to the pavilion, one with a wound to his head that could only have come from the hand of another person, could not be kept quiet.

"Fetch your father—"

Rhys broke off to see Gareth already shouldering his way through the crowd, which gave way to him easily. An audible murmur of relief swept among them to know *their* man had arrived. They trusted him. Even Cadwaladr nodded at Gareth as he passed, to which Gareth managed a guttural, "my lord," before arriving at Rhys's side.

Seeing the body on the ground, he allowed himself an aggrieved sigh.

"We are very glad to see you, Father," Dai said in a low tone, "we've had an eventful evening," he shot a glance at the prince, whose back was again turned away from them so he could speak to some of the men in the crowd, "even before this."

Gareth let out a low laugh that conveyed no amusement. "I'm almost afraid to ask what that might be about, because, quite frankly, so have I."

17

Day Two
Gareth

"What do we know?" Gareth settled into a crouch beside the dead man and reconciled himself to a long night.

Before this moment, his investigation had been narrowly focused on Helen and the events in the guesthouse. She, however, was alive. With this death, right next to the king's pavilion, his attention needed to shift dramatically. Even if he could have used him right now, he was glad he'd already sent Llelo on the trail of the guesthouse intruder. At least until he sought Gareth out again, someone would be pursuing that line of inquiry.

"Nothing more than you see here. I heard Cerys scream and came running." Dai gestured to the people behind Cadwaladr, all craning their necks to get a better look at the form lying on the ground.

Gareth placed a hand on the dead man's back, praying it might rise and fall, praying for a miracle. "Are you able to talk, Cerys?"

"What do you need to know?" She sniffed weepily and still had her head on Dai's chest.

Dai was standing poker straight, trying to comfort her while at the same time endeavoring not to actually touch her. He knew the perils of standing too close to another man's wife, no matter the circumstances. If Cerys's husband saw him, he would be irate. It didn't matter that Cerys was really the one holding on to him. The only person who didn't know Cerys was unhappy in her marriage was her own husband, who hadn't even bothered to put aside his mead and get up from his seat in the pavilion to find out what the commotion was about. If he had, he would definitely not have liked the way Cerys's arms were wrapped around Dai under his cloak. Then again, Gareth didn't like the look of it either. Somehow Gareth was going to have to get over the fact that his sons were men. It didn't look like he was going to manage that any time soon.

"Talk me through how you came to find him, Cerys. What were you doing in the field?"

It was time to turn the man over and start the process of grieving. Up until now, nobody had said out loud who he was, though Gareth was pretty sure he knew. Judging by the mop of black curls that normally framed his handsome face, this was Marc, King Owain's manservant. Of course, his death made all the sense in the world, given what lay hidden in the guesthouse.

But until they rolled him onto his back and acknowledged his identity, the man they'd known could be alive a little longer. Gareth had never thought a circumstance could exist where a man could be both alive and dead at the same time.

"I needed a moment by myself so I went for a walk."

Gareth almost blurted out *really?* in a sarcastic manner but caught himself at the last instant. Nobody could be surprised Cerys wanted time to herself, but nobody would also be surprised to learn she had intended to meet another man, maybe even the dead man.

So instead he said, "Alone?"

"Yes, alone." She was certain. That didn't mean Gareth believed her. "My eyes were on the ground as I walked. With the moon and the light from the pavilion, I could see well enough. I wasn't planning to go far—just far enough to get some fresh air."

Gareth gave way, deciding for now maybe she could be believed. It would be brazen of her to plan a liaison in the next field over from where her husband sat feasting. Then again, people did mad things when they were in love and desperate, or miserable and lonely. "And then what?"

"I stumbled over the body." She swallowed hard. "I-I-I touched him. He wasn't breathing. I can't believe he's dead. Who would do such a thing to him? That wound—" She returned her face to Dai's chest. Her comment had been revealing in the sense that she also knew who he was.

Dai shrugged and answered Gareth's question before he could ask it of him. "I heard her screams and came running. I didn't even know why she had screamed until she pointed out the body to Abbot Rhys."

Gareth was opening his mouth to ask something about where Dai had been before then, and how it was that he had been first on the scene so conveniently, thinking that Cerys could have intended to meet *Dai*, when Abbot Rhys nudged his elbow and spoke low in his ear. "He'd been with me." The way he spoke, with a dark overtone in his voice, closed Gareth's mouth.

"I see." Gareth didn't, but if Dai was in league with Abbot Rhys, Gareth wasn't going to question them in public. He could only think the more time Dai spent in Rhys's company, the better. He couldn't imagine a better influence.

At that point, Cadwaladr planted himself in their little circle, having proudly done his duty in keeping back the crowd. "Who's dead?" He glared down at the body, his hands on his hips.

Gareth couldn't stomach an actual reply, so he motioned for Abbot Rhys to help him, and together they carefully rolled the man over.

At which point he took in a great, shuddering breath.

They all reared back, and Cadwaladr was the first to let out a shout of surprise, "He's alive!"

Gareth found himself gasping, relieved beyond measure, though he didn't leap about with joy as Cadwaladr was doing.

Cerys left Dai's embrace in order to throw herself on top of the hapless manservant. "I can't believe you're alive! I thought you were dead! We all did!" Her joy was palpable too.

Marc, for his part, coughed and sputtered, and took some more heaving breaths.

Gareth reached down and tugged Cerys away. "Give him space. He was dead a moment ago."

"What happened?" Marc found his voice, blinking at the ring of faces looming over him. He tried to sit up but arrested the movement with a moan and a motion towards his wound.

Cadwaladr was back to being in charge. Raising a hand above his head, he shouted to the crowd, "Get the healer. Now!"

Meanwhile, Rhys had gone down on one knee on the other side of Marc, opposite Gareth, and the two of them helped to raise Marc's head and shoulders off the ground, at which point Cadwaladr saw them and motioned Rhys out of the way. "I'll do that." He ended up bracing Marc into a sitting position on the grass. Gareth had honestly never seen Cadwaladr so helpful before.

"Thank you, my lord." Marc was still coming around, his breathing having gone from effectively nonexistent to heavy and somewhat labored.

Gareth didn't think it wise to constrict Marc's chest by having him lean too far forward, but the healer who tended him wouldn't thank Gareth for filling his wound with mud and grass from the field either.

The wound itself looked so similar to Helen's, even as the physical surroundings were very different, that Gareth struggled not to make assumptions. If he himself, who had long experience with murder, had assumed Marc was dead, whoever attacked him had to have believed he'd killed him too. *Just like Helen.*

Cadwaladr, meanwhile, was reveling in his role as investigator and began the questioning, "Who hit you?"

Gareth probably wouldn't have started in on Marc quite so soon, but since Cadwaladr had asked, he decided he was happy to hear the answer.

"I don't know! He came from behind me. I didn't see him. I didn't even hear him!"

Though only in his early thirties and not a knight or a warrior, Marc had been raised in the king's court and spent his life in King Owain's service. He would not have been an easy man to surprise—certainly not to the point of allowing someone he didn't know to sneak up behind him and fell him in the middle of a field.

Gareth studied him. "Do you know who *I* am?"

Marc tsked. "Gareth ap Rhys."

"Can you tell me where you are?"

Marc opened his mouth to answer, and then frowned, though doing so appeared to hurt his head since his hand went to his wound again. "Er ... a field?"

Cadwaladr inserted himself once more, "What were you doing in this field?"

Marc's eyes crossed for a moment, and then he frowned, "I was ... getting some air?"

That was the second answer he'd ended with a questioning tone. It was sounding more and more to Gareth as if Marc was trying to give them answers he thought they wanted to hear. "Do you know *where* the field is located?"

Marc looked around at the faces gazing back at him. He seemed to feel no surprise at their owners. He knew them as he'd known Gareth. For a moment his gaze sharpened on Cerys, who nodded encouragingly. "Tell them."

Then he latched onto Abbot Rhys, who was standing next to her. "We are at St. Kentigern's monastery." This time, his tone was certain and as confident as Cerys's had been when she'd told Gareth she'd intended to be in the field alone.

Cadwaladr made a sound that implied to Gareth he was about to tell Marc he was wrong, but Gareth moved his head slightly as a way to ask him not to. Amazingly, the prince understood and changed course. "Let's get you up."

Marc's entire life had revolved around accommodating the requests of King Owain, and although this was Prince Cadwaladr, his response was no different. He immediately moved his legs to get his feet under him. Using Gareth's shoulder as a crutch, he pushed himself upwards to the point of reaching a standing position. But then a wave of revulsion crossed his face, his entire body spasmed, and he leaned forward to vomit into the grass.

The look on Cadwaladr's face was, quite frankly, priceless, since the spray was dispersed enough to coat his boots.

Once Cerys had left his arms, Dai had been hovering on the margins, and his face was perfectly readable, even in the low light: *Hasn't he ever encountered someone with a head wound before?*

Then Dai said out loud, which had to be one of the few times he had ever spoken in the presence of Prince Cadwaladr, "We probably should wait for the healer to come before we move him, my lord. Maybe he'll remember more once Saran gets here."

The boy was getting bold, perhaps too bold, but Cadwaladr simply waved a hand. He was more interested in getting one of his lackeys to wipe the vomit off his boots than slapping Dai down. And as was typical, one of his many underlings, this time Geraint, hastened to give him a cloth from his own purse.

In truth, Dai had said only what was obvious to everyone else. With Cadwaladr otherwise occupied, they got Marc back down to the ground, at which point, Gareth felt it was appropriate to ask, "Do you know *why* you left the pavilion?"

"No. I'm sorry." But then Marc gazed at him in such a steady fashion Gareth suddenly thought this was the one question he *did* remember the answer to, but also the one question he didn't want to answer.

"So you have no idea how long ago you came out here?" Dai asked, in an impressively innocuous tone.

"No." He attempted a shake of his head, before arresting the movement since likely it hurt. "I can't remember anything before—" His eyes crossed as he thought, "—I remember eating." And then some understanding seemed to pass through his mind. "We aren't at St. Kentigern's. This is Holywell."

"Yes." Gareth sat back on his heels, feeling increasingly confident that Marc was going to remember more as time went on, though he might never remember the exact moment he was injured. The mind worked strangely that way. Eventually, Gareth might have to press him on the lie he'd told about why he was in the field, but that shouldn't be done in public or right now. Gareth was quite sure he was here to meet someone. The question was if that person was Cerys or someone else.

He patted Marc's shoulder. "Do not worry. It will come or it won't. We will talk later."

He stepped away to allow Saran to take his place. The crowd had parted for her with complete willingness, much as it had for Gareth himself, an indication of their respect for her manner, her skills, and her discretion, all of which had earned her the deference they paid her. In her role as healer, she knew far more about what was really going on at court than anyone in the king's retinue, including him, Prince Hywel, Gwen, or Abbot Rhys. She guarded her reputation fiercely too, with the tenacity of a priest. In truth, she treated what people told her when she helped them with the same care a priest might take to the confessional. She was his stepmother-in-law, but Gareth already knew she would tell him nothing about Marc, even if she knew.

Saran had only to look at the situation to start shaking her head. "I shouldn't be doing this in the middle of a field. It would have been better if you hadn't raised him up at all. He could have had a neck injury which you would have made worse!"

Gareth took his chastisement with good grace, not explaining that Marc himself had been the first to try to sit up nor that Cadwaladr had been the one to attempt to get him to his feet.

Dai, on the other hand, was offended on their behalf and not afraid to speak his mind to his grandmother. "We thought he was dead, and he started breathing again only after Tad rolled him over!

Once he was alive again, we didn't want his wound to get dirty in the mud."

Saran lifted a hand to Dai. "I stand corrected, *cariad*."

Dai instantly knelt beside his grandmother and wrapped his arms around her shoulders. "Sorry, Nain. I didn't mean to sound so abrupt. We really did do what we thought was right."

"I know you did, as you always do." She patted Dai's hand. "Well, he's awake now."

Once Dai released Saran, he, Rhys, and Gareth stepped farther into the darkness, leaving the field, literally, to others for now.

"Are you going to tell us what happened to you earlier?" For the first time, Gareth noted the unlit lantern Dai held at his side. "Where did you go?"

"That is a story too."

Gareth allowed himself a laugh. "It's more than a little ironic that Marc would have been among the first to know all about it if he hadn't been half-killed in this field."

"Or maybe ironic isn't the right word," Abbot Rhys said. "Would a better one be *deliberate?*"

18

Day Two
Gwen

With Nest and Sister Efa promising to stay behind to watch over Helen in Cristina's room, Gwen encouraged Taran to come with her into King Owain's. He'd been reluctant to leave his love, but he was concerned that the trunk had been left unlocked, and he went through the ledgers one by one, paying as close attention as he could manage when his mind was really in the next room. If the intruder was interested in Gwynedd's accounts, he'd had full access to those records, but he hadn't taken any of them with him.

While Gwen tidied the room, Taran also expended a modicum of attention on the loose scrolls and documents, most of which were legal agreements for land disputes. There should have been ninety-three and, after careful counting, there still were. "If I'm going to unroll each one, I'll need the ledger that lists every document in this trunk. We brought that with us, but I need space to lay out every item and mark it present. That will take time I'd rather not spend, and quite honestly, don't see any need to spend."

"But the trunk should have been locked, right?"

"Should have been." He shrugged. "I see no sign of tampering. Why would anyone risk his life for a few documents?" Again, his eyes went to the wall between the two rooms, and Gwen understood his attention had wandered again to Helen. He wanted to be with her, and Gwen was keeping them apart.

She still didn't let him go. They both knew they could trust Abbess Nest to care for Helen, even protect her with her own life, if necessary. That was the iron will behind the gentle smile. It hadn't taken very long, no more than a short conversation, for Gwen to see it and understand how her husband could admire the woman so much, beyond the fact that she'd taken him in at the lowest point in his life.

What Gwen needed from Taran in this moment was information. When Gwen didn't fill the lengthening pause with the news that he could go, he gave her a nod that indicated he knew what she was about and sat wearily in one of the chairs near the low fire. Marc would have ensured it was going well by the time King Owain retired for the night, but he remained absent, so it was Gwen who poked and prodded it to a fuller flame. Then she poured Taran the last cup of wine from the same carafe from which Sioned had drunk.

Taran was unhappier than Gwen had ever seen him, but he wasn't incoherent, and while he took the cup readily enough, he didn't down it in one gulp as Sioned had. Taran was not one to indulge to excess anyway, and Gwen was not worried about getting the information she needed from him, with or without the lubrication of wine. Helen wasn't dead, and while Taran was devastated to see her unconscious body on the bed, his mind was perfectly capable of turning to who might have hurt her and why. While everything could possibly be explained by her being in the wrong place at the wrong time, Taran's demeanor so far had made it clear there was more to the story than he had told.

The Taran who could tell her that story was the one Gwen needed. The sooner that version of him returned, the better off not only would he be, but potentially all Gwynedd.

And because of that, she didn't begin by saying, "I am so sorry, Taran," but instead took a more straightforward approach. "Gareth and I—and every one of the people who love you—will do everything in our power to discover who did this to Helen. But you know as well as I that we need more to go on. I am ready to listen to whatever you have to say to me. You know me. You can trust me."

He took another sip and nodded, not even reluctantly. "I do know you." He gave her a small smile. "You were such an inquisitive child from the moment you opened your eyes and looked around the room. So many nights your mother had such a time getting you to sleep!" He put out a hand. "Don't get me wrong, you were as sweet as the day was long. You still are."

Gwen sat very still. He had spoken musingly, as if he had forgotten why they were there as he'd been talking. He had never spoken to Gwen of her childhood or her mother, in all the years she'd lived at Aber. She had observed him, but it had never occurred to her that he would have paid attention to her as a child. And while Gwen often thought about her own mother, her memories of her were colored by the long years of caring for Gwalchmai that had resulted from her death. For many of those years, Gwen had been angry at her mother for dying.

Now that Gwen was a mother herself, she knew without a doubt that her mother would never have willingly abandoned her. At ten, that had been an impossible understanding. She knew only that she'd *been* abandoned.

Unusually for him, Taran was so absorbed in his own concerns he didn't seem to realize how his words had affected Gwen. "I know you will do your best for her, and I am trying not to think about what happens if you fail, or if she—" His voice cracked, but he immediately took another sip of wine to steady himself. Taran's story was one Gareth would have liked to hear firsthand, but it seemed important to get it out of him right now, before he changed his mind or thought better of sharing the truth in the light of morning.

"I need you to begin at the beginning, if such a thing is possible, Taran. I don't know what information you have that might help, but right now I know nothing."

"We met so many years ago." Taran's expression turned inward as he settled into memory. "Owain and I were wild then, sowing our oats." He suddenly rose to his feet and began straightening the room in an entirely unnecessary fashion, since Gwen had already fixed everything she could fix, piling the bandages on the floor in the corner to await the arrival of Marc or a servant to take them away and removing the bloody bedcurtains and blanket. Apparently, the extra blanket with which she'd replaced the bloody one wasn't quite as square as he desired. "Or rather, the king was. I was standing watch outside."

"Like Gareth with Hywel." Gwen hadn't ever heard Taran say King Owain's given name in public, or if she had, she couldn't remember. The two men had been friends their whole lives, and she imagined Taran really did call the king *Owain* in private. She would not ever have assumed *private* would include her.

Taran laughed ruefully, acknowledging a truth. Owain had been the son of a king and Taran merely his friend. Their mutual status had been set from birth, and neither had questioned it in all their fifty years of living. "Helen was never one of his women, not that the king didn't try." His lips twitched in a smile. "Owain has apologized since."

"Everyone was young and foolish once," Gwen said, thinking of a similar conversation with Hywel about which Gareth had told her.

Taran drew in a breath. "But I was unacceptable to Helen's father. That was clear from the moment I stepped into his presence. He laughed at me when I asked for her hand. *Laughed.*"

Gwen was truly astonished. "How could you have been unacceptable to her father? You are a lord yourself, she was illegitimate, and you were offering her, in a sense, legitimacy."

"He still had eyes on a bigger prize."

Gwen's eyes narrowed. "Not the king!"

"King Henry certainly had a roving eye, as you well know, and many children over many years, but no, not that. She was never pretty enough for him." He shrugged. "Even I can admit Ranulf made an advantageous match for her. His name was Roger Fitzroy."

Gwen stared at Taran, almost more daunted by this news than any other tonight. "Her husband was an illegitimate son of King Henry?"

"He isn't important except that he gave her access to the highest levels of court."

"How did you meet her?"

"It was right after King Henry bestowed the earldom of Chester on her father, Ranulf. He'd installed him as quickly as was seemly after the White Ship went down, specifically to keep Gwynedd in check. Owain and I went with our fathers to a conference—" He permitted himself a little laugh, "—much like this one, but with Ranulf at the Dee. It was supposed to be about peace between England and Wales. And it did result in peace, after a fashion."

The White Ship, which had gone down in the English Channel with all passengers but one, had been carrying not only the heir to the throne of England but Richard d'Avranches, the Earl of Chester at the time. King Henry and Ranulf, Helen's father (and the father of the current earl) had already been close companions for many years. Once Henry's son died, and the former earl with him, it was natural for the king to turn to Ranulf. In so doing, he increased Ranulf's power ten-fold.

"If I'm correct about the timing of your meeting with Helen," Gwen said, "ever since then, Gwynedd hasn't even attempted to gain any land east of the Dee. At most, we've managed a few raids."

Taran nodded. "We were confined to contesting the very lands on which we stand now; In truth, old King Gruffydd had no attachment to Cheshire. Those lands are held by Saxons. He could not rule them, and because Gwynedd was neutralized as a threat to anywhere beyond the Dee, Ranulf was able to spend most of his subsequent years in Normandy."

"And took his daughter with him?"

"To court, anyway," Taran said. "And there she married, and there she stayed."

"And then, with Henry's death fifteen years later, England went to war with itself," Gwen said.

"By then Helen was ensconced at court."

Gwen knew as well as Taran the intrigue, deaths, famine, and hatreds that had been sparked by the simple fact that two people could not both sit on the throne of England at the same time. The conflict between Maud, Henry's daughter, and Stephen, Henry's nephew, had torn England, and the people of England, apart. That history also explained so much about how they'd arrived here tonight: Helen's status, the secrecy of her presence in Gwynedd, and her father's refusal of Taran.

Taran had managed to entirely gloss over his actual meeting and interactions with Helen. They were none of Gwen's business anyway. She was almost embarrassed it had taken her as long as it had to realize where this conversation was going. "She became your spy!"

"Not mine—never mine—or maybe only fleetingly for a night or two at a time over the years. It was Owain she served faithfully through her connection to me, and her marriage was most helpful in that regard—more helpful than one to me would have been! Until today, Owain and I have been the only ones who even knew she existed. I am quite certain neither her father nor her brother has ever been aware that the attachment to me we formed over those few days was real, not even after I asked for her hand."

"How old were you when you met?"

"Just past twenty. She was eighteen."

Gwen felt a surge of pride at the young man Taran had been. Welsh and the companion of the future King of Gwynedd, he'd had the confidence to stand before Helen's father and lay bare his heart.

"What happened after Helen's father said no?"

Taran scoffed. "He barely heard me out, seeing my love for her, and hers for me, as nothing more than a passing fancy. And if in the subsequent days and weeks Helen railed at her father, he laughed her away. To him, Helen, along with every other noble woman, born illegitimate or not, was simply a coin to be spent. He wasn't going to waste her on a love match to some Welshman whose name he forgot within moments of hearing it."

Not for the first time, Gwen was grateful she'd been born a bard's daughter and a Welshwoman. Her father had refused several suitors' hands, Gareth's among them, but he'd looked carefully at every suitor's character, not just at the station he held. He had also not sent her to a land far from where she was born because of some perceived political advantage her marriage to a foreign lord would give him.

Now Taran let out an audible sigh. "King Gruffydd forbade me to pursue her and, God help me, I obeyed him."

"She never forgot you, though."

"She did not." Taran bent his head. "Nor I her."

Gwen thought Taran was giving himself too little credit. From the outside, it looked as if Helen had served Owain all these years because she loved Taran, even if she couldn't have him. "From the way you're behaving, and the fact that you asked her to marry you, I'm guessing she's a widow now?"

"Yes." So much history and love and longing was carried in that one word. "Her husband died last year. As the wife of Henry's son and the daughter of the Earl of Chester, she moved with ease throughout the royal court. She was a friend to both Empress Maud and Stephen's queen, Matilda. In fact, the two queens often used her to send messages between them."

Gwen found her mouth opening in surprise. "Maud talks to Matilda?"

Taran frowned. "Of course. They're cousins, both grand-daughters of King Malcolm of Scotland."

Gwen mostly kept the complicated lineages of English royalty straight, but only the broad strokes. They'd been at the court of King David of Scotland, now revealed to be uncle to both Maud and Matilda, only last May for the knighting of Maud's son, Prince Henry. She had known David was Maud's uncle, but had not remembered he was also Matilda's. Her son—King Stephen's son—Eustace, was equally Malcolm's great-nephew. David could just have as easily allied with Stephen as Maud. He'd chosen as he had for political reasons and issues of power. He thought he could get more from Maud than from Stephen.

The current Earl Ranulf, though not royal himself, had married the daughter of another illegitimate son of King Henry, Robert of Gloucester, and therefore tied himself equally into this family dispute. Anyone who'd hoped these ties would ensure Ranulf's allegiance had been continually disappointed over the years. Ranulf served himself and always had. In that, he was a lot like Cadwaladr, albeit less frenzied, more calculating, and slightly less selfish, though admittedly that bar was very low.

"That's how you so often have had some warning as to how things are faring in England. She sends word."

"Not often, and very carefully," Taran said, "but yes."

Love was a funny thing, as Gwen well knew. So was loss, which laid one low in ways that made a girl want to cry out years after someone was gone. It didn't matter how many loved ones were lost either. Grief and love were simply two sides of the same coin; it was impossible to have one without the other. Taran was on the edge of grief now, hoping against hope that he hadn't loved so long for nothing. He'd envisioned a glorious future with Helen, a future that for decades he had been hoping to see and feared he never would. Now he feared its loss, and his hopes and dreams were carried along with every rise and fall of Helen's chest.

In Gwen's experience, suffering filled the space between what a person wanted to have happen, and what did happen. The solution might be to want nothing, or to love nobody. Certainly, the impulse was to shake a fist at the sky and beg to never feel this way again, much as Gareth had been doing this past year, ever since Cadwaladr had returned to Gwynedd. But one always felt grief again. Those who were strong enough survived to carry on and even love again. After Rhun's death, Taran himself had said as much. She would not presume to say any of it back to him now.

"You said she told you she would return, ready to finally marry you. How is it we found her in Queen Cristina's room?"

"I have no idea."

For thirty years, Taran and King Owain between them had kept secret an entire world. But even knowing how much Taran still hadn't told her, in this, Gwen believed him.

19

Day Two
Gareth

"Look out." Rhys spoke low in Gareth's ear. "We are being invaded by spies."

Gareth turned to see Iwan, King Owain's old friend, but a man about whom Gareth knew distressingly nothing, heading towards them. Mari's father, Ralph, walked at his side.

Gareth swung around to Rhys. "You use the plural. They are both spies, then?"

"Yes." It was a profound admission.

"I wondered. Tell me quickly what you know."

It was a command Rhys did not question. "Iwan has been serving in King Stephen's court these last ten years."

"Like Ralph."

"Yes, except Ralph has always served Maud."

"As did you."

"Except, unlike me, Iwan has always belonged to Owain."

"How did Hywel not know of him?"

"That I couldn't say."

"But Iwan is Welsh?"

"His mother was Welsh. His father was the brother of Bernard, the Bishop of St. David's."

Gareth gaped at Rhys, so surprised his breath caught in his chest. "I have heard of this man. Bernard was an advisor to Matilda, King Henry's wife, and this nephew has been an ambassador from the bishopric since he came of age. But his name was—"

"Jehan." Abbot Rhys said the name as if they were speaking French instead of Welsh. "John of Pembroke to the English." These were all the same name, just pronounced differently according to the language being spoken: Jehan, John, Iwan.

Gareth barked a laugh. "Of course. I'm a fool not to have made the connection."

"Never a fool. There was no way you could have known."

"Why is he here with us, as if he were one of us?"

"He has decided to come home."

And then there wasn't time for any more conversation because the two men had arrived. "What can we do?" Ralph's tone was anticipatory, even excited, a sentiment mirrored in Iwan's face.

With his newfound knowledge, Gareth had a moment of insight that the two men may have become spies out of obligation, but they had continued their service in the way they had all these years for the same reason Abbot Rhys had left it: because they *loved* what they did. In the end, Abbot Rhys had decided such a love was unhealthy for him and had become a monk.

Regardless, these were two extra hands Gareth hadn't expected, and also experienced ones that might be useful. He had the Dragons at his disposal too, and he had every intention of using every one of them he could. He'd already put Steffan and Iago to work. But with two attacks in a single night, the rest of the Dragons were right where they were supposed to be: guarding Prince Hywel. Even if Gareth might have other tasks for them later, like using them as scouts or to pursue whoever had done this, he wouldn't be sending them out tonight in the dark. If nothing else, he had no clear idea in which direction to send them.

Gareth longed for the long days of summer when the sun was in the sky almost too many hours. Tonight, a torch gave him light to see by, nominally, but it still wasn't enough to prevent him from stumbling about in the dark.

Now that a stretcher had finally arrived to carry Marc to the abbey infirmary, he and Saran were able to leave the field. With their departure, so went the interest of the king's court, and of Cadwaladr himself. The prince had no desire to do investigative work if it meant mucking about in the field in the dark. With him in the lead, the onlookers trooped back to the pavilion to drink more mead and speculate as to how and why this had happened.

Giving Ralph and Iwan important work was also an effective means of heading off any curiosity they might have been experiencing regarding Gareth's earlier absence. So he sent the two spies in an ever enlarging circle pattern around the field, with the spot Marc had lain as the central point. They were to look for anything that might help them identify his attacker.

Then he turned to Rhys, who was, of course, another spy. "I need you too."

"I am here to serve."

Gareth laughed. He couldn't help it. Rhys had spoken in that deadpan tone of his that was at one and the same time serious and mocking. But the truth was, he had spent his life serving others. The middle of a muddy field was no different. That was not to say he wouldn't feel differently when he knew exactly what Gareth was asking. "Do you know what I need you for?"

Rhys wet his lips. "Are you asking for help with more than the investigation?"

Gareth's expression was rueful as he made a motion towards where Ralph and Iwan were walking, bent over with their eyes on the ground. After such a huge crowd had come to gawk, many footprints had disturbed the scene, and what might have been crushed grass had given way to mud. Gareth didn't expect them to find anything of use, but he needed someone to look.

Rhys's chin came up, and as he was still holding the torch, Gareth could see his expression clearly. "You want me to keep an eye on *them*."

"I'm sorry. I know it's wrong even to ask." Gareth was uncomfortable about what he was asking Rhys to do as Rhys might be about doing it. "I simply don't know them."

"And I do."

It was an enormous relief to have Rhys understand what Gareth was asking without him having to say much of anything at all.

Gareth had many close friends and family, but few men could see what was in his mind as well as Abbot Rhys.

"It's all right, Gareth. Those men have been my friends, if friendship is possible amongst spies, but I can see as well as you they are taking excessive joy in aiding your investigation. Neither strikes me as the type to fell a man in the middle of a field, but they are practiced in deception. They could just as easily be chortling about how they're pulling the wool over your eyes. I will join them, and then we'll see which it is."

"Thank you. I know King Owain trusts them—"

Rhys made a gesture to cut him off. "You don't have to apologize to me. In point of fact, I'm glad to see you trusting your own instincts and methods again." And then at the quizzical way Gareth tipped his head, he added, "It wasn't only Gwalchmai who lost a step a year ago. You did too. Nobody was murdered and you thought you'd failed anyway."

A moment earlier, Gareth wouldn't have said he was right, but now that Rhys had spoken, he knew it was true. And Gwen would know exactly what he was talking about.

"It's Cadwaladr. Every time I look at him, I feel like raising a fist to the heavens and shouting *curses be upon him!*"

Rhys's expression was understanding, but not pitying. "You are wise not to speak of this to anyone but me. I suppose it's futile to say you shouldn't let him upset your center of balance. That would be like telling the wind not to blow when it rains."

Gareth wet his lips, unable to remember the last time he'd blurted out a truth like that. Even Dai had more self-control these days. "Perhaps we can talk of this later—"

"We have prints." Ralph spoke from where he'd come to a halt on the northern side of the field, some twenty yards away, by a gate in the wall. His voice was just loud enough for them to hear but not loud enough to draw the attention of any of the guests in the pavilion. The last thing they wanted was Cadwaladr realizing there was something interesting to be seen after all and trekking into the field again with his followers. Fortunately, the pavilion lay behind them to the south.

"I've got another set over here." Iwan had straightened from where he'd been doing his own circuit, next to the field's eastern wall. "This was someone wearing too big shoes. A boy doing a man's job, is my guess."

Gareth was happy to have a discussion of his feelings interrupted by a genuine find. Two people had been attacked tonight, and he didn't have either the time or the inclination to worry about what was going on inside himself. "I would be very interested to hear how you know that."

Iwan held his torch low to the ground over a boot print. "This person was walking on his heels. You can tell that from the way the toe of the foot is lightly impressed into the soil, while the heel of the foot goes deep. It's an odd way to walk. An impossible one, really, for any distance."

Gareth crouched to study more closely what Iwan was showing him, and then thanked him for the instruction. He could have been offended that Iwan felt the need to tell him his job, but he decided not to be. He hadn't actually seen something like this before. In the dark, he didn't know that he would have noticed what was special about these particular prints.

Iwan continued, "The prints don't go anywhere near Marc's position, so they might not really be what you were looking for. They come from where Ralph is standing by that gate over there."

With Rhys still holding the torch, they went together to the gate where Ralph was waiting.

"Here are two sets of prints." Ralph lifted a hand like he was a bard directing a chorus. "They came through this gate together from the north, practically right on top of each other, and then separated once they were in the field. One continued on to where we found Marc. The second set is the one Iwan showed you, which curved away."

"Those that go to Marc aren't going to be useful to us," Rhys said. "They're Dai's. As you recall, he said he had only just arrived at the field when Cerys started screaming."

Gareth swung around to eye the distance from the middle of the field, where Marc had fallen, back to the gate, where he now stood. Then he walked a few paces beyond the gate, heading north. As Ralph had said, the prints were clear, at times practically on top of one another and in other places side-by-side. If the owner of one set really was Dai, then he had followed after whoever had made the other prints.

Rhys answered his unasked question. "Dai was coming from the north because he and I had been at the mill together. He followed these very prints and had reached the gate when Cerys began to scream. By the increased distance between his steps once he entered the field, you can tell that he had begun to run."

Iwan's face had a dubious cast to it, and he opened his mouth, potentially to cast doubt on the scenario Rhys had just described. The abbot overrode him before he could. "Before that, he was with me. I can assure you he had nothing whatsoever to do with Marc's injury."

What was astounding to Gareth, in this moment, was the knowledge that Rhys himself wasn't being entirely honest. Or to be more charitable, since Gareth could perfectly well believe the order of events he was relating, Rhys was speaking of something he could not know about firsthand. From his own explanation earlier, he had arrived in the field after Dai and from the opposite direction.

It was a good reminder that if Abbot Rhys could mask the truth—out of necessity, instinct, or habit—so could every other person here.

20

Day Two

Dai

Dai headed into the pavilion, having heard a brief summary of what had happened in the guesthouse, and was now under new orders from his father to question anyone he could about everything he could. His first encompassing glance told him only the most hardy and serious drinkers remained. That didn't bode well for getting answers to his questions. Sometimes drink made a man more talkative and sometimes it made him morose. Once a man was deep in his cups, one never knew which of the two was going to rise to the fore.

Given the late hour, Dai wasn't really surprised to find so few still awake. By the time the sun set, half of eastern Gwynedd had turned up for the feast, so the pavilion had been crowded all evening. Now that the music had stopped and the excitement appeared over, the revelers had dispersed to their beds, whether here at the encampment or in their own homes within a few miles of the abbey.

For Dai, naturally, the excitement was still in full swing.

He glanced to where Sioned slept with her head in her arms, her last cup of mead still half-drunk by her left elbow. While Cristina had taken King Owain off to bed, she appeared to have forgotten about her maid. Although they'd never had a conversation about it, Dai knew Sioned had been married once, but her husband had died, and she had no living children who ever visited her. In short, she had nobody to care for her at a time like this.

Whatever else, it was too cold to be sleeping outside. After moving her cup a few feet farther down the table so she wouldn't knock it over if she startled, Dai gently shook her awake. "You need your bed."

Sioned looked up at him, initially with no recognition. Then she blinked and the corners of her mouth turned down. "Where?"

Dai frowned. "Don't you have a room—"

"I'm not going into that guesthouse ever again!"

"I'm so sorry," Dai said quickly. "There must be an extra pallet somewhere?"

He was embarrassed to think how little he knew about where people like Sioned might be sleeping. The Dragons had their own tents, of course. The encampment servants had theirs. The men of the garrison had theirs. His family had their wagons, and otherwise were on the ground floor of the guesthouse. Dai himself had multiple options for where to lay his head. In order to accommodate everyone, the king's court routinely traveled with wagons full of gear and supplies, to account for any weather and circumstance.

Sioned was recovering, and perhaps hadn't been as drunk as all that in the end. "Don't worry about me, Dai. I'll manage."

Between one breath and the next, her manner transformed to exactly the opposite of her earlier incoherence. She was speaking clearly enough, in fact, that Dai deliberated asking her questions about the investigation.

But she was already rising to her feet, focused on leaving, and he decided the morning was soon enough to ask her what she remembered.

Neither Marc nor Helen were dead, after all. While his family would still be pursuing with the full force of their abilities those who had attacked them, their hearts were less heavy. In fact, they all had a bit of hope inside that everything really could be well in the end. Dai had never started an investigation feeling so cheerful.

That wasn't to say the matter before him wasn't urgent. Helen was lying in the guesthouse and Marc in the infirmary from wounds they hadn't inflicted on themselves! Danger loomed around any corner.

He thought about calling Sioned back after all, to escort her to the encampment and use that act as a cover for questioning her. At the very least, the last thing they needed was for someone walking alone to be attacked, especially the queen's maid.

But she was already gone. Having failed utterly with Sioned, and since his charge was to interview whomever he could, Dai decided to move on to the remaining Dragons. That way, he'd have something to show for his evening of effort. They were trained to respond well to the type of questions he was charged with asking, would know why he was asking them, and would already be champing at the bit to help. In addition, they all had been friends and companions of Dai's father for years now, so had participated often in these investigations. If anyone knew death, and the relief at its absence for one more day, it was these men.

All of them, including the prince, were still sitting at the same table as when he'd last seen them. Hywel himself sat between Gruffydd, the captain of the Dragons, and Cadoc, the best archer in Gwynedd, if not Wales, and a former assassin. Cadoc had seen Dai coming, so by the time he sat amongst them, they had taken thoughtful last sips of their mead and were looking at him expectantly. None were drunk, of course. Gruffydd would have kept a tight rein on his men if necessary, but were any of them inclined to overindulge, they wouldn't have been chosen to be Dragons from the start. It was a good thing Dai had learned that lesson or he might have ultimately been rejected from their company.

Steffan and Iago were the only ones missing, but he knew from his father that he'd already sent them to guard the guesthouse. Dai wasn't sorry to know some of his own companions were keeping his mother and siblings safe.

Prince Hywel began, as was his right. "Don't bother relating what happened in the field. We already know: Marc was felled by an unknown assailant. Cerys screamed when she stumbled upon him." It made sense they would know about it, since Evan sat among them. Not only had he helped keep back the crowd around Marc's body, but he had assisted Gareth on many occasions before now. Because of him, the Dragons might know more about the scene than Dai did. "He is not dead, thankfully, so what do you need from us?"

It was somewhat gratifying to Dai that Hywel hadn't said, "What does *your father* need from us?"

So he got straight to the point. "I can't imagine it's a surprise to you that I need to hear anything unusual you might have seen tonight. Someone hit Marc on the head. He has no idea who might have done it. If Marc's attacker followed him from the pavilion and then returned, maybe one of you saw him."

"Are you thinking this was before or after Gareth left with your brother and you followed Cadwaladr?" Trust Aron to be the one to voice that question. He was the Dragon who saw connections others missed. "Does one have anything to do with the other?"

None of the Dragons would know yet about Dai's sojourn at the mill. He wanted to tell them, but this was not the time or place. "We don't know the exact timing. While Saran doesn't think Marc could have been lying in the grass for hours, he could have been there for an hour, slowly weakening. Eventually, he would have woken on his own or he would have died." Then Dai hesitated, wondering how much was safe to say. He felt he had to say something. Resisting the urge to look behind him, he dropped his voice to a whisper. "We have actually had *two* attacks tonight." He almost laughed to see how unsurprised they looked. "They may be related. They may not. At this moment, we are sure of nothing. The other occurred in the guesthouse, which is where Steffan and Iago have gone, in case you were wondering."

Gruffydd grunted. "You say *attacks,* but not murders. Nobody is dead?"

"Not yet."

"And we won't borrow trouble worrying about the possibility, eh?" Evan barked a laugh. "You sound more like your father every day."

Aron, who was sitting to Dai's right, nudged his elbow. "He means that as a compliment, you know."

Dai grinned, accepting their jesting for the relief it was. If someone *had* died, they would still be making jokes, but these would have been much darker.

"Who was attacked?" Prince Hywel asked.

"I can't talk about it."

"Can't ... or won't? And what does the queen have to do with any of this?" Then Hywel scoffed as Dai pressed his lips together. "I know for certain it was she who sent your father on his way. I saw it."

Prince Hywel had been delighted to insert Dai's family into Cristina's household. He didn't trust his stepmother any more than Dai's parents did. Dai's single useful thought had been that, while Prince Hywel wanted them to spy on Cristina, perhaps Cristina also wanted to use them to look into the prince's mind. He was the heir to the throne, after all. Cristina's eldest son wouldn't come of age for nine more years. Though King Owain wasn't elderly, per se, he wasn't exactly *young* anymore either. If King Owain were to die before Dafydd became a man, Cristina would lose her position as queen. No wonder she was doing everything in her power to solidify her standing. If that meant wooing Dai's parents away from Hywel or simply as a way into Prince Hywel's heart, so be it.

"My lord—"

"Leave the poor boy be, my lord." Gruffydd gave Dai a wry smile. "Gareth told him not to say anything, and he's attempting to be obedient. He would tell us more if he could or we needed to know it."

Hywel tsked. "Fine. We will do as he bids. For your insolence, Gruffydd, you get to go first."

Gruffydd shrugged. "I am ashamed to say I didn't see anything that seems useful. Dozens of people entered and left this evening. I don't know even half of the people here. Many are local. If I made assumptions, it was that people were leaving for reasons that were their business and none of mine."

Dai leaned forward, intent now that the answers were coming. "Can you identify anyone at all who behaved in a manner you thought unusual?"

Gruffydd shook his head. "I hate to just pick someone unfairly. But if I had to, Cristina's maid has been behaving oddly."

"She was with Cristina in the guesthouse."

Gruffydd waved a hand. "I meant before that."

Dai interest sharpened. "When exactly was this? What do you mean *before*?"

"This was before Gwen left." He frowned. "Sioned sloped into the pavilion and found a seat amongst the other servants as if she'd been here all along. My guess? She was with a man."

"Marc?" Dai asked.

The others laughed, and Gruffydd said gently, a bit like Dai should have known the answer without asking, "Marc fancies himself a gallant with the ladies, and Sioned is older than me. No. She definitely wasn't with Marc."

Aron nudged him. "There was no reason you should know that."

Dai appreciated his kindness, but he was embarrassed to have misunderstood the way things were. He had a job to do, and his father was trusting him to do it. "Anyone else?"

"I was heading to the latrine when I bumped into two monks," Aron said. "It was so dark on the path, I didn't see them until I was upon them. One almost knocked me over, and when I flailed out with my hand, he caught it to steady me. In that moment, I felt his ring. Even at the time, I thought the fact that he was wearing one odd, since monks give up their possessions when they join their order. I've never seen any monk but an abbot wear a ring. Regardless, they apologized and headed away. I forgot about them until now."

"Which latrine was this?"

Aron's chin wrinkled, as if he was embarrassed. "The one associated with the monks' dormitory. That's why I thought it was odd to see them leaving the abbey instead of going to the church or to bed."

"Aron likes his privacy." Evan clapped a hand on his back. For once, Dai didn't care much for the Dragons' teasing. He could understand Aron's sentiments.

Aron merely shrugged. "It wasn't really that much farther to walk, and with Compline ended, the monks should have been in bed. Or so I thought. I was alone in the latrine."

Compline was the last holy office of the day. The residents of the encampment had attended Vespers, a mass held at sunset, but all the monks and nuns would have continued their daily round of holy offices. This included Abbess Nest, who'd had a seat at the high table for the meal, but had not returned to the pavilion after Compline. Just as well, really, since she was available to bring to the guesthouse after Helen was attacked.

"Could you get a sense of what kind of ring it was?" Dai asked.

"The setting was flat with an engraving, so I'm thinking it was a signet. I felt it under my thumb, but I couldn't tell you what it pictured." Aron had a reputation for being not only observant, but the most clever of the Dragons. He was looking contrite now, as if he should have been able to make out the image just from feeling it under the pad of his finger for a single heartbeat.

Cadoc leaned into Dai and said in his ear as if he were conveying a secret, but nonetheless spoke loudly enough for everyone to hear him. "Don't mind him. He's distracted. A girl, you see."

Gruffydd grunted. "Lord Hywel has given you permission to ask Lord Ifon for her hand! What are you waiting for? Get on with it and stop moping about. You're a Dragon! It's unbecoming."

"I will. In time. When I'm ready." Aron's eyes skated for a moment to Hywel, who looked on, amused.

Dai had never known Aron to be so timid, but then, Dai himself had never been in love. He looked around at the other Dragons. "Last thoughts?"

Prince Hywel pursed his lips. "I should be able to tell you something, since I, among everyone here, was facing the crowd when I was singing, but I confess I'm at a loss."

"Nid bob dydd yr ydym yn lladd mochyn," Gruffydd said. *It's not every day we slaughter a pig.*

Hywel was one for old sayings too. "Llwm tir a boro dafad." *Bare is the land where sheep graze.* "You might ask Meilyr and Gwalchmai. They were up on the dais longer."

Taking Hywel's suggestion as something of a command, Dai thanked the Dragons and then made his way to the dais where Dai's grandfather and uncle were talking quietly on a bench, working on a new song, as they would be.

"Taid, are you aware of what has happened?"

"You mean Marc? Is he dead? Saran hasn't returned, so I was hoping he would be all right."

"He's alive, as far as I know." Dai hastened to reassure him. "Did you see anything that struck you as odd tonight?"

Gwalchmai rolled his eyes and answered first. "Other than *everyone's* behavior?"

"What do you mean?"

"I saw Llelo leave with Gareth, and then you went after Cadwaladr." Gwalchmai made a gesture to encompass the pavilion. By now, it was all but empty. Even the Dragons were making their way to the exit. "I see the way a married woman looks at a man who isn't her husband. I know who drinks too much, who beats his wife, who gambles more than he can afford to lose. I know that Aron is in love with a cousin of Ifon of Rhos and she with him. What I don't know is why he hasn't asked for her hand already."

"All that from the dais?"

"Especially from the dais."

"Can you tell me anything about Marc ... and Cerys?"

Gwalchmai let out a thoughtful *humph*. "If they are together, they've been very careful. But then, they would have had to be since her husband is a jealous man."

Dai turned to survey the pavilion. "Anyone of interest here now?"

"Not that I can see. And why would there be? Whoever felled Marc is long gone or is blending in, one of us." Then Gwalchmai gave Dai a mischievous grin. "And let me just say, I'm quite sure father and I can be glad we weren't planning to sleep in the guesthouse tonight. Are you going to want space for yourself in our wagon?"

21

Day Three
Gareth

It might be past midnight, but it was long past time Gareth's family was able to talk to each other in the same place. His family, in this case, included Abbot Rhys and Abbess Nest. He wasn't entirely sure at what point Rhys had gone from close acquaintance to like an uncle. But it was in the same way that Nest had filled the gap left by the mother he didn't remember.

Without him realizing it had happened, his family had expanded yet again.

Nest, however, was a new addition for everyone but Gareth. That she was included was a reflection of the love and trust Gareth felt for her. Nest had given him a surety and confidence he hadn't had before he'd met her and, quite frankly, changed his life in ways for which, to this day, he was grateful. He was quite sure Gwen wouldn't ever have become his wife if not for Nest.

Those who knew of his early years thought Gareth must have been supremely confident to have refused to obey Prince Cadwaladr.

But in Gareth's heart, he knew how easily he could have made a different choice. Not that he would ever have cut off that boy's hand. But he might have found a less publicly defiant way to refuse. While that moment had transformed his life too and set him on the path he continued to tread, it had been merely the first step in making him the person he was today. These days, those who knew the story acted as if Gareth's character had been fully formed at that point. In truth, he'd been a boy, reaching to be a man in the best way he knew how. Like Llelo and Dai were now, Gareth had been balanced on the knife edge of maturity. The wrong sort of push could easily have sent him falling.

When they'd arrived at the abbey, Gareth had greeted Nest with a bear hug that had flushed her cheeks. She was looking her age, more so than a few years ago, as if the cares of running this abbey were visibly weighing on her in a way her responsibilities hadn't in the past. But her eyes remained bright with the same intelligence and forthrightness they'd always shown.

They'd pulled chairs close together around the fire in the guesthouse common room, and were working to keep their voices low. Other than the sleeping children and their nannies, they were the only ones in the guesthouse, but they were all feeling the pressures of the evening and didn't want to be overheard.

Dispensing with any niceties other than a hearty dollop of warm mead in everyone's cup, Gareth began: "This night has witnessed four events that occurred at almost exactly the same time. To have King Owain's room invaded, Helen attacked, and then Marc, the very man who cares for the king and his possessions, almost killed with a similar blow to the head as Helen, *cannot* be a coincidence. While I would prefer not to consider a conspiracy until I have to, I feel like I already have to. I realize I have always been the one to urge you not to assume anything, but we can go too far in the other direction."

"We don't have to assume these events are related to consider it," Gwen said. "In addition, it would certainly be a mistake to assume they *weren't*. As always, we will take the evidence as it comes."

Gareth gestured that Gwen should begin with her tale of finding Helen attacked in the guesthouse, outlining the details as succinctly as she'd told him and Llelo earlier, followed by a summarized version of her conversation with Taran. Gareth had already heard the complete story, but how Taran felt about these events could be kept private.

For his part, Gareth couldn't help feeling that for both Helen and Iwan, not to mention Ralph, to have decided to return home at nearly the exact same instant was an extraordinary coincidence. Then again, all three were of a certain age, with their time left in life growing short. And perhaps the situation in England was such that they saw the moment was right to flee a sinking ship. If so, that was something Gareth would like to hear more about all on its own. As it was, Gareth had a thousand more questions, but he could ask none of them. Iwan and Ralph had done good work with the footprints, but Cristina's orders to keep their circle small were still in effect. Gareth was quite sure she would not want anyone involved beyond his family of investigators. Since that was Gareth's inclination as well, he didn't choose to fight it.

Abbess Nest put up a hand. "You said *four* events? That sounds like three."

Her words were followed by complete silence, finally broken by Gareth, who coughed and laughed at the same time. "The fourth is not my tale to tell. I don't even know the entirety of what happened."

"Father, are you sure? Since this is about Cadwaladr..." Dai allowed his voice to trail off and tipped his head in Abbess Nest's direction.

"I can leave." Abbess Nest rose to her feet, not for a moment mistaking Dai's concern. "I don't need to be here if you don't want me here."

Gareth put out a hand. "That's not necessary. You should stay." He took in a breath. "I think you need to stay. As Dai intimated, this has to do with the king's brother, Cadwaladr."

From a standing position, Nest looked one by one into the faces of those who gazed back at her. Gareth found himself meeting her eyes, even knowing she could see right through him. On the one hand, he was embarrassed that Dai had forced them to reckon with this issue. And yet, his son was growing up, and he had a legitimate right to ask if they were sure of the wisdom of sharing what they knew about Cadwaladr with someone who was, to him, a stranger. Gareth had already decided not to share far more with Ralph and Iwan.

Gwen was looking at Gareth. "The question is more whether it's *fair* to include her in what we know."

"It will affect her future; it is her abbey." Gareth talked directly to Gwen as if they were the only ones in the room. "If events unfold adversely, she might be at a disadvantage if she doesn't know."

"But once she knows the truth, she can never go back," Gwen said.

Dai inserted himself again. "And we'll be giving her knowledge about Cadwaladr she didn't ask for—"

"We will be speaking the truth," Abbot Rhys interrupted. "Without the truth, we cannot make proper decisions. You would not be telling her what you know out of a sense of glee or a desire to gossip. You would be telling her because the safety and sanctity of her house might depend upon her knowing. There have been times mine has."

While they had been talking as if she wasn't there, Nest had slowly resumed her seat. "I realize I am new to your circle, but I am not entirely ignorant about what has gone on in Gwynedd these last years. It was my hand, as you may recall, that brought you the Book of Kells. I have been to Aber. I know at least something of why you say *Cadwaladr* with such weight! But you don't have to tell me anything you don't think I should know."

"He is directly responsible for the death of Prince Rhun," Dai said flatly.

"Not to mention the King of Deheubarth," Llelo added.

Nest accepted both statements as calmly as everything else they'd said so far.

"If knowing in any way helps ensure this abbey's survival, you want to hear it," Abbot Rhys said. "Another war might mean the end of you, especially if King Owain loses it. That is one reason I have so strongly supported this peace conference and King Owain's quest for Welsh sovereignty of this region. If the Normans regain these lands, control of this Welsh holy well will go to the Hen Blas monks. What we discuss here now might really be crucial to ensuring that doesn't happen."

Nest looked at Rhys, and then her eyes met Gareth's again. In that moment, he thought he saw tears. Then she looked away, and by the time she spoke again, her tears had been replaced by her more usual serenity. "I will listen quietly, and if I have questions, I will ask them."

But he'd seen her doubt and fear and grief, and once seen, they couldn't be forgotten. Just like the information they were about to convey to her about Cadwaladr.

"Tell us, Dai," Gwen said softly.

Dai suddenly turned rueful. "Despite this long preamble, I'm suddenly feeling what Abbot Rhys and I saw tonight might be the *least* important of these events."

"If only that were true." Gareth couldn't help feeling a little proud of this family. Honesty was the coin in which they dealt, and they all had a hand in that. "Just tell us."

So Dai talked, Abbot Rhys joining in at appropriate moments.

"When Cadwaladr came out of the mill, we split up," Dai said. "I entered the mill."

"While I followed Cadwaladr back to the pavilion. He returned as directly as he went, albeit with a detour, finally, to the latrine."

"Which one?" Llelo sat up a little straighter.

Rhys didn't ask why he wanted to know. "The one at the back of the men's dormitory."

"Aron ran into two monks, coming from that latrine," Dai said.

"Did he?" And then Llelo said, "Steffan and I followed footprints from the guesthouse to the latrine. We lost them at that point with so many comings and goings. We saw no sign of the missing bed slat either. If that was, in fact, the weapon used on Helen, it's gone."

Gwen sat up a little straighter. "I don't think it's a stretch to suggest that Aron's monks are the same as Cristina's, though she met them nearer to the guesthouse."

"Intruders disguised as monks?" There was horror in Abbess Nest's voice, as well there might be.

"We will look for more evidence in the morning." Gareth then gestured again to Dai, who picked up the story of what he'd found in the mill, followed by what he'd learned from the Dragons.

"Cadwaladr always looks far too pleased with himself, but his look was particularly satisfied as he left the mill," Abbot Rhys said.

"Why would he have been there if not to meet someone?" Gwen asked. "Was he carrying anything in his hands when he left?"

"No," Abbot Rhys said. "Definitely not."

"A message was passed; I'm sure of it," Dai said.

"It could be the spilled grain *was* the message," Llelo said. "Grain spilled could mean, *proceed as we discussed* or something like that."

"That is not at all comforting!" Dai rubbed his chin, though he had little beard to smooth. "But it wouldn't be so different from communicating by tying a piece of ribbon of a certain color around a tree, or moving a candle from one side of a window to another. Odd to go all the way to the mill for it, though."

"These methods have been used by spies since spying began," Abbot Rhys said, "and it may be that, if Cadwaladr wasn't supposed to proceed, the meeting would have been longer."

"We found your footprints and those of the person you followed in the field, Dai," Gareth made sure his tone was approving. "Or rather, Iwan and Ralph did."

He didn't need to look pointedly at Abbot Rhys for him to realize he was asking without speaking about the loyalties of the two spies.

Rhys gave a somewhat uncharacteristic shrug. "I stayed with them afterwards. They seemed content with their contribution to the investigation. The three of us chatted about what we'd found and then retired for the night. They treat me like an old friend. Maybe I'm exactly that—old—but I can't help feeling that what we are seeing on the surface may be all there is to see with them."

Nest put up one hand. "The implication from the footprints is that whoever went to the mill was disguising the size and shape of his feet, meaning they are naturally smaller than the prints."

"Nothing we know precludes the person who met Cadwaladr being a woman." Gwen let herself laugh. "In fact, if he'd stayed inside the mill longer, we would have assumed he was meeting a woman. Cadwaladr does seem to have a knack with them."

"We do have a dozen half-grown boys here, not to mention a dormitory full of nuns." Abbess Nest had grimaced at the thought. "That said, none were missing from the holy office at Compline and, from what you've all said, that is the relevant hour when so many of these events occurred. I can assure you we had a full choir tonight, every man and woman accounted for. And every one in his or her bed afterwards."

"My apologies, Mother, but you're that certain?" Gwen asked.

"Every member of the abbey has a set place in the choir. Either I or my prior makes sure at every holy office that none are missing, and if any are, they are soon found. Our infirmary is even gratifyingly empty at this time."

"You have eased my mind, Mother. Thank you," Gareth said. "Not that we can be happy those two so-called monks Aron and Cristina saw were imposters. But at least we know now not to look within the abbey itself for our culprits."

"We can't lay the act of felling Marc or Helen on Cadwaladr either," Rhys said. "I followed him back to the pavilion, where he resumed his seat as if nothing was amiss. As it stands, I don't see how he is connected to the events in the guesthouse or in the field."

"How can the attack on Marc *not* be related to the one on Helen? They *have* to be." Not uncommonly, Gwen couldn't help skipping ahead to the *who* and *why* of a matter when Gareth wanted to focus only on what they *knew*. "It's too much of a coincidence to have Marc laid low just when the king's room is invaded. And with a similar wound! Could Cerys herself have been the one to attack Marc? Or both of them?"

"We found no weapon nearby," Rhys pointed out. "There's no evidence she isn't what she seems either."

"All she would have had to do was fling it away and then start screaming," Dai said.

"So what message was Cadwaladr receiving at the mill?" Llelo asked. "And what might he have wanted from his brother's room? And how are these two things related?"

"Taran says nothing is missing either here or in the king's pavilion in the encampment, not that he can find," Gareth said.

"Alternatively, could something have been put there and then retrieved without his knowledge?" Dai asked. "Just as with Cadwaladr's foray to the mill? Maybe someone put something amidst the king's things and then came to retrieve it."

"Or it's still here." Gareth looked up as if he could see through the ceiling to the king's room.

"And Helen came upon them in the act." Gwen nodded. "They ran out of time. That's why Cristina's room was ransacked. They were looking for something. The question we have to ask is, *did they find it?*"

With those words, a silence fell among them, broken in the end by Nest. "I see why Dai was hesitant to include me in this consultation, and I understand why what we've said here can't go beyond this room. Please know you have my complete discretion."

"It's already too late to keep out the Dragons and Prince Hywel," Dai said, "and likely Saran, Meilyr, and Gwalchmai."

"We need them anyway, if only so they keep doing what they've been doing." Gwen looked at her husband. "I assume my stepmother told you nothing of what she knows about Marc?"

"She has not." His conversation with Saran on the matter had gone exactly as Gareth had predicted. "She was forthcoming enough to say she had heard the same rumors I had about Cerys. Whether or not Marc confessed anything to her specifically will remain, forevermore, between them."

Dai nodded, equally unsurprised at the news. "I will make sure the Dragons know Cadwaladr needs to be watched now more than ever."

Abbess Nest put up a hand like she was blessing them at the end of a service. "I can see that all of you would like nothing more than to catch Prince Cadwaladr in an act of treachery that would rid you of him forever, but please don't forget your main objective."

"To find who hurt Helen and Marc?" Llelo asked.

"Justice, son," Rhys said, to an appreciative nod from Nest, "as always."

22

Day Three

Mold Castle

Ranulf

As the years had gone by, the aches and pains from old wounds and an occasional distressing bout of gout had kept Ranulf from sleeping. His enemies would have claimed it was shame, but Ranulf didn't have any remorse about how he'd lived his life. He knew he'd done what was necessary for the continuation of his House. If anything, he should have taken advantage of more opportunities that had come his way. Regardless, it was normal for him to be up well before dawn, and he cursed his aching toe as he hobbled across the bailey to the stables.

And cursed again, though this time inside his head, when he found the King of Powys already there. Though it had a large bailey, Mold Castle was relatively small as castles went, so Madog and his men had been staying in an adjacent encampment. Even had Madog risen to ride as Ranulf was intending, he should have been combing out his horse's mane in his own domains. He definitely shouldn't have come inside the castle to disturb Ranulf's morning.

Ranulf should have known it was no oversight or coincidence. Instead, as he entered, Madog spoke directly to his concerns. "Any word?"

He was talking about Cadwaladr. They were always talking about Cadwaladr. "I would tell you if there had been. We must give him more time. Owain fears to trust him, so he is being watched. Cadwaladr wants to stay on the good side of his brother as long as possible. We can't blame him for that; I would too."

If Madog had expected anything less, he was far more naïve than any king should be. Admittedly, for all his appeasement of Madog, Ranulf was growing more concerned too. As long as Ranulf had known him, Cadwaladr's vision of the world had been colored by his personal wants and desires, and his endeavors had always been bent towards shaping his surroundings to his will. That wasn't unusual in a prince, of course, nor even a commoner. Every man wanted the world to be a certain way and at times railed against all the ways it wasn't. In Ranulf's experience, the world generally refused to conform to the way things *ought* to be. But Cadwaladr had a rare talent for *believing* things were the way he wanted them, all evidence to the contrary. In short, Ranulf had never met a man with a greater capacity for lying to himself.

And that was saying something, given the company Ranulf usually kept. What was truly amazing, as well as disconcerting, was how Cadwaladr kept getting his way in the end. The world *did* often conform to his wishes. And now he was back in Owain's good graces, perfectly situated to be the man they needed in Owain's camp. Ranulf was doing his best to keep that thought in the forefront of his mind.

Madog's expression contorted. "What about the Danes? Any more news from that quarter?"

Ranulf blinked. This was an unexpected salvo, and he cursed yet again at whatever impulse had prompted him to tell Madog about those particular plans. It had been a moment of weakness, out of a misplaced desire to create a sense of camaraderie between them so that Madog would be more inclined to do Ranulf's bidding. *There* was a regret to satisfy his naysayers. In truth, Madog was hard enough to control as it was.

But it was a mistake Ranulf wouldn't be repeating. "They say they are on their way."

"Those Dublin Danes are not the allies you think they are. According to Cadwaladr, their ties to Gwynedd are strong."

"Perhaps." Ranulf endeavored to keep his expression impassive. He didn't care to disagree with Madog, not because he thought he was correct—or incorrect, for that matter—but because he didn't want to discuss the task Prince Godfrid had agreed to do.

Ranulf could have told Madog that all alliances contained elements one came to rue. These days, Ranulf himself was regretting almost every aspect of his current alliance with King David and Prince Henry, not just the part that would have given Owain suzerainty over Wales. Because of that loyalty, Ranulf himself had attacked Lincoln for a third time as a way to distract King Stephen's forces, who'd spent many weeks after the aborted meeting in Carlisle chasing Prince Henry the length of England to Gloucester. They'd almost captured him three separate times, with Henry in the end escaping the clutches of Prince Eustace only by blind luck and the grace of God. Henry was safe in France once again, but his survival had been in question for much of the summer. While Ranulf was glad to retain the backing and support of King David of Scotland, he'd had to give up his claim to Carlisle without getting nearly as much as he should have in return.

Madog had no such misgivings. "Bastard Danes and their empty promises. They were supposed to have taken care of Eustace for us. They and Cadwaladr are two peas in a pod."

Ranulf thought the *us* in Madog's comment was interesting, as if he genuinely cared who ruled England or thought anyone in England cared one whit about him. Madog hadn't been part of the *us* in that meeting at Carlisle. In fact, King David had made it clear that if Owain had turned down the opportunity to join their alliance, his place would not have been offered to Madog. If Madog were honest with himself, which in truth he was only slightly more often than Cadwaladr, he was not suited to ruling all Wales. He had neither the temperament nor the vision.

And really, he'd only ever shown an interest in keeping his small patch of earth for himself. "I happen to agree with you that we can't truly trust them. I will believe they are coming when they stand in front of me."

"In the same way, we will believe Cadwaladr will come through for us when we see his message arriving." Madog practically whinnied the thought, as if he was the horse whose reins he held.

Ranulf eyed his ally, resigned to the discussion. "These two situations are hardly the same, Madog. You can't blame the Danes for what happened with Henry. That first ambush by Stephen's men occurred a matter of days after his departure from Carlisle. Even for a Dane, it would have been impossible to sail to Dublin and return with a sufficient number of men to capture Eustace. King Stephen knew about the meeting at Carlisle, and his forces were lying in wait. We had a traitor in our midst."

But Ranulf could see his words didn't make Madog any less irritated. It was time to distract him some more. Everybody needed to forget that meeting in Carlisle as soon as possible.

"I am committed, Madog. You should have no doubts about me. Are you yourself having second thoughts? Is that why you chose to meet me here at this hour?"

"Of course I'm not having second thoughts!" He snorted. "I'm just worried about all we don't know."

"The natural solution, as I told you the other day, is for you to send *someone* to Holywell. Owain cannot be suspicious of you; he cannot start to wonder if you are insincere or suspect you aren't really coming. *We* have come too far to turn back now."

The Powysian king grumbled under his breath, focused on his woes and speaking more to his horse than actually to Ranulf. "I already told you I won't go."

"I said *someone*. It doesn't have to be you. Send your son. Send your wife. She can tell her brother you are on your way, but the weather still delays you. Invent a malady that slows your progress." Ranulf spoke forcefully, overriding Madog's sour expression. His relationship with his wife, and his wife's with her brothers, was a sore point. Perhaps Ranulf had been unwise to mention her, but her loyalties had always been personal rather than political. She *was* the perfect person to send. "She is at your hunting lodge at Ewloe. It's a short ride from there to the abbey."

Madog abruptly turned away to pace towards the doorway of the stable. Because of the palisade surrounding the fortress, there wouldn't be much to see. Just a bailey with the usual accoutrements to a castle: craft works, kitchen, barracks, laundry—and not much activity at this hour of the day regardless.

He stared out for a long moment, his hands on his hips, and when he turned back, he did not appear angry. In fact, his face was devoid of expression. Ranulf didn't know whether to be relieved or worried when he spoke in a totally calm voice. "I already sent word to her that she must ride to Holywell. She will obey."

Ranulf didn't cast doubt, since this had been his idea too. A wife was obligated to obey her husband, but Welsh wives sometimes were less quick to do so, and Susanna had a mind of her own. She knew about the peace conference, but had been told to wait for Madog, who was supposedly visiting his holdings in the south, before she joined her brothers. It went without saying that the messenger Madog sent would be well-skilled in lying.

"Good." Ranulf paused, considering how to end the conversation. It was time to act, not talk.

Madog, however, was all confidence. "A single smile from her in Owain's direction will remind him of how much he loves her. She can always get him to do what she wants. I've seen it before. He won't suspect a thing." He waggled his head. "I also instructed her to discover what Cadwaladr isn't telling us."

Ranulf felt as if he'd been dunked into an icy river. He took a step towards Madog. "What did you suggest she say?"

"Do not worry yourself." Madog made a dismissive gesture, one that left Ranulf hunching his shoulders. He hated being dismissed. "I did not tell her anything she doesn't already know—or think she knows."

Unlike with Owain, Ranulf thought it much more likely that *Susanna* would give Cadwaladr what he wanted, but he held his tongue. Not every truth needed to be stated, especially with allies, and especially because Madog was taking most of the risk in this endeavor.

"Leave the matter to me, Ranulf. Our men are ready." Madog continued speaking, all of a sudden disturbingly overconfident. The man did love to boast. It also made Ranulf uneasy. He hadn't achieved his current station by boasting. "Our plan cannot fail."

Ranulf studied him, calculating all the ways Madog was entirely wrong, and understanding more fully why it was that Madog had always failed to defeat Owain Gwynedd in all the times they'd met, either on the battlefield or in council. "Are you marching with your men, Madog?"

A surprised look crossed Madog's face. "My son Llywelyn will lead them. I would only get in his way." He hesitated. "Are you?"

Ranulf's own heir was just three years old, so he was hardly a viable candidate to lead an army. Ranulf himself was never one to lead from the rear anyway, so he had indeed been planning on riding at the front of his men. But Madog's demur had him suddenly suspicious. Madog was like Cadwaladr in that he was ever one to have plans within plans. With Ranulf occupied with battle, what might Madog be doing instead? And then there was this damn gouty toe. "I'm sure my captain feels the same way. Perhaps it's best if we let the young ones have their sport."

23

Day Three

Llelo

"How was the watch?" Llelo stopped at the entrance to Gwynedd's encampment in order to speak to the guard. All of the men posted on the perimeter overnight had been warned of the possible danger to the king and queen. They'd put extra men on the outskirts of the abbey as well. To do so had been instinctive, and probably not very helpful, beyond stopping an overt coordinated attack, which hadn't come anyway. Still, if they had not acted and something had happened, it would have been far worse than inconveniencing a few of their men. This was their job, after all.

"It's been quiet." The guard pointed towards the field where Cerys had found Marc. "Your father passed by a moment ago. He said something about letting you and your brother know he was headed to the mill. He did not tell me why." The guard's brows drew together. "Is this about the attack on the king's manservant?"

"It is." Llelo replied in the affirmative even though he didn't actually know enough to answer at all. He was more than a little bit pleased that his father hadn't managed to rise much earlier than he had. While they both were feeling the pressure of having too much to do and too little time in which to do it, they needed their sleep too. "Dai will be along shortly, I'm sure."

A quarter of an hour earlier, Llelo had sat bolt upright in bed, realizing it was well after dawn and cursing himself for not already being at work. Dai had still been asleep beside him. They'd gone to bed very late, so Dai had chosen to share Llelo's room in the guesthouse rather than make his way back to the encampment where the rest of the Dragons were sleeping. Even before the attack on Helen, when it had just been Llelo, he'd had his own room. There were some advantages to being on the good side of Queen Cristina. It honestly would have been just like her to refuse one to him on a matter of some unspecified principle and thus leave empty rooms in the guesthouse.

The disadvantage of having his whole family sleeping in the guesthouse, of course, was that Gwen had been the only available person to respond to the queen's screams. Although Llelo wanted to protect his mother from danger, he had to admit her presence had been for the best. Because Gwen had been there, they'd been able to keep the attack on Helen a secret, which everyone seemed to want, though not all for the same reasons.

Cristina didn't want anyone to know Helen had been found in the guesthouse because people would think she herself had lost favor with her husband. In truth, she wasn't wrong about the threat to her station and that of her sons, though Llelo didn't think the number of the king's bedfellows would have any bearing on her future in the end. Owain had a dozen sons. Once Hywel became king, it was his own family that would be preeminent. Cristina would have dowager rights, but as she wasn't even Hywel's birth mother (and despised him to boot), her privileged status would effectively end.

In turn, Taran didn't want anyone to know about Helen because he was worried about her safety. If the attacker knew she was still alive, he might come back to finish the job.

Finally, Gareth didn't want word to get out because the fewer details the general population knew, the easier it would be to catch the attacker, whom they thought might still be close by. All of them agreed they needed to keep the matter of what had gone on in King Owain's room to themselves. That someone had entered it without his knowledge, and possibly stolen something, though they didn't know what, made him look weak. That was the last thing the king needed with his opponent on the way.

Thus, for now, everyone outside their small circle still thought Marc was the only victim. Even if people knew the king and queen had rooms in the guesthouse—and how could they not, given the way Cristina had gone on about hating to sleep in a tent—they knew she was fickle too. For her to spend two nights in the guesthouse and then decide to sleep in the encampment wasn't entirely out of character. The only way anyone was going to know about Helen was if one of their few talked. His parents had taught Llelo to always put the needs of his king and prince first, so that person wasn't going to be *him.*

For that reason, Gareth had been wary of how exactly to pursue inquiries into the attack on Helen. Marc was a different matter. That investigation needed to be public.

Which was where Llelo came in.

As his father's apprentice, people would expect to see him out and about, asking questions, following footprints and what have you. Last night, once they'd reviewed the events of the evening one last time, Gareth had given Llelo his morning's task: to reinvestigate the happenings in the field next to the pavilion. It wasn't that his father thought he and the others hadn't done a thorough job, but it had been dark. He wanted fresh eyes—Llelo's eyes—on the scene, to search for anything the older generation had missed.

Before Llelo could swell too much at his own significance, Gareth had given Dai the job of tracking the footprints outside the guesthouse, the ones Llelo had followed and then lost once they reached the men's dormitory latrine block.

It was a good thing Dai and Llelo got along so well together and probably good as well that they were pursuing different careers. It meant they could work together, but not get bogged down in brotherly rivalry. And because Helen's and Marc's injuries were so similar, any questions about their activities could be passed off as pursuing Marc's assailant.

Also good, and in this case against all odds, it hadn't rained in the night. All the footprints might still be visible.

Llelo didn't expect to learn anything new from the area where Marc had fallen because so many onlookers had churned the earth with their boots when they'd come to observe his recovery. The investigators had done a great deal with footprints last night, including linking Dai to the boot prints coming from the northern gate, and Helen to the prints outside the guesthouse. Llelo had taken one of her boots, removed during Sister Efa's care for her, and matched it himself.

But by the light of day, any hope of distinguishing one print from another in the middle of the field had to be put aside.

In truth, it had been put aside from the moment Cadwaladr had brought a host of onlookers from the pavilion. And even if Llelo happened to find some token on the ground amidst the mud and grass, who was to say it belonged to Marc's attacker? It could just as easily have been dropped by one of the revelers. From the way the grass had been disturbed, the festivities in the pavilion might as well have been held right here. It looked like the village green at Aber whenever the boys were *playing at ball.*

Llelo looked anyway, digging about in the mud and dew-soaked grass, at first with the toe of his boot, and then with his hands. Sheep had grazed here recently, so the grass was relatively short. Of course, the sheep had left their droppings too, normally something so common as to be ignored, but given his current task, he was trying not to get any on his hands.

He saw nothing of interest immediately where Marc had lain, but a few feet from the central point, he discovered a rounded stone lying in the grass. It was so smooth it was almost polished, and was slightly bigger than a robin's egg. He stared at it for a moment, and then put it in his pocket. He didn't know if it was important, but he liked the feel of it and saw no sense leaving it where it was.

As he'd been told to expect, the footprints he was meant to follow began some distance from where Marc had lain, though in truth mostly what Llelo saw amounted to crushed grass. Here and there, the ground was muddy beneath the grass, and he could make out an impression of a toe or heel. Unlike Gareth, Llelo had not been raised to be a hunter. Before the age of twelve, he'd certainly never tracked any creature, much less a man, through the woods. He'd been happiest, in fact, when his birth father ignored him.

But Gareth had been teaching him this new trade since the day they'd met, and Llelo had learned a thing or two in the intervening years. He could easily make out at least five different treads near the gate on the north end of the field, three of which should belong to Gareth, Iwan, or Ralph. Every man wore down his boots in his own way, and boot prints could be as individual as the way a man spoke or his mannerisms, distinguishing him from his fellows even in a crowd. For example, Llelo walked on the outside of his feet more than the inside, and every time the bootmaker had to replace Llelo's soles, he shook his head over the uneven wear.

To ask every man here to lift his feet and show the state of his boots would both be intrusive and an odd invasion of privacy which his father would resist until he wasn't given a choice in the matter. The idea that the person who'd gone to the mill had worn too big shoes (maybe even someone else's shoes) would put off the need for that line of inquiry even further.

With the sun up, albeit not actually visible due to the continuing heavy cloud cover, Llelo followed the footprints that curved from the north gate to the eastern wall of the field. Coming from the path to the mill, the prints initially went straight towards where Marc's body had lain. Then, when the person had been about twenty-five feet away, he'd veered east.

Llelo could imagine their owner spying Marc, whether upright or already on the ground, and deciding not to continue in that direction as had been his original intent. It could even be that he'd witnessed the attack and then fled to save himself. Ignoring Dai's footprints, Llelo followed these others to the eastern wall, around which numerous other prints were again clustered. What nobody had mentioned last night was that the footprints belonging to their culprit ended at the wall, in exactly the same manner Dai had described at the mill.

Llelo hadn't thought to ask if Ralph or Iwan had followed the prints beyond the wall. As far as he knew, they hadn't, even though the wall itself wasn't that much of an obstacle. It rose only to chest height and wasn't so high that anyone, especially an agile boy, couldn't have climbed over it. Maybe now that Ralph and Iwan were old, they hadn't considered it.

Llelo, on the other hand, was soon crouched at the top. The wall was plenty wide enough for him to walk along, which he began to do since he couldn't make out any footprints in the grass on the other side. Unlike the field in which they'd found Marc, the grass in this field had been allowed to grow long and was unmarred by either the feet of men or sheep.

Discovering what the culprit had done next was the very question that had prompted his father to make this Llelo's first task, and he intended to determine this morning whether or not the prints eventually led to the pavilion. To that end, he stayed on the top of the wall, first heading north, just to see if the culprit had backtracked that way, and then turning to face south again, towards the encampment.

He'd walked a matter of twenty feet before he spied any footprints at all, though when he found them, they looked nothing like the ones in the field. Those had been made by a man's boots, but these were the result of a shoe with a flat sole, with no ribbing, tread, or heel, much like common folk wore in the winter. Only a knight needed a heel on his boot in order to keep his foot in the stirrups.

Llelo had heard about a strange shoe, worn by wealthy residents of London, which were elevated several inches at both the heel and toe to keep feet out of the muck of the street. Llelo couldn't imagine any circumstance that would possess him to wear such a shoe. Certainly, they would be impractical and absurd anywhere in Wales.

Somewhere in his tracking lessons with his father, Gareth had told him about men escaping detection by walking for a time in a stream or creek, so any tracker would have no idea where their quarry had come up the bank. This person appeared to be to operating on the same principle, with the wall substituting for the stream. That he'd also planned for a means of evading detection by wearing too big shoes when he went to the mill indicated he was no stranger to intrigue. And he'd done a good job too. By taking off his shoes first at the mill and then at the wall, he'd made himself very difficult to track.

Normally, Llelo didn't know many people with the wherewithal to hide themselves so deftly. But with all the spies about this week, plus a court accustomed to hearing of his father's investigations, altogether too many people could think like a villain.

His confidence growing, Llelo leapt from the wall and followed this new line of footprints across the grassy field until he reached a gate that allowed entry onto a track that curved around the encampment. There, the prints disappeared among a hundred other prints embedded into the dirt of the road, which over the last few days had been churned continually by feet and hooves. Llelo couldn't help thinking the owner of the footprints had also known that if he could reach the dirt track he'd be safe.

Nonetheless, Llelo kept looking, following the footprints through the gate. At that point, he made one final discovery, one that once again changed everything: hidden amidst the weeds and tall grass just off the road lay a discarded shepherd's sling.

Llelo stared at the weapon for a long moment, telling himself shepherds were everywhere in Wales and any one of them who worked in and around the abbey could have lost it. In truth, it looked like any other sling he'd ever seen, consisting of two long strings with a pouch tied between them.

But in this place, at this time, the sling was far from ordinary. With near trembling hands, Llelo pulled the smooth stone from his pocket and placed it into the sling's pouch.

It fit perfectly.

24

Day Three

Gareth

On first approach by the light of day, the mill appeared no more exciting than the field where Marc had been attacked. Abbess Nest had said she would ask the miller to meet Gareth before entering, not because she didn't trust Gareth per se, but because Brother Francis would be affronted to have his domain disturbed, and she was conscious of the sensibilities of those in her charge. It was a small request as far as Gareth was concerned, though if Brother Francis was involved somehow in Cadwaladr's intrigue, he could have come and gone at any time since she'd spoken to him and nobody would have been the wiser.

Being an investigator made a man suspicious. Sometimes too suspicious. Gareth would see what he thought about the miller once he met him.

Gareth had risen later than he had planned, but even so, hadn't awakened his sons, knowing full well that they might feel affronted he'd started work without them. In this, however, Gareth was exercising his prerogative as their parent. They were their own men, and Gareth respected that, but in too many of their investigations, nobody got remotely enough sleep. As lead investigator, Gareth hadn't deemed such deprivation necessary today.

He hadn't disturbed Gwen either. It didn't take six years of marriage to know better than to do that.

Gareth crossed the yard, as Dai said he himself had done after Cadwaladr had gone on his way, and approached the door. He was careful to tread lightly on the stoop where the residue of Cadwaladr's muddy boots was still visible, the earth dried now and falling apart into smaller clumps.

Once past the dirt on the steps, Gareth set down the lantern Dai had taken from the mill, wanting to make sure it was returned to its rightful place. Then he stood off to one side, lifted the latch, and swung the door inward. Cadwaladr had entered and left openly, with no concern for where he put his feet. They knew he'd been inside. What was at issue was *why?* It would have been so much simpler if they could just ask him.

But that was something they could never do. According to Gruffydd, who as Gareth had passed had been yawning from a prime position near the pavilion, hot porridge in hand and affecting a casual attitude, the treacherous prince remained asleep in his tent alone. Even if he'd been wandering about the encampment, Gareth wasn't worried about him returning to the scene of this particular crime, if that's even what this was. What was more concerning was if Cadwaladr's own spies were watching the mill—or watching Gareth. It was impossible. Heaven knew how anyone could remain loyal to Cadwaladr through all his treachery, but even now he had his supporters. And as had been the case since the beginning of time, the proper allocation of money could encourage a man to betray any virtue and sacrifice any friend.

Gareth couldn't worry about it, or rather, *shouldn't*. Maybe he should even assume Cadwaladr knew he was being watched, which was why he'd gone to the mill so openly, in hopes someone would follow him. Gareth had seen Cadwaladr afterwards, and he would have said he'd spent the rest of the evening in good spirits. Certainly he'd been as officious as possible when he'd come to the aid of Marc in the field, in the manner of someone who was particularly pleased with himself.

Gareth knew by now that when Cadwaladr was pleased, something truly terrible would surely follow.

And yet, if the entire trip to the mill had been a ruse, there wouldn't have been anyone coming to leave the strange footprints Dai had found at the back door. It wasn't as if Cadwaladr had removed his own shoes. In fact, he'd shown no care whatsoever about leaving his traces in the mill. Gareth thought that was unusual, even for Cadwaladr. While he could be so focused on what he wanted that he ignored both the needs of others and his surroundings, he had to have known what he was doing wasn't normal. Maybe he truly just didn't care.

Gareth's internal dialogue had an answer for everything, and he very much felt like he had an angel on one shoulder preaching righteousness and a devil on the other inciting iniquity, just like in a priest's sermon. He had to remind himself that Cadwaladr had the possibility of both within his character too, as all men did, even if it was the devil who had the most influence over him.

Just as Gareth was deciding he might as well enter the mill alone, with or without Brother Francis, the monk in question hurried up, breathing hard and holding his chest. "My apologies, my lord. A conversation with the baker ran overlong." Francis was quite stout and short, giving him more than a passing resemblance to a barrel and explaining why he was so out of breath.

Gareth remained on the threshold, waiting to enter until the miller was standing beside him.

The miller rewarded his patience with a harrumph. "What is this?"

"This is why Abbess Nest asked you to meet me here this morning," Gareth said. "I'm guessing from your expression that the floor was clean when you left the mill yesterday afternoon."

"Of course it was!"

"Were you the last to leave?"

"I was." Francis's initial comment had been defensive, but now he frowned, understanding why Abbess Nest had asked him to delay the start of the workday and that it hadn't been on a whim. "I locked the doors, both front and back. Nobody could have opened either without a key."

"Where is the key kept?"

"On my person. Or, when I'm not at work, in my cell on a hook—" Now his expression showed dismay. "Nobody would have taken it! I would have noticed!"

"None of your underlings have a key?"

"If they are working without me, or opening or closing for the day, they get the key from me and return it when they're done."

"There are no other copies at all?"

"Well," Francis had a very expressive face, and it contorted again, "Abbess Nest has one. It goes without saying she would not have unlocked the mill to allow a stranger inside to muddy my floor!"

"Of course not," Gareth said. "I would never think it."

The miller smiled. "I see you know her as well as I."

"She saved my life when I thought it was at an end," Gareth said simply. It was no secret, and as he talked about it routinely, he saw no reason not to speak the truth.

"I had heard that." Brother Francis canted his head. "There you go. It is impossible that anyone could have entered the mill last night."

"And yet ..." Gareth let his voice trail off.

Brother Francis looked at him blankly.

When he didn't see where Gareth was going with the rest of his sentence, Gareth filled it in for him. "We know for certain some-one did. He entered through this door with mud on his boots. He was seen doing it."

"Impossible!"

Gareth didn't bother explaining that Dai and Abbot Rhys, as witnesses, had impeccable credentials. "How else do you explain the footprints?"

Brother Francis really didn't want to admit anything could have gone awry last night. Gareth found it astounding the way bare facts didn't always penetrate an individual's consciousness, even when they stared him in the face. At the very least, Gareth had been standing in the open doorway when Brother Francis arrived. Gareth wasn't blaming Francis for the fact that someone had entered the mill. Nor was it a reflection on him. Abbess Nest certainly wasn't one to lay blame where it wasn't warranted either, but maybe he didn't know her yet as well as all that.

Finally, Gareth sighed. "Keys can be duplicated."

"Well, of course, but—" Francis eyed the clumps of dirt Cadwaladr had left inside, and then he skirted them to reach the big shutters, in order to open the window and flood the mill with light.

Gareth, as an investigator with an inquiring mind, knew of several ways to duplicate a key, especially if the duplicate was intended for a single use. Easiest was to borrow a key and impress it into wax for an exact copy. Likely that's how the second key the friary currently possessed had been created in the first place.

Having followed Brother Francis further into the mill, Gareth inspected the grains of unmilled oat that had fallen to the floor, as Dai had said he'd done. He found nothing within the sack either, any more than Dai had, though Francis let out a little gasp of horror to see Gareth plunging his hand into it.

Gareth glanced back at him. "Were these grains on the floor when you left?"

With a somewhat chastened expression, Francis shook his head. "No." He paused. "That sack wasn't positioned there either."

That news was more definitive in a way than anything else Francis could have told him. It could even be that the sack and grains were a message, per their discussion last night.

Gareth straightened. "Where did the sack come from?"

"These are our oats." Brother Francis was frowning now. "I could have told you that by the quality of the grain alone, but the symbol on the sack says so too." He bent in order to sift the grains through his fingers. Then he turned the bag slightly to show Gareth the sketch of a well painted on the side. "I'd have to check my records but, as I recall, this sack was among the first to grind today."

"Are sacks of grain always stored right here?" Gareth gestured to other bags that lined the wall under the window.

"Just until one of the men can bring them up to the loft."

"I'll see that next." Without waiting for permission, Gareth went up the stairs to the level above them.

The miller followed, if somewhat reluctantly, huffing again with every step. "This is where most of our unground grain is stored, in preparation for it being put into the hopper and carried down to the grinding stone below. These have already been dried."

"Who sleeps there?" Gareth pointed to the bed placed against the far wall. The blanket was folded neatly and laid at one end. "I thought nobody stayed overnight in the mill?"

"Sometimes someone does. We can work long hours. I myself have closed my eyes there a time or two. On top of which, if a farmer wants to pay one of us to protect his grain until it's ground, I'll keep a man here."

"Can you explain how that would work? Would you leave him a key?" Gareth was trying very hard to phrase his question so he didn't overtly contradict what Brother Francis had told him earlier.

"Yes, when he stays here, I leave him mine."

"When was the last time a man stayed the night?"

The miller frowned. "That would have been the first night you were here. Market day."

"From the way you're speaking of him, that man isn't a monk?"

"No, he is not. He lives in the village but works at the abbey. When the numbers of our abbey were in decline, we had more work than men to do it. Now that Abbess Nest is here, the situation has improved, but she still employs those same workers because she didn't want to deprive anyone of his livelihood."

"What's his name?" Gareth asked, all the while thinking Brother Francis could have been more forthcoming with this information from the start and not required him to draw every little detail out of him.

"Cadell."

Gareth filed the name away for later inquiry. "Does this space resemble how you saw it last?"

The miller turned slowly on one heel and then, as he came around again, nodded.

Back downstairs, Gareth inspected the flight of steps to the bottom level. As Dai had said, the floor was clean. Once through the back door, he was able to see the footprints Dai had found, toes still facing the wall. By their clarity, the man could have been standing there all night and just left.

No small part of Gareth was pleased to find the scene exactly as Dai had described. Though not apprenticed to Gareth like Llelo was, Dai had played a vital role in many of their investigations, and he was a Dragon now to boot. Clearly he had retained a great deal of what Gareth had taught him, even if he didn't intend to use it formally like Llelo. After Dai railed at Gareth about not waking him, Gareth would tell him so.

As Gareth and Brother Francis stepped out the back door and headed around to the front of the mill once again, a monk entered the yard from the road. Spying Gareth with the miller, he pushed back his hood, revealing himself to be close in age to Gareth, in his middle thirties with brown hair and beard.

"Hello, Brother Francis." The newcomer bobbed his head. "My lord."

"Brother Iolo." Brother Francis was huffing again.

Iolo looked past Gareth to the mill, his brows furrowing. "Why is the mill not in service? Did something happen?"

"That's what we are trying to discover." Gareth replied with as vague an answer as possible while still answering. "May I ask your purpose here?"

From beside him, Brother Francis managed something of a heaving laugh. "Save your suspicions for those who deserve them, my lord. Brother Iolo oversees the granary. Without him, we would not know how much to grind in our mill."

Iolo smiled obligingly. "I hoped I'd find you here, Brother Francis. I came by earlier but the mill was empty. And unlocked!"

Brother Francis looked sheepish. "My apologies, brother. Lord Gareth asked us to delay our opening this morning."

"Really? Why would that be?"

"Have you not heard?" Francis asked.

"What would I have heard?" Brother Iolo's expression turned stern. "You know I don't listen to gossip."

Gareth had let Francis take over the conversation while he observed the other brother. In some instances, he would have wanted to control the flow of information, but he had already decided it was going to be impossible to keep the news that someone had been inside the mill last night a secret, not with Iolo already knowing the door had been left unlocked. Someone would have to sweep the floor, and that wasn't going to be Brother Francis, who was looking increasingly red-faced and distressed. Gareth was really starting to worry that his heart might give out at any moment, so he gently suggested Francis should sit down on the front steps of the mill.

Almost immediately, Francis's color improved.

Still keeping a wary eye on the miller, Gareth turned back to Iolo. "Do you not sleep in the dormitory with your brothers?"

"Three of our number take turns keeping watch at the granary. Last night was my turn."

Gareth felt like this was just one more bit of useless information in a morning of useless bits of information, but he threw out one last query, just in case. "By chance, did you see anything unusual last night?"

Iolo blinked. "I did see something. In fact, that was what I was coming to talk to Brother Francis about."

25

Once her head had hit the pallet, Gwen slept solidly, so much so that she hadn't even noticed Young Taran waking in the night. For him to want to nurse at least once was more usual than not. Regardless, as the light filtered through the cracks in the shutter above her head, it showed him still asleep.

Gwen loved this moment of the day, brief as it often was. Knowing all her children were asleep at the same moment, with these two within touching distance of her, gave her a feeling of relief. Now that Llelo and Dai were men, the four children slept under her roof less often. She had to be content knowing the older two were with others she trusted. And still, every morning she sent up a prayer of thanksgiving that all of them were alive to see the dawn.

Today, Gwen's feeling of relief couldn't last long, since her husband was already going about the day's business. And if she guessed right, her boys would soon be too. Long gone were the days when Gwen might have resented being left behind. She knew she was a valuable partner in their investigations. But her role was different now, less dealing with the immediacy of a crisis, though that had certainly been her job last night, and more focused on interviewing witnesses and thinking through the details.

Leaving Taran and Tangwen asleep, she carefully extricated herself from the covers and carried her dress and boots into the corridor, where she dressed quickly. From the quality of the light visible through the windows in the common area down the hall, the sun was fully up now. That made it mid-morning at the very least, with perhaps only a few hours to noon. The sun rose so late this time of year that they had hardly more than eight hours of daylight. Her family had a great deal to see to and too little time in which they could actually *see* it.

The children's nanny, Marged, was already awake. As Gwen entered the common room, she gestured to the food on the table. "They brought enough for an army." Gwen gave Marged a smile of thanks, which the older woman uncharacteristically did not return, and then fell upon the meal like one starving. In truth, until she'd smelled the fresh bread, she hadn't known how desperately she needed to eat.

Marged, meanwhile, hovered, straightening what didn't need to be straightened, in a manner not dissimilar to Lord Taran last night. Gwen watched her for a moment and then set down the piece of honeyed bread she was about to stuff into her mouth. "What is it, Marged?"

"Nothing, my lady."

Gwen's eyes narrowed. "It clearly isn't nothing." She waved a hand. "Stop fiddling with the cushion and come here."

She rarely gave Marged orders, but it seemed to be called for in this case. Marged obeyed, if with somewhat hesitant steps, and ended up standing on the other side of the table, shifting from one foot to the other and wringing her hands. "I'm so sorry I didn't hear any of the terrible things happening right above my head last night. How could I not have realized?"

Gwen took a sip of water, wondering how this conversation had suddenly become one that might have done better with breakfast mead. "I'm not sure what you mean, Marged. When could you have heard anything? It was all over by the time we arrived."

Marged bit her lip. "Not—" She paused and swallowed. "Not exactly."

Gwen felt like swallowing hard too. She was trying to question the other woman in something of a matter-of-fact tone, since Marged was anxious enough for the both of them.

Then the nanny began to blush. "We would have gone to his tent, but it was in the middle of the encampment. We aren't wanting anyone to know about us just yet."

"What exactly are you telling me?" Now that Gwen thought back, she realized she had seen Marged at the feast near the beginning and then only at the end when it was time to put Tangwen and Taran to bed.

Marged's job as the children's nanny was, in many respects, to raise them as her own. At the same time, she was not responsible for the children every hour of the day and night. In particular, Gwen worked very hard not to call upon her continually except when she was helping Gareth with an investigation. Tangwen and Taran were Gwen's responsibility, and nobody could care for them as well as their own mother. In that, she agreed with Queen Cristina.

But by now, after two years of employment, Marged was a member of the family, along with her son, Cian, whom Gwen *had* seen at the feast. He had taken on the role of assistant to Meilyr and Gwalchmai. Gwen had a private thought that his proximity to the best bards in Wales brought him female attention in excess of what he might otherwise attract. He had also become Gwalchmai's closest friend, especially in the absence of Iorwerth, who was a year married and expecting his first child. And not here.

Marged still wasn't explaining more, and while Gwen was working very hard to rein in her own anxiety, the more Marged hesitated, the more worried Gwen became. "Just tell me what this is about."

Marged was still struggling to say, and the inner war with herself was visible on her face. "You won't like it."

Gwen feared she was right but was equally determined, no matter how bad the news, to contain her dismay if at all possible. At the very least, she knew Marged hadn't formed a liaison with Cadwaladr himself. "How do you know I won't?"

"Because sometimes I'm not sure I like it."

"Now you really are starting to worry me." Gwen was hoping to elicit more information without turning Marged into a weepy puddle on the floor. "Tell me who he is, and then we'll both know whom we're talking about."

"Geraint."

The name fell between them like someone had pushed a boulder down a mountain to start an avalanche. Marged had known it would, which was why she'd been reluctant to say anything at all.

"The look on your face." Marged shook her head. "That's why I didn't tell you sooner."

Even prepared, Gwen had given away her dismay—and distaste—without meaning to. Underneath the table, her hands clenched, and her fingernails momentarily dug into her flesh. Then, flexing her fingers and shaking out her hands as a means to ease her immediate tension, she managed to sort out her expression too. With the best smile she could muster, she reached across the table, palm out, for Marged to take. "I can tell you're in love, and I am happy for you in that."

At this initial comment, Marged obliged by grasping Gwen's hand, but then Gwen couldn't help but add, "You must know, Marged, that he has served Cadwaladr for many years. You know the role he played in Prince Rhun's death."

"He has confessed his sins, his mistakes." Marged immediately released Gwen's hand, indicating clearly, if her behavior hadn't been obvious enough, the depth of her commitment to Geraint. "He has served his lord, as Gareth serves Prince Hywel. He went where his lord pointed."

Gwen eased herself back in her seat. "You are right, of course, Marged." She wet her lips. The need to say more was rising within her, even as she didn't know if she should, or could, without alienating Marged entirely, something she very much wanted to avoid. "Does he know how you feel and are your feelings returned?"

"They are!" Relieved of her guilt and shame and finally able to speak the truth, Marged in the last few moments had been transformed into a woman twenty years younger. "Whatever you've heard about him, I assure you, he is a *good* man."

Up until this moment, Gwen would have said Marged was a reserved person, if not staid, as well as possessing above average intelligence. But as Gwen gazed at her children's nanny, all those formerly dominant qualities were overridden by infatuation. And really, she *could* believe Geraint wasn't a bad person. She even believed he had attempted at times over the years to rein in Cadwaladr's excesses. But once it was clear he couldn't divert his lord, he had gone along with him, if not aided and abetted him in the worst ways. Gareth had left Cadwaladr's service and had been taken on by Prince Hywel precisely because he *hadn't* been able to do that and live with himself.

That was Gareth, of course. Nobody else was like him, and she couldn't expect anyone else to be exactly like him. It certainly was nice when they came close, however.

"Do you have to tell Lord Gareth?" Marged was back to wringing her hands, worried, as she should be, about how Gareth might react to her liaison. That was the reason for the honorific. She feared the result.

"I do, Marged."

Marged's shoulders sagged. "I'll go pack my things."

"Wait." Gwen half-rose from her seat. "Marged, no. *Stop.* Who you love can make for a tense conversation around the dinner table but you are still part of our family and the children's nanny. I am not asking you to leave us."

The hope in Marged's face wrenched Gwen's heart. "Do you mean that?"

"Of course I mean it. We will work this out." Even as Gwen spoke, she wasn't sure how, but she wasn't sorry she'd said it. "Does anyone else know?"

"No!" Marged was horrified at the thought.

"Cian?"

"Least of all him."

Gwen wasn't so sure. Cian was an observant young man. But she understood a mother's reluctance to reveal a new attachment. It wasn't just that Marged was in love with Geraint, but that they had found themselves a quiet room in the guesthouse while everyone else was at the feast. They weren't waiting until they were married to be together.

"Cadwaladr?"

"Definitely not. His reaction to Geraint loving me would be no better than yours has been. We have been discreet. *You* didn't know, and you know everything."

Gwen didn't know that she believed her, because it was perfectly within Cadwaladr's character (she didn't know enough about Geraint's), to be pleased about having a spy in Gareth's camp, and thus Prince Hywel's. In that, he was no different than Cristina.

So Gwen took in a deep breath, letting it out as she reoriented her thoughts back to what had brought them to this point in the first place. "You were in the pavilion during Gwalchmai's singing when I was rocking Taran. Now that I think about it, I hadn't seen you much before that. How long exactly were you in the guesthouse?"

"Almost the whole feast. It was just three more songs before you and I left with the children." Again the rueful expression, though there was a pleased smile around Marged's lips too at the memory.

Gwen put the reason for it from her mind. *That* was something she didn't care to think about. "So you were in the guesthouse the entire time up until then?"

Marged nodded.

"And Geraint?"

"The same, of course. He left moments before I did."

"Where did he go?"

"He returned to the feast. I saw him there, seated with Cadwaladr's men."

Marged wouldn't know that Cadwaladr himself had left the feast not long after she and Gwen had gone to put the children to bed. It might even be that it wasn't Gareth's departure that had prompted Cadwaladr to leave but Geraint's return. Gwen had a very hard time believing Cadwaladr didn't know his man had been gone all that time. Gwen's only consolation was that, ever since the fateful ambush where Rhun had died, Geraint had been one of several men upon whom Cadwaladr relied, rather than the main one. Ostensibly, this was because Geraint had been injured in that battle, and it had taken him too long to recover. The unspoken reason was Cadwaladr blamed the men beneath him for that mistake (he certainly never blamed himself!) and had demoted them all accordingly.

"You saw nothing? Heard nothing?"

"No. Just-just each other."

Gwen gave Marged what she hoped was a sincere smile. "Thank you. If you could stay here and keep an ear out for Taran and Tangwen, I would be grateful." She stood.

Marged was back to looking anxious. "Where are you going now? Please tell Lord Gareth that Geraint is not the man he thinks him to be!"

Gwen made sure her tone was gentle. "As Gareth is busy with our investigation, I will not trouble him with this immediately. You have a reprieve for now."

Marged's relief might have been comical under other circumstances. Gwen herself was somewhat shocked by the transformation in her nanny. *Had she been that empty-headed in the first blush of loving Gareth?* Certainly she'd worn out her father and brother going on about him. Well, he was worth going on about.

It was a good reminder of how motive wasn't always what it appeared at first. The attacks on Helen and Marc had been vicious, but they could just as easily have been a product of love as hate. It wasn't as if they hadn't seen it before.

26

Day Three
Gareth

"What did you hear?" Gareth asked Brother Iolo. His heart wasn't exactly beating faster in anticipation of what the monk might say. Still, with so many incidents taking place in a single night, he had to tug on every thread that presented itself. He counted himself fortunate he had no bodies to see to in the laying out room. No bodies *yet*, anyway. He'd preferred to keep it that way.

Before his visit to the mill, Gareth had stopped by Cristina's room to see how Helen and Taran were faring. When he'd arrived, Sister Efa had just come to check on the patient as well and had remarked that she very much wanted to see Helen wake up today. With every hour that passed with her still unconscious, her chances of a full recovery became more remote. Fortunately, Taran had stepped out of the room briefly at that point, so hadn't been there to hear her.

By some amazing series of circumstances, they'd managed to keep the fact that Helen was unconscious, or that such a person as

Helen existed at all, out of the general knowledge of the residents of the abbey. They hadn't even had to lie. She wasn't normally present in their lives, neither in the village nor at the peace conference, so nobody knew to miss her.

Except Taran, of course. He had slept on a pallet, if any sleeping had been done at all, beside her bed. The man was in love. Last night in the pavilion, he'd been full of hope, anticipating Helen's return. Now he was despairing that all his patience would have been for nothing. Gareth could understand how he felt. He loved Gwen that way, and he was pretty sure she felt the same way about him. There truly was nothing more magnificent or transforming in a man's life than knowing his love was returned in full measure. All the more reason to learn if what had happened at the mill had any connection at all with Helen.

"I'll tell you what I heard: men talking in a language I don't know, though here and there I understood a word I thought to be French."

The miller looked surprised. "I didn't know you spoke French, Iolo."

"I don't." Iolo chuckled. "But Abbess Nest speaks it, and occasionally she has given me a word or two to mull over because I like the sounds."

Iolo appeared to be a jovial fellow, which was lovely for him, but Gareth was ready to get back to the matter at hand. "How many men did you hear, and where were they?"

"I don't know how many for certain. At least two. They were walking along the road by the granary."

"To or from the abbey?"

Iolo's eyes narrowed as he thought. "From."

"Do you remember the words they said?"

"One in particular, an insult that one man was calling another. *Imbecile*. He sounded so angry!" The idea seemed to be a difficult one for Iolo to grasp.

Gareth found it interesting to learn that *imbecile* was one of the words Abbess Nest had taught Iolo. "And another?"

"*Sang*."

Sang meant *blood*, or even *gore*.

"You're sure?"

Iolo nodded his head vigorously. "I remember specifically because he spat on the ground after he said it."

"You were that close?"

"I heard them coming down the road and, as I said, they were arguing, far louder than I would have thought sensible so late at night. Sound carries well at night." He nodded, as if giving Gareth a piece of information he might not have otherwise known. "That gave me warning and time to peek my head out the window, though with a tree growing between the granary and the road, I couldn't see much."

"Could you see what they were wearing?"

Here his brow furrowed. "Dark robes? Cloaks? As I said, I couldn't really see them. It was night, and they had no torch."

Gareth's heart skipped a beat. "Could these have been monks' robes?"

"I suppose they could have." He seemed surprised by the notion. "I don't know what monks could have been talking in French on the road last night, though. Maybe they were from Hen Blas. Many of them are French."

That was an entirely new thought, though Gareth wasn't going to tell him so. He certainly wasn't going to cast aspersions on the Hen Blas monks without more evidence. Anyone could put on a robe. "Was there any chance they could have seen you?"

"They gave no sign." Iolo shook his head, although with something less than surety, and qualified his answer. "I don't believe so."

"Nonetheless, it might be best if you told nobody else about this." Gareth put a hand on Iolo's arm to emphasize his words. "Nobody but your abbess."

Iolo clearly didn't understand why secrecy was important, and Gareth could tell already, even on such short acquaintance, that keeping secrets wasn't in his nature. He also didn't yet know about Marc, and certainly wouldn't know about Helen. Given Iolo's garrulousness, he must feel stifled on the nights he slept in the granary. Then again, perhaps it was easier for him to stay away than have to keep quiet during readings and prayer times.

Gareth now returned to the miller. "You are free to begin work. I apologize for the delay this morning. I know it was unusual and unsettling."

Brother Francis bent his head. "I would not deign to second-guess Abbess Nest, and I'm thinking now what you learned might have been helpful?"

"Indeed it was."

"May I set things to rights?" It was this last item that clearly was most important to the miller. Brother Francis wanted his domain back in order. Maybe that lack was all that his racing heart and huff-ing had been about. Nonetheless, when Gareth next went to the in-firmary to look in on Marc, he was going to mention his concerns about the miller's health to the healers.

"As you wish." Gareth felt an urgency rising within him, not about the mill itself, or the miller, but about these strangers Iolo had seen. He set off at a fast walk back to the abbey. He didn't like that he was going in the wrong direction, but he knew better than to search for these strange monks alone. At least now he had some idea where to look.

27

Day Three
Gwen

It was almost noon by the time Gwen left the guesthouse. In the end, Marged had become so unsettled by her confession that Gwen hadn't felt she could leave her alone and had stayed until the children woke, were dressed and fed, and had played in the garden. Gareth hadn't yet returned, so Gwen decided the best use of her time was to seek out Queen Cristina and Sioned for another chat.

Those noble intentions were diverted almost immediately, however, by a commotion near the entrance to the encampment. A man in his early forties, whom Gwen didn't recognize, was bobbing and weaving with some level of discomfort in front of the current guard on duty, who was very determinedly not letting him through.

"I must speak to Lord Taran. It is very important. I have urgent news for him." The newcomer fidgeted with his hat, which he spun around and around in his hands. He was dressed as a workman, in rough clothes an indeterminate shade between gray and brown, and spoke Welsh with a heavy French accent. Foreigners weren't unknown in Wales, particularly in the king's court and the border regions of Wales. But still, that any Frenchman would put in an appearance at the encampment of the King of Gwynedd was enough to make Gwen turn to the man with interest.

She wasn't the only one either. Already they were drawing the attention of those gathered in the nearby pavilion, many of whom had nothing better to do than start in on the mead and watch their neighbors.

The high table, meanwhile, was empty. Some of the more noble diners could have come and gone already, but given the late night, Gwen wouldn't be the only one who'd delayed her appearance until noon.

"Lord Taran is indisposed." The guard had a stubborn set to his chin, indicating he had been told a certain thing, and he was not going to go against it, no matter the provocation. "Be off with you."

"Perhaps I might be of some assistance?" Gwen put a gentle hand on the soldier's arm. "I'll take care of this, Gronw. I have Lord Taran's ear today."

Gronw immediately bent his head and gave way. "Of course, my lady."

That he acquiesced so quickly was an indication that whoever had told him not to allow anyone to see Taran had also told him Gwen had authority in the matter. Perhaps that was even her husband. In other words, Gronw wasn't being stubborn for its own sake but because he thought that was his job.

She made a motion with her hand that the newcomer should step away from the pavilion so nobody else could hear them. At the moment there was nothing she could do about them being observed. "What is your name, friend?"

Like the guard, she spoke to him in Welsh. He had an accent, but she had understood him and she hoped he could understand her. She could always switch to French if need be.

"Henri de Tours." The name rolled off his tongue, confirming she'd been correct about his origins. "I need to speak to Lord Taran immediately." For a moment, he was quite forceful.

"Gronw was correct that he is indisposed at the moment. My name is Gwen. My husband, Gareth, is steward to Prince Hywel. Can you tell me something of what this is about?"

"Lord Gareth is your husband?" Henri sounded hopeful. "I could perhaps speak to him."

If she was being honest, Gwen was growing impatient with his hesitancy. She wanted to snap at him that talking to her was just as good as talking to Taran or Gareth, but Gareth wouldn't thank her for scaring Henri off, nor would she, once she'd settled down.

So she tipped her head towards the abbey. "Please come with me. I will take you to him."

Gwen hadn't seen Gareth at all today. She knew he'd gone to the mill, but she didn't know if he was still there. Regardless, she expected he would check in with her soon. Since he wasn't visible in the pavilion, rather than spend an hour wandering about looking for him, it would be better for her to stay in one place and wait for him to come to her.

That appeared to be good enough to get Henri moving. They walked slowly, since he moved with a pronounced enough limp, favoring his right side, that she couldn't help but ask him about it. "Is it hurting much?" Other than the limp, he was well-built, even handsome, beneath the simple exterior.

"Not so much, except when the weather's bad." He grimaced slightly. "Which it often is in January." Now he patted his hip. "War wound."

"I'm so sorry. Where were you fighting?"

He gestured generally east. "I haven't always lived here, you see."

That was, of course, obvious, given his accent, and he was hardly the first man to come home from war with a permanent injury. It was equally true that living in Holywell was hardly a recipe for avoiding war.

"I heard someone was attacked last night. Is that true?" As they approached the entrance to the abbey, several people passed them going the other way. This seemed to make Henri more nervous than ever. Once through the gate, his head kept swiveling this way and that, like he was afraid someone would leap out at them at any moment.

"Yes, it's true."

"Is he all right?"

"He is going to be."

At last they reached the guesthouse door, at which point she heard Gareth's voice coming faintly through an upstairs window. From the lack of children's voices, Tangwen and Taran must still be on a walk with Marged. She had no notion as to where Cristina's boys had gone. There had been some talk of convincing one of the garden-ers to put up a rope swing.

"Please wait inside," Gwen opened the door for Henri. "You are welcome to serve yourself a cup of mead."

Henri's eyes widened at the offer, and he ducked his head. His timidity was even more pronounced, and he was back to worry-ing at his hat. Gwen would have done more to put him at ease, but she didn't know how. Fetching Gareth appeared to be the only solu-tion, so she trotted up the stairs and down the corridor to what was now Helen's room.

There she found Gareth and Taran sitting together, confer-ring quietly and not necessarily about Helen. She distinctly heard mention of *Ceredigion*. Helen remained asleep on the bed, just as when Gwen had last seen her.

"I have a man here who says he has important news for us. He wanted to speak to Taran first, but then settled for Gareth."

Gareth pushed to his feet. "Did he say what it was about?"

"He refused to tell me anything. Just that it's news we would want to hear. He's French."

"French!" Gareth moved so quickly he practically threw him-self out of the room and down the stairs.

Gwen followed a little more slowly, uncertain as to why the fact that Henri was French had made Gareth so excited. She arrived to find her husband looking around the common room in puzzle-ment, his hands on his hips. "You said he was waiting here?"

"He was here a moment ago." First Gwen poked her head down the corridor towards their rooms and then went to the guesthouse door, thinking Henri might have felt too uncomfortable in the common area to stay and decided to wait outside. He hadn't poured himself any mead either.

Once outside, she even followed the path that led to the closest gate in the wall, the one they'd come through, looking for any sign of him. As had been the case when they'd come from the pavilion, it was unmanned.

That didn't mean people weren't about, and she hastened to where Iwan, Ralph, and Lord Ifon were just leading their horses from the stable, to all appearances about to enjoy a ride. "Did you see a man leave the guesthouse just now? He would have been dressed roughly."

Ralph frowned. "I don't think so."

Iwan shook his head. "So sorry."

Gwen nodded and let them go, in this case out the main gate, with a wave of hands to the red-headed monk who guarded it.

Gareth had followed into the yard. "A monk overheard two men talking in French late last night as they walked down the road past the granary where he was sleeping."

Gwen didn't bother wishing she'd known that earlier. There was no way she could have. "Well, this was only one man, and his Welsh was passable enough to be understood." She paused. "He did have a limp. He said it was an old war injury."

Gareth was chewing on his lower lip. "Did you get his name?"

"Henri de Tours." Gwen then hesitated, thinking back over everything he'd said—and not said. "Unfortunately, I realize now that I don't know a single other thing about him."

28

Day Three

Llelo

Llelo was trying to hold the sling and stone in such a way that nobody looking at him would think, "He's holding the murder weapon!" Not that Marc was dead. Nor Helen, for that matter.

He managed to make it all the way to the abbey without anyone stopping him or looking askance and arrived to find his parents standing outside the guesthouse, hands on their hips, mirror images of each other, which seemed like the perfect opportunity to announce what he'd found.

"I know how it was done," he said without preamble, holding up the weapon.

Gareth took the sling and examined it while Llelo told them about his morning's adventures.

He concluded, "If Marc's attacker really is the person who left a message for Cadwaladr at the mill, it doesn't feel like his attack on Marc was planned. From that distance, it might not have been possible to know who was being hit, not with Marc silhouetted as he must have been against the lights of the pavilion. The lights also would have made him an easier target."

"Whoever this is, he can think on his feet," Gwen said. "He planned his trip to the mill and his escape from it, and then was prepared to change course when things went awry."

"Most murders are not premeditated," Gareth said, "and you may be right that Marc was felled in a heat-of-the-moment impulse as the result of an unexpected encounter. Whoever attacked Marc hoped for a clear path back to the pavilion and didn't get it."

"He might not have intended to kill him either," Llelo said. "He needed him out of the way *right now* and ensured it by use of whatever lay to hand."

"His sling. Which he just happened to have brought with him because he planned ahead." Gwen wrinkled her chin. "Are we flat-out accepting that the culprit is a boy, like Iwan suggested?"

"Based on the footprints, now that I've seen them, I would say *yes*," Llelo said. "I've heard of a trick where a horse's shoes could be put on backwards to hide the direction of travel. For humans, too big shoes sounds like the next best thing."

"I'll need you to show me what you found, Llelo," Gareth said, "before it rains."

"I think the prints will be obvious, once you know where to look, though in the end it hardly matters. They led to the road and no farther, at least that I could tell. Maybe you can see more." He shrugged apologetically.

"Don't apologize. You did good work," Gareth said. "If not for the fact that all these machinations allowed him to get away, I would have said he was too clever for his own good."

"So are we wrong about the connection between what happened in the guesthouse and what happened to Marc?" Gwen was tapping a finger to her lip, speculating again and receiving a sour look from Gareth because of it. "Until now, I thought Marc was attacked because he served King Owain, and the intruder wanted to make sure he was unable to interrupt him or discover what he took."

"I would have said so too," Gareth said. "Sadly, we aren't getting any help from either Helen or Marc. If Marc was lured into the field in order to keep him from the guesthouse, he has no memory of it. According to him, he left the pavilion some time before we found him, but doesn't remember anything after that. Saran says he could have been lying there for an hour or more, slowly dying, until we turned him over. It certainly doesn't seem possible for the person who was at the mill to have also ransacked the king's room and attacked Helen. Despite the fact that Helen and Marc have similar injuries, the timing is too tight."

"When you look at it closely, while they were both wounded in the head, the method of attack was entirely different," Gwen said. "Marc was laid low by a stone from a sling. Helen was stabbed and then hit on the head."

"Have we found that weapon yet?" Llelo asked.

"No."

"Or have any idea why any of this happened?"

"We know why it happened." Gareth's lip curled. "It was done for the same reason in both cases: out of desperation."

Llelo truly couldn't understand how any man could attack a woman, but his father was right, and he'd seen enough desperation in his life to have an idea of how the events of the night could have unfolded. "No sign of the dagger either?"

"No," Gareth said, "and between you and me, I don't know that if I had a hundred knives in front of me I could match any one in particular to the wounds on Helen's body, even if Sister Efa would let me get close enough to do so. The cuts are also healing, which can only be good for Helen, but we aren't going to catch the one who hurt her that way."

"And then there's Henri," Gwen said.

Despite his find, Llelo had been feeling more and more disheartened as the conversation had gone on. Now his ears perked. "Who's Henri?"

His parents filled him in on what little they knew. Gareth had been about to set out on a more concerted effort to look for him when Llelo had arrived.

"I'll come too—" Llelo broke off at the arrival of his brother, who grinned when he saw them. "Oh good. You're all here."

Last Llelo had seen him, Dai had been asleep in their shared room. He'd obviously been out and about today too, and his bright eyes told Llelo he had good news before he spoke. "We found the weapon used on Helen."

29

Day Three

Gwen

"I must have dreamed about the footprints too because I awoke thinking about monks and latrines. Tad had left without waking us, so I got a late start."

"I was late getting up too," Llelo said.

"As was I," Gwen said.

Gareth took the (admittedly mild) censure of his sons in stride. "Nobody was late. We needed to sleep."

Dai led them through the abbey, his brother at his side, both boys talking as fast as a horse could gallop. Llelo was pleased to relate his successful engagement with footprints and a weapon, at which point Dai explained that he'd followed those Llelo had found—with a similar result.

"It was just like you said, Llelo." He had their full attention and was reveling in it. "Two sets of prints in particular stood out to me, with none of the peculiarities of those in the field. Just the impressions of men's boots. What you couldn't see last night was the drops of blood." He grinned. "I lost them on the road after the latrine block. But they definitely went towards the mill."

Gwen glanced at her husband. "Have we just tied off some of our loose strands?"

"It would be nice to think so." Just as Gareth spoke, they came through a gate in the western wall of the abbey and took a path towards where a half-dozen monks and nuns were clustered. Although Holywell Abbey was located above the Holywell Stream, it was fed by numerous rivulets that came down from heights that were higher still. One of these had been diverted to run right through the center of the abbey, providing fresh water as well as a means to remove waste from the kitchen, laundry, and latrines. Ultimately, all the separate channels came together at this point to enter the river here: the main drain.

As their little group approached, the circle of people at the drain opened to reveal a man wearing little more than a loincloth, despite the cool air, standing ankle deep in the channel. His skin was very white, but he otherwise appeared oblivious to the cold. Just upstream from where he stood was the metal grill that acted like a portcullis over the drain's exit from the abbey.

Abbess Nest gingerly held out a three foot length of wood, which Gwen didn't have to look at very hard to recognize as the missing bed slat. "Brother Petr found it floating in the drain."

One of the nuns asked, with an element of eagerness in her voice. "Was this the weapon used on that injured man, Marc?"

It was a good reminder that nobody was yet to know about Helen. "We don't know, but it is an interesting find, and we appreciate your efforts. Do you always check the contents of the drain as it leaves the abbey?" Gwen asked this because she wanted to know but also in an attempt to deflect further questions along that line.

"We do check it frequently, but to look today was your son's idea." Abbess Nest gestured to where Dai was trying to look modest and failing. "While the holes in the grate are large enough to allow general waste and water to pass through, they're small enough to catch objects of any significant size that might have been discarded by mistake."

"Or, in this case, on purpose," Gareth said.

Dai took the bed slat from Nest to show his parents. "Even having been put through the sewer, a bit of blood and hair remained, caught within a splinter at the end."

To Dai's credit, he had stopped preening. They were all sickened by the image of the bed slat connecting with Helen's head.

"Why not just dump this in the trees?" Llelo asked. "We have no way to link it to any particular person, regardless of what we think it was used for."

Gwen didn't wait to hear what answer Gareth came up with, whether something definitive or a suggestion that they not speculate until they could find the culprit and ask him. To her mind, the attacker had dropped it in the latrine shaft because he didn't want to be seen carrying it through the monastery. Why he'd brought it from the guesthouse in the first place also remained a mystery, though she could guess that he had seen what a useful weapon it could be and didn't want to discard it in case he needed it on the way out.

She didn't say any of that, not that she could, since everyone else other than Abbess Nest thought they were talking about Marc. Instead, she turned away, and began walking determinedly back the way they'd come. Dai took a few hurried steps after her to catch up. "Are you all right?"

"I'll be fine."

"Do you need me to come with you?"

Gwen looked back to where Llelo and Gareth were still talking with Abbess Nest, and then forward again about twenty yards to where Abbot Rhys was just crossing the path. At the sight of her looking at him, and the cluster of people beyond her, he stopped. She lifted a hand to tell him to wait and then turned back to Dai. "I'll be fine with Abbot Rhys. Right now, your father needs you more than I do."

That might be the truth, but the real story was that the stench from the drain had been impressive. Gwen needed to get away from it as quickly as possible, rather than endure the smell when she didn't have to. She could feel Dai's curious eyes on her. Normally Gwen had an iron stomach, but this brief encounter had her on the verge of vomiting for a second time in recent days, the first being in the guesthouse when she'd first seen Helen's wounds.

It wouldn't be startling to learn she was pregnant. That said, she had thought she might be pregnant at least eight times in the last two and a half years since Taran's birth, and been wrong every time, so she herself was still of a mind that it could be something she'd eaten. Time, as always, would tell.

Regardless, in this moment, Gwen was simply not capable of standing around an open sewer, and the matter of Henri's disappearance had to be pursued. She had no idea why he had left before he'd had the chance to speak to Gareth. At the encampment, he had been worried and insistent. His news had been urgent, or so he'd said.

Something had made him change his mind. She couldn't know what that was until she found him again, and that was a mystery which seemed within her ability to solve—especially when so much else about this investigation eluded her.

And it seemed to her that Abbot Rhys might be the one man, other than her own husband and sons, who was best able to help her solve it.

Because of his foreign accent and appearance, she was confident someone would know Henri and where he lived the moment she described him. This region of Wales, known as Tegeingl, had been fought over for decades, but the people who lived here remained the same, no matter how many times their land changed hands from one lord to another. They would know any time a stranger lived among them.

Rhys had waited for her to send Dai back to his father, and when she reached him, greeted her with a quirked eyebrow. "You have a look of determination on your face. Tell me what you need. Do we have a mission?"

"We do, if you're willing."

"For you, anything."

Gwen came to an abrupt halt. They were far enough away from the sewer channel that she couldn't smell it anymore. "Really, anything?"

Rhys smiled gently. "Since you would never ask me to do anything untoward, I feel I have made a safe offer."

Gwen eyed him as they fell into step beside each other. "I don't mean to take you for granted."

"I know that. Again, safe."

She let out a little laugh. Already her stomach was feeling better. "To the village, then. We are tracking an informant named Henri."

"A Frenchman? Here?"

"Yes to his origins and his location. He came to the encampment with news for us. I took him to the guesthouse to speak to Gareth, since he wouldn't speak only to me, and he left before I returned with Gareth."

"And you think he lives in the village?"

"I have no idea where he lives, but the village seems like a reasonable place to start. He was dressed in workmen's clothes."

Their first stop was with the red-headed monk who watched the front gate of the abbey. He was young and twitchy, in that he kept moving various limbs like he had ants crawling on them. His job wasn't really to guard the front gate—it wasn't as if he carried a weapon or even had a portcullis to drop—but to warn the Abbess when someone important arrived.

As soon as Gwen described the man she'd seen, the monk nodded vigorously and pointed down the road towards the village. "He's staying in his cousin's house, though his cousin married a girl from Denbigh so he doesn't live there anymore. Henri comes through every now and then, stays in the house, and gets himself hired on for food and a bed."

"Hired on by whom?" Gwen was in a hurry, but it seemed a question worth taking the time to ask.

"Anyone. Whoever needs help. Last year he was one of the men to rebuild our latrine blocks."

"How long has he been in the area this time?" Abbot Rhys asked.

"Maybe a week."

King Owain's party had been at Holywell Abbey for three of those days. "Did you speak to him today?"

"Not today. I can't understand a word he says anyway." The monk shrugged. "He keeps to himself, and he's a good worker."

"What work has he been doing recently?"

"He was mending roofs yesterday. The day before, I think he helped track down a lost lamb. Wherever he's needed, as I said."

"Thank you for your help. If you see him again, please waylay him and send for me." Gwen spoke the last words over her shoulder as she and Rhys headed down the lane. She appreciated that Rhys had left it to her to talk to the monk. He was the authority figure more than she was, but he had held back, just smiling and being as unintimidating as he was likely ever to be.

The entrance to the village was a matter of a hundred yards from the abbey gate. They took the distance at something close to a run, without actually running. Rhys too seemed to have been infected with her sense of urgency, since she had to take extra steps to keep up with his long strides. At least she was no longer feeling sick to her stomach. Instead she was feeling her heart race with a rising excitement.

Once in the village, all she had to do was ask a young boy, who was using a stick to corral a pig, "Can you tell me where Henri might be?" The boy knew whom she meant and pointed them to the far end of the village.

Rhys didn't have to be told twice, and she again had to take multiple extra steps to catch up with him. It wasn't until they had crossed the green that she saw what had caught his attention: the door to the cottage to which the boy had directed them had been left partly open. As they arrived on the threshold, low curses in French came from within.

They'd come to the right place.

Rhys put up one finger to tell her to wait while he snuck around the back. Gwen was honestly amused to see a man of Rhys's stature and character *sneak*. She gave him the count of ten he asked for and then put her shoulder to the door to ease it open all the way. "Henri? Are you here? It's Gwen, Gareth's wife."

While the muttering ceased, small movements continued. Gwen stepped into the room, blinking at the transition from the daylight outside to the relative darkness within. As her eyes adjusted, she spied Henri loading a wrapped brick of cheese into a satchel. A water skin was already looped around his shoulders.

He didn't even look up. "I'm leaving. Don't try to stop me."

"I don't understand. Why did you come to the encampment if you were only going to leave again before you told us anything?"

"I can't talk about it—" He broke off as the back door opened to reveal Abbot Rhys framed in the doorway.
"Why hello ... Henri, is it?" Rhys said with a remarkably gentle smile under the circumstances. "It's been a long time."

30

Day Three

Gwen

"You!" Henri reared back at the sight of him, and then turned, perhaps thinking to run. His expression appeared genuinely panicked.

Gwen blocked his way in the other direction. "Perhaps you'll be willing to talk to us now."

"Wait." Henri pulled up short and glanced from Gwen to Abbot Rhys and back again. "He's with *you*?"

"Of course he's with me. That surprises you?"

Henri swung around to look Rhys up and down more fully. "I would have thought disguising yourself as a priest was beyond even you."

"It would not have been, back in the day, but these days it is no disguise. I am a priest. I am also the Abbot of St. Kentigern's monastery."

Henri gaped at him. And then he laughed out loud. And laughed again. "I thought you died."

"You were meant to think it."

Completely gone by this point was the nervous laborer. Of course, that he knew Rhys and Rhys knew him meant he couldn't sustain it. "I imagine so. You have never failed at anything you set your mind to." His laughter gave way to a disdainful snort. "So anything I say to you will have the sanctity of the confessional?"

"It would if we were in a church and I were your priest, which we aren't and I'm not."

Henri grunted, accepting Rhys's comment and no longer afraid. "I must leave. Don't follow me."

"Please don't go." Gwen had no idea what was really going on, other than the obvious fact that the two men knew each other well enough for Henri to know so much about Rhys's character—and Rhys about his.

Henri scoffed. "Who is going to stop me? Him? You?"

"We are just the ones who've come inside." Gwen so rarely lied, but somehow the false words easily came to her in this moment.

"What did you want to speak to Lord Taran about?" Abbot Rhys added his voice to Gwen's.

"It doesn't matter now."

"It matters to us. We would hear it." Gwen was hoping if she said the same thing over and over in different ways, it would eventually have the outcome she wanted.

But Henri's chin stuck out. "Why should I say anything? I have done nothing wrong, so you can't keep me. I know Welsh law. What does it matter that I came to the encampment to speak to Lord Taran and then left before I could? That is not a crime."

"You are correct, of course. But we are in the midst of an investigation, which you are hindering."

"How so?"

"It's clear you have information we need. Tell us what you meant to say, and then we will let you be on your way."

Then Abbot Rhys added, changing tack, "You aren't here in this village by chance, are you?"

Henri ducked his head, much in the manner he'd done back at the guesthouse when she told him to wait for her. It worried her a bit, since he'd otherwise discarded all the workman's mannerisms he'd expressed when they'd first met. She wondered if it was the manner of a man considering not telling the truth. You would think after so many years of investigating, she would be better at knowing when she was being lied to.

"Here is the truth. I was looking for Lady Helen." He met Gwen's eyes, maybe for the first time. "I see by your face that you know her. Have you spoken with her?"

"We have not." It wasn't even a lie. As when she had lied earlier, Gwen wasn't sure where the instinct to hide the truth came from, but even at this late hour, she was sure she still needed to keep Helen's presence in the guesthouse a secret.

Henri subsided. "She and I were to have met last night. She never came."

Abbot Rhys nodded, as if this news was only to be expected. "You were her informant."

"For many years." Henri looked down at his feet for a moment, and when he looked up, his expression was rueful. "I would have called her friend, even."

"When did you arrange to meet?"

"I saw her nearly two months ago in Chester, for the first time in many years." Henri appeared to have capitulated completely. "Against my better judgment, I agreed to help her again. I move about a great deal, and I hear things. I am not so well off I would object to a few coins now and then for what I know. We arranged to meet again last night."

Two months ago sounded like when Helen was on her way back to court, after Taran had last seen her and after he'd asked her to marry him.

"*Where* were you supposed to meet?" Gwen held her breath, truly hoping the man would say "the mill on the Holywell stream", which would tie their multiple incidents together.

"At the Travelers' Rest, near Garreg Ateb." He meant the Answer Stone, an ancient marker perhaps a mile to the east of Gwenffrewi's holy well.

"What time was this to have been?"

"As the bell tolled for Compline."

Things were starting to make more sense, and Gwen was a little annoyed that she wouldn't have known any of this if they hadn't tracked him down. They'd already determined that Compline must have been about the time Helen was encountering whoever had hurt her. Gwen had started back to the guesthouse to put her children to bed not long after.

"Why were you so reluctant to tell us this?"

"My apologies. Earlier, I was trying to ask about Helen without asking overtly. I didn't know who you were. I didn't even know if Helen had come to the abbey or had just been delayed. But I did hear that someone had been attacked, and I was worried it was she. Lord Taran, as King Owain's steward, seemed to be the most likely person to know about it. That's why I asked for him."

"How long did you wait at the inn for her?" Abbot Rhys said.

"All night." His voice cracked, and as he looked back to Rhys, his expression was imploring. "And all morning. I tell you, something is very wrong here. At the very least, those two other Frenchmen are up to no good."

It was as if he'd lit a flame in a dark place. "What two other Frenchmen?"

"Have you not encountered them? I'm very worried they had something to do with why Helen never came to see me!"

"What do you know about them?" Gwen asked.

"Nothing." His jaw worked. "Or at least nothing much. I encountered them a few days ago on the road. They asked me for directions to the abbey." His eyes widened. "Come to think on it, I was walking to the Travelers' Rest at the time, and they were going the other way!"

As the realization hit him, it was as if that same fire had just been lit under him. He shoved a spare shirt into his satchel and swung it on his back. "It's been safe for me here for a very long time, but now it's clear that every moment I stay, I am in danger. Someone might even try to make it look as if *I* have done something wrong.

You thought so! I can't help you more." His gaze went to Rhys instead of Gwen. "I will disappear. Start over. Like you did."

"What someone are you talking about?" Gwen said. "Whoever it is, we can protect you."

"Nobody can protect me. Not from *him*."

Once again, the tenor of the conversation had changed. "Who's *him*?"

But Henri was back to looking at Abbot Rhys, who was still effectively blocking the rear door. And if Henri was going to leave by the front, he would have to get past Gwen. She wouldn't tackle him, but she took a step to center herself in the doorway, and pushed the door closed.

It made the room much darker, to the point that Gwen struggled to make out Henri's expression. Maybe that was what Henri had needed, that small way to hide himself from her gaze, to find the courage to speak.

"You said you wanted to know why I fled the abbey just now? I'll tell you why. It's because as we were entering the guesthouse, I saw another man from those days, one who knows I have the power to ruin him. I've been running from him for a long time." Henri spoke quickly, the words tumbling over each other to get out of his mouth, almost as if he knew that if they didn't, he wouldn't say anything at all. "Those Frenchmen must be working for him. I think Helen might even have wanted to talk to me about him."

Gwen waited. That was no explanation at all, but if Henri needed to tell the story in his own way, she was going to let him. Maybe they were finally getting at the truth.

"What are you talking about?" Rhys spoke sharply. "One of the monks?"

"Not a monk. You may be the only one who can affect that kind of transformation." Despite the tenseness in his frame, Henri's mouth quirked. "This is a man in King Owain's retinue. He may not be going by the name he had when I knew him any more than you and I are." He gestured to Rhys. "Rhys, is it?"

Rhys's glance in Gwen's direction showed wariness—and maybe warning. She didn't want to put words in Henri's mouth so instead she said, "Can you describe him?"

"Heavy jowls. A full head of gray hair. He was known at court as Jehan."

As Rhys drew in an audible breath, Gwen sagged a bit against the edge of the nearby table. "That name becomes Iwan in Welsh. He has served King Owain for many years."

"So you say." Henri scoffed. "I'm leaving, and you can't stop me." He made for the front door, apparently having decided Gwen was the softer target. He was right, of course. She couldn't stop him, not unless she was willing to use her belt knife, and even then, he had one of his own.

And, of course, they hadn't brought anyone with them, as Henri would discover the moment he walked out the door.

Gwen could still try to delay him with more talk. "What do you know about him?"

"More than you!" He glanced back at Rhys. "Either of you."

"So tell us," Rhys said calmly, with the unspoken rest of the sentence *if you're so certain.* "If you do, we'll let you go."

Henri glared at Gwen. She still had her back to the door and wasn't going to move without more provocation than a glare. Henri seemed to realize that too because he took the bargain Rhys had offered. "I saw him kill the last man who discovered the truth about him. He has never served Owain like he pretends. He is King Madog's spy and always has been."

31

Day Three
Gareth

At first, the finding of the bed slat had made Gareth feel as if he was *too* lucky, but then he reminded himself that he had trained his sons to be investigators, even if Dai had chosen instead to become a Dragon. Both sons were smart and capable and sometimes had ideas of their own that led them to places he hadn't thought of or hadn't made a priority. Last night, Dai had become involved inadvertently and entirely on his own accord, and today Gareth was almost embarrassed at how he himself hadn't thought to wonder why the intruders had used the latrine on their way out of the abbey. The truth was, he'd been so focused on Cadwaladr, he'd had no space in his head for anything else.

That was a giant flaw in his process, he knew. He tried not to let his hatred of Cadwaladr get the better of him, but it was as if the man were a monstrous beast he couldn't stop staring at. If he was anywhere near, or the threat of him was, he was all Gareth could see.

Fortunately, Gareth did have people to rely upon to keep him from wandering too far from the main point, and he just had to be grateful for that. Having asked whatever questions he'd thought relevant of the gathered monks and nuns, in hopes any of them had seen anything useful (none had, not that they could remember), he'd thanked everyone profusely, and set off with both boys back to Gwynedd's encampment. It was long past time he shared what he knew with the king and Hywel. Between the bed slat and the sling, he had real physical evidence for the first time.

He could also take a moment to avail himself of a meal. If the rumbling in Dai's stomach was any indication, he needed to eat too.

But almost before these resolutions could be confirmed, the ripple of excited voices of a great crowd rose up ahead of them. Having come around a cluster of bushes, they all pulled up short at the entrance to the field in which they'd found Marc last night. It was suddenly full of people setting up tents.

Llelo, who was in the lead on the narrow path, spoke with horror in his voice. "What are they doing? They're destroying the crime scene! I didn't even get a chance to show you what I found!"

Gareth put a hand on his shoulder, in case he intended to launch himself at the closest worker. "Look at the banner."

Dai recognized it first. "Powys." Then he frowned. "But that isn't Madog's banner. The king hasn't come. Isn't that—"

"Yes. That's Susanna's standard."

Not all queens had their own sigil, but upon her marriage to Madog, Susanna's father had given her a banner showing both the red lion of Gwynedd and the black one of Powys. It was meant to indicate an alliance and a merging, in a very real sense, of the two kingdoms. When Madog's daughter Marared had married Owain's son Iorwerth, Madog had done the same for his daughter, with slight variations from Susanna's banner, though again with the two lions.

Not that Madog for one moment intended to give up any real power. Both he—and old King Gruffydd before him—saw these marriages as an opportunity to increase the power of his own kingdom at the expense of the other man's. Unfortunately for Madog, for the last thirty years since Susanna had married him, Gwynedd's star had been on the ascendancy, regardless of Madog's desire to ensure a different outcome.

"The question remains as to why Madog didn't come with her. Owain will be happy to see his sister, but I confess, I'm not." Dai's awareness of the nuances of politics had become increasingly sophisticated this past year.

"I, for one, prefer her smile to his," Gareth said.

Dai nudged his father's elbow. "Llelo and I will be with the Dragons if you need us." The two young men left by a less public avenue to find their companions, while Gareth continued straight on, arriving at the entrance to the pavilion just as Owain kissed his sister's cheeks in welcome. Knowing his place, Gareth moved closer still, behind and to the left of Hywel, who stood next in line for the queen to greet.

"So good to see you well, Hywel." That was as fraught a comment as any she could have made, considering the fact that her husband had tried to murder Hywel when he'd last visited Dinas Bran, after Rhun's death.

Rather than take offense in any way, Hywel grinned. "Always a pleasure, aunt."

Gareth was next, and at her initial sight of him, Susanna's face fell. Nonetheless, he bowed over her hand. "My lady."

"Sir Gareth, please give my greetings to your lovely wife."

"Of course, my lady."

Her eyes skated towards the dais where Gwalchmai and Meilyr were preparing to sing, and some of the tension left her. She didn't outright ask how Gwalchmai was faring. Even she didn't have the gall. She'd almost killed him a year ago, regardless of what her actual intentions had been, so her reception could only be cordial, never effusive, with anyone in his family. The irony was if she hadn't just arrived, Gareth might have wondered at her culpability in the felling of Marc or Helen, since she had hit Gwalchmai on the head with a plank not dissimilar from the bed slat they'd just recovered from the drain.

Gareth thought Gwalchmai had genuinely forgiven her, even if the rest of them were still finding it hard to do so. That was probably one reason why both Llelo and Dai had made themselves scarce upon her arrival. Better to absent themselves than to have to look her in the eye, even from afar, and pretend they were happy she was here.

Once Gareth moved away, Susanna was back to smiling, and soon the whole family, wives and children as well, were ensconced at the high table, having a joyful reunion. At times it appeared as if they were all talking at once. Susanna wouldn't have seen any of them since the previous year at the wedding of Marared (her stepdaughter) to Iorwerth.

And then Cadwaladr arrived. "Susanna!" He bellowed the word across the pavilion, and Susanna rose to her feet in order to go to him for a very public embrace.

"Is she telling us Cadwaladr is the true brother, the one in favor with Powys, or is this just familial affection?" Evan delivered the words low in Gareth's ear. Gareth himself had been thinking along similar lines. By going to him rather than waiting for Cadwaladr to come to her, Susanna had made herself appear the lesser of the two.

"I don't think there's any *just* about it. Really, it's both. She loves him the most and always has, *and* she is showing us how in favor he is with Powys. Neither trait is likely to endear him further to Owain, but that was never going to happen anyway. I do think Susanna is telling Owain he must tread carefully."

"All that from a hug." Evan shook his head.

"Or she's just happy to see him and didn't want to put up a fuss by denying him the embrace he wanted."

Evan laughed.

He wasn't the only one. The laughter continued in the pavilion, moment to moment. Susanna's arrival had increased the merriment, which hadn't exactly been absent the last three nights, but had maybe been a little forced or muted at times. They'd all been waiting for Powys to come, wondering if it even would. She wasn't Madog, but her arrival meant they hadn't traveled all this way for nothing.

Even though the sun hadn't yet set, Gwalchmai and Meilyr sang from the dais, wine and mead flowed, and what food was ready was served early, with the roast pig that was intended for the evening meal still coming later. Even Hywel was enlisted in the festivities. Susanna was his aunt, and she could always get him to do what she wanted.

For his part, Gareth was feeling something less than jovial. He might even have called himself morose. Llelo had found himself another post upon which to prop his shoulder, and Gareth made his way across the pavilion to set himself on the opposite side.

"Have you seen your mother?"

"Not since we found that bed slat."

"Do you have any idea where she went?" Gareth's stomach was suddenly tight, and he was glad he hadn't eaten more than a few bites of mutton and parsnips. Something wasn't right, no matter how happy everyone else seemed to be.

"You could ask Dai. He went with her initially, but she told him to stay with you."

Gareth was suddenly furious. "He let her go alone—"

"She was with Abbot Rhys."

That was better. But still, something deep in Gareth's gut told him to find his wife *right now*. While she drew him to her normally, this felt different. He decided not to fight the impulse, not after the few days they'd had. "Where?"

"Last I saw, they were walking towards the abbey's main entrance."

Gareth was heading away from the pavilion before his son had finished talking. By the time they reached the road, he had Dai,

Evan, and Aron with him too. He didn't know where they'd come from, but he would never object to their presence.

They stopped first at the priory gatehouse where a red-haired, wide-eyed monk pointed them in the direction of the village almost as soon as Gareth opened his mouth. Gareth proceeded to take the distance toward the village at a flat run, urgency a goad in his belly. The others kept pace.

They had reached the green when the front door of a house at the far end was wrenched open to reveal a man with a satchel over his shoulder.

A shout emanated from behind him. "Henri!"

"That's Abbot Rhys's voice!" Dai broke into a run towards the man, who froze on the doorstep, conflicted between going forward or turning back.

But then Abbot Rhys and Gwen appeared on either side of him.

As Gareth ran up too, Gwen made a motion with one hand. "You said you wanted to meet my husband, Henri. Gareth, this is the man I was telling you about. It seems he had a great deal to say to us after all."

32

Day Four
Gareth

It had been not quite dawn, so still gray outside, when Gareth had found Hywel just coming out of his tent. At long last, he was able to lay before him what he needed to know.

"What is Madog up to, sending his spy into our midst as if he's a friend—and then sending his wife to lie for him?" Gareth was hunched over, his elbows on his knees and his hands clasped before him. What he really wanted to do was punch something. Or someone (Cadwaladr, or maybe Madog).

"We already knew he was up to something. We just didn't know what. I suppose we still don't." The prince's demeanor was the same as if he was sitting around his father's council table instead of on one of the beds in Gareth's wagon, his little home away from home.

"My apologies for that, my lord." Gareth sat on the other bed, which, like the one Hywel occupied, was raised up off the floor to allow storage underneath. Over the fortnight of their journey to Holywell, Gareth had learned to love his wagon, almost more than was reasonable, after decades of laying his head wherever it came to rest at whatever *llys* or castle his lord willed. To know that every night he was going to sleep in the same place, no matter in which *place* he found himself, was almost too good to be true.

Except, of course, because of Cristina's demands, the wagon was currently being used by Gwalchmai and Cian, Marged's son. For now, having booted the young men out of their beds, it was a convenient consultation spot. Evan was loitering outside, keeping watch for eavesdroppers. The canvas walls were hardly sufficient to block the sound of their voices if anyone got close. They didn't care if Evan overheard. In fact, Gareth was assuming he would hear most of what they were saying so Gareth wouldn't have to go over it all with him again when he and the prince were done.

Hywel's look was almost pityingly. "None of this is your fault."

"I do know that."

"Madog does what he does, and even if a new agreement came out of this peace conference, we were never going to put off conflict with Powys for more than a few years. Though, admittedly, I was hoping for at least a few months. For now, hold yourself to determining what Henri and Iwan and Madog have to do with Helen and Marc—and Cadwaladr!"

"I regret how little we still know," Gareth said. "The two attacks, plus Cadwaladr's meeting in the mill occurred nearly simultaneously. One person could not have been present at them all, even if he had planned everything out in advance."

"While you've been keeping all this from me for two days," this comment was accompanied by a glower, "has it also been kept from my father?"

"Yes." It was a dangerous truth, but Gareth couldn't pretend otherwise.

"How did you manage to convince him not to enter his own room all day yesterday?"

"We didn't have to convince him of anything," Gareth said. "He doesn't like sleeping in the guesthouse anyway. And he had other things to think about."

Hywel's eyes narrowed. "Surely he missed Taran."

"Cristina told him Helen had arrived, and that he was with her. My apologies again, my lord, but your father has been assuming, since Madog isn't here anyway, that they have been enjoying each other's company."

Hywel snorted. "He would accept that, wouldn't he, even at his age?"

"For once, Cristina has encouraged that kind of thinking."

"And now you tell me your nanny is sleeping with Geraint, who is Cadwaladr's man. So for who knows how long, we've had a spy in our camp."

Gareth nodded. "I am so sorry, my lord."

"I can hardly blame *you*. Cadwaladr is *my* uncle! What does Marc remember?"

"Nothing."

"And we can hardly blame him for that, can we?"

Gareth looked at him curiously. "Do you think he's hiding something?"

"Oh, they're all hiding something. The question is what? And we have barely touched upon the snake we let into our midst, who is truly the most pressing matter."

"Your father loves Iwan and trusts him," Gareth said. "Henri appears truly terrified of him and believes your father will see any accusation against him as his word against Iwan's."

"Henri's not wrong about which one my father is going to believe. He has known Iwan for decades—seemingly since childhood—and we met Henri yesterday. If only Helen would wake! Maybe she could tell us what is really going on here."

Gareth acknowledged the difficulties.

"Still, perhaps it isn't as disastrous as all that." The prince sighed. "What could Iwan have learned since we came from St. Kentigern's that Madog doesn't already know? That we have no love for Powys? That is hardly news."

Gareth was far less complacent. "My lord, while I admit I have less experience thinking as a spy, I can see how it could be much worse than that. How much could you or Mari have told her father that Ralph might then have told Iwan, as an old friend. He is discreet, but he trusts Iwan. This betrayal is as profound as any I have ever encountered."

Hywel grimaced. "So where is Henri now? Did you let him go?"

"We did not. He has made more than clear that he wants to run but, if he did, we wouldn't have his first-hand testimony about

Iwan's allegiances. Even if your father takes Henri's word over Iwan's, he isn't that trusting, not even if it's Gwen and Rhys testifying. We had to keep him close. That said, Henri refused to stay in the abbey or the village a moment longer than he had to. Thus, I have a plan to borrow Aron and Dai from you this morning and send them with Henri to the Travelers' Rest, which is the inn where he was supposed to have met Helen. If those on duty recognize him as having waited all night for her that night, we will know at the very least that he cannot be responsible for anything that happened at the abbey. That will help your father believe what he says."

"Well, that's something." Hywel rolled his eyes. "We'll be able to eliminate the one man who came to us and offered what he knew to be the truth."

"To be fair, he did run away once already," Gareth said. "I neither trust nor distrust him, which is why we have not told him that Helen was attacked and remains asleep in the guesthouse. If he had anything to do with what happened to her, he must be very worried by now as to where she went."

Hywel grunted his understanding. "Meanwhile even now Iwan is sleeping within our encampment, sure of his place in our retinue. How could my father and Ralph have trusted him all these years? How could they not have known?"

"That is always the question: *how could you not have known?* Sometimes signs were missed, and sometimes there was no way to have known." Gareth looked intently at his lord. "You can't tell anyone about the investigation yet either, my lord, especially not Mari and Ralph."

"Of course I won't tell them." Hywel tsked under his breath. "Sometimes you may have greater insight than I, but I was doing this before you. I *trained* you."

Gareth was content to admit that was true. Though, to be fair, Gwen's role in Gareth's education had been as influential as Hywel's. "They have known Iwan a long time. They are going to be devastated when the truth comes out."

"If." Hywel made a face. "If the truth comes out. We are going to have to think about how to tell them, and even if we tell them. It might be better to leave Iwan exactly where he is."

That was true spy thinking, something Gareth was still slow to get his head around sometimes. "How attentive were you to everyone's comings and goings in the pavilion that night?"

"Not enough, apparently."

"I feel the same," Gareth said. "How many could have been gone for a quarter of an hour or even an hour and we wouldn't have known? How many *more* traitors do we have in our midst?"

"I agree with you that the window of opportunity was relatively small. What seems most likely to me is that the two monks Cristina saw and Iolo overheard were in my father's room, and it is they who attacked Helen."

"I agree, and neither of them is Iwan. Equally obvious is that they are working for someone. Maybe Iwan. Henri thinks so."

"That means all of them are working for Madog, then."

Gareth bent his head. "With your permission, I intend to send out your *teulu* to find these two Frenchman. There can't be that many places they could be hiding. You will be safe enough here within the encampment with the rest of the Dragons."

Hywel made a *pouf* sound with his mouth that itself was very French. "You are very free with my men!"

Gareth knew Hywel wasn't really offended. "It feels like we are running out of time. We have to act. We can't wait for events to unfold."

Hywel's eyes brightened. "You have an actual plan?"

Gareth nodded, solid ideas forming in his head even as they spoke. "I have several."

33

Day Four
Gwen

The previous morning, Gwen had endured a painful confession from Marged, one she was still regretting. This morning, by contrast, she slipped out early, without giving Marged a chance to explain or apologize again, if she was looking for the opportunity to do so. Gwen suspected she had seen Geraint again in the night, which made her all the more careful to be awake and waiting when Gwen awoke, so she could mind the children.

Marged was trying to be perfect. That couldn't continue if she was to stay on as their nanny, but Gwen wasn't going to deal with her troubles now. Besides, Marged's relationship with Geraint would resolve one way or another. If it didn't last, Gareth and Gwen could continue to employ her, and if it endured, Marged would go with Geraint to wherever Cadwaladr was living. Gwen saw no point in borrowing trouble. She would think about finding a new nanny if it became necessary.

It was thoughts of the investigation, and Marged's liaison in particular, that had Gwen rising so early today. Rather than thinking about footprints, as Llelo and Dai had done, she had been considering all the ways in which royal courts, as much as villages and towns, were composed of fallible people, who pursued what they wanted, often impulsively, without thinking through the consequences. This fact applied to murder, but it also applied to relationships.

Within Welsh law, a wife could divorce her husband on the grounds that he was unfaithful, and vice versa. Even so, while divorce was rare, infidelity was not. Most of the time, Gwen endeavored to know every secret and all the gossip, while also ignoring it. That was a fine line to walk, but one Hywel had asked her to tread before she'd married Gareth.

Thus, when she found Cerys sitting by herself in the pavilion, staring down at her food without eating it, Gwen sat on the bench opposite and began filling a plate for herself. "What were you really doing in that field, Cerys?"

Cerys jerked up as if she were a marionette pulled by a puppeteer's strings, but after a single blink, had herself in hand again. "What I told your husband. I was finding time for myself."

Gwen believed her now no more than she had when Gareth had told her about it. "I let that lie stand for a whole day, and I would have let it stand forever if it wasn't so urgent we know the truth at least of this. I wouldn't want you accused of harming Marc if you didn't do it."

Cerys let the hand that was bringing a piece of bread to her mouth drop in astonishment. "I wouldn't! I didn't lie!"

"Not about that, perhaps. Gareth and Dai took you at your word, as all men seem to, but I have known about your on-and-off liaison with Marc for months." At Cerys's next attempt at denial, Gwen put out a hand. "I haven't shared this knowledge with anyone, not even Gareth. I endeavor to ignore what isn't relevant. Now it is."

"I don't know what you're talking about." Cerys pressed her lips together.

Gwen reached out a hand, less stern than before. "I will keep your secret if I can, and I understand why you lied, but this is an investigation." In truth, and less flatteringly to Gwen, she also wanted Cerys to know she hadn't pulled the wool over *everyone's* eyes. Most of the time, Gwen tried to keep herself above such petty matters, but in this moment she was feeling burdened by her secrets. The list of spies at this conference had to include her too.

At the furtive way Cerys looked around, Gwen added, "Nobody is close enough to hear us. But if you're that worried, all you have to do is nod or shake your head in answer to my question. Were you in that field to meet with Marc?"

By way of reply, Cerys rose to her feet, gracefully and entirely contained. "I have nothing more to say."

But then she paused and, with a bard's sense of the moment, *nodded*.

"Thank you."

Cerys didn't acknowledge Gwen's reply, instead walking quickly away from the table. Gwen let her go. It was enough to have persuaded Cerys to admit the truth.

She was just settling back down to the food on her plate, when Sioned slipped into Cerys's place. Once again, she was weeping. With everything else that had gone on since the attack on Helen in the guesthouse, Gwen had given Cristina's maid no further thought.

Now Sioned clutched at Gwen's hand, fat tears coursing down her cheeks. "I lied! I lied!" Great sobs burst from her. "It's all my fault!"

Gwen had been the receiving ear of more than one spontaneous confession in the midst of their numerous investigations, but she never looked for it, and it wasn't always clear from whom one might come. Unlike Marged's revelation yesterday, Gwen was happy to hear whatever Sioned had to say.

But not here.

It was early enough that the only other residents of the pavilion were at least twenty paces away. Even so, it would be impossible for any of them to miss Sioned's distress, as she was making a spectacle of herself. Hopefully, thanks to previous experience, they would assume Cristina had done or said something to upset Sioned, and Sioned had come to Gwen for solace.

With a rueful smile at the various members of the court who were looking openly at them, Gwen urged Sioned out of the pavilion and up the pathway to the abbey. Once inside the gate, she moved at first towards the guesthouse, but Sioned dug in her heels. "I'm not going in there!"

"Of course. I'm so sorry. Please forgive me." Gwen thought the squeamishness ridiculous, but she was more interested in finding a quiet corner to talk than upbraiding Sioned for her misplaced sensitivity. They ended up instead next to the laying out room by the laundry. Unusually for an investigation, it was the one place they hadn't had to use.

Yet.

With the thought, Gwen immediately touched the wood of the door. Investigations were no place for superstition, but sometimes she couldn't help herself. Then, as Sioned continued to weep, Gwen mentally threw up her hands and pushed open the door. The room was empty, clean, and turned out to be a sensibly constructed laying-out room, with a gap between the top of the wall and the eaves to let in fresh air. It was chilly, but no more than standing outside would be.

Gwen kept a grip on both of Sioned's arms. "Tell me what this is about."

"It's that woman who was attacked!"

Her voice came loudly, making Gwen all the more glad they had retired to the laying-out room. Sioned had always been the weak link in keeping the attack on Helen a secret. It would be even more difficult if Gwen couldn't calm her now. "How is that?"

"I should have been there!"

Gwen had already lost the thread of the conversation. It felt like talking to Marged all over again. Or maybe Henri. "Did you yourself attack Helen?"

The question shocked Sioned into a sudden gulp and the cessation of her sobs. Staring at Gwen through watery eyes, she said, "No! Of course not!"

It was a genuine denial, one Gwen had no trouble believing, in the same way she'd believed Cerys when she said she hadn't attacked Marc. The tears were real; the guilt and shame were real. But none was because Sioned herself had hurt Helen. Gwen had no idea why Sioned thought any of this was her fault, and she worked to find a question she could ask that would bring understanding. "Where were you when she was attacked?"

"I was with ... with ... with Cadell!"

Gwen blinked, surprised that her first question had produced an answer and also narrowing her eyes because she'd heard that name before but had no recollection where. "Who is Cadell?"

"He helps out at the abbey. He is so gentle and kind!" Stars appeared in Sioned's eyes, amidst the tears.

Gwen couldn't help thinking the last thing she needed was another besotted middle-aged woman. "He's a monk?"

"Oh no! He lost his wife a few years ago, and Abbess Nest gave him work. He lives in the village here, but didn't feel he had a calling as a monk."

That Gwen could understand. Taking in strays was what Abbess Nest did. She'd helped Gareth too and who knew how many others. Of course, Gareth couldn't have joined the community he'd been protecting then, since at the time it was composed entirely of nuns.

"How does this make you responsible for what happened to the woman in the guesthouse?"

"I wasn't supposed to be with him. I was supposed to be preparing the queen's room for her, and then I was to wait at the guesthouse for her to return from the feast."

Understanding was creeping in. "So when the queen explained how she'd followed me shortly after I left the feast with my children, and implied you were with her, you weren't?"

"Oh I was! I met her there and told her I had finished and thought it best to escort her, since this was a strange place. She was *pleased* at my attentiveness." This last statement was accompanied by renewed sobs.

Gwen would have to confirm with Cristina, but the queen was a worldly person, married to a man who was routinely unfaithful. Gwen suspected she had no illusions about what Sioned had really been doing. Gwen would leave the sorting out of Cadell and Sioned to her, but if Cristina didn't want to lose her maid, the king might end up with a new handyman when he left Holywell.

How ironic that Sioned was upset she hadn't been in the guesthouse to hear the attack on Helen, when Marged, who *had* been there, even though she wasn't supposed to be, was upset because she'd been there and had heard nothing.

By extension, this also explained Sioned's extreme shock two nights ago when they'd found Helen on the floor of the queen's room. At the time, Gwen had thought her reaction excessive for the occasion. Now she knew why.

Gwen rubbed Sioned's arms and convinced her to look directly into her face as she spoke. Sioned needed calming down and, if it was within Gwen's power, absolution. "The attack was not your fault. You didn't know it was going to happen, you didn't plan it, and you were entirely uninvolved. If you had been in the room when the attacker arrived, you might have been hurt or even killed. The person who did this was very determined and desperate, and that made him vicious."

Sioned blinked, her tears starting to dry now. "I hadn't thought of that."

Which was another mark in her favor. Gwen was exposed all the time to the worst in people, and she hadn't thought much of Sioned up until now. But it seemed that when Sioned had looked down at Helen's body as she lay slumped against the wall, she hadn't thought *that could be me*, but instead had felt guilt that she hadn't been there to stop it. Honestly, other than the propensity for tears and histrionics, Sioned appeared to be a very loyal servant. Cristina would be wise to keep her.

"You have a kind heart. I will say as much to Cristina, though if you want to be with Cadell after this week, you should tell her the truth."

"I can't." Sioned's head bent, and her shoulders slumped, indicating dejection and probably exhaustion.

"You must." Gwen squeezed her hand. "Do you love Cadell?"

"Yes!"

"Does he love you?"

Sioned nodded vigorously. "He says he does, but he has very little to his name. He doesn't see how he can provide for me."

Gwen waggled her head. "In the end, I think that matters less than love. Gareth had nothing when he asked for my hand the first time and my father refused him. He was saved by Abbess Nest too. Tell the queen you love the man and then bring him to her. But don't go to her like this. Have the courage of your convictions. You might find things aren't quite as dire for the two of you as you fear."

Cristina might not do the right thing. It was within her character to deny Sioned what she wanted simply because she could. If that's how things fell out, Gwen decided then and there to expend whatever favor she had in Cristina's eyes on Sioned's behalf.

34

Day Four
Llelo

Llelo's task this morning, as given to him by his father, was to sit with Helen. On the surface, it might appear to be a fruitless waste of his time, but he'd accepted that *someone* needed to be there when she woke, if she woke, to not only care for her but hear immediately if she had a story to tell and what it was. Taran was so far gone by now, Gareth didn't trust him to relay anything clearly. It was doubtful whether he could even stay awake for one more hour.

Sure enough, when Llelo arrived in Helen's room, he found Taran on his knees beside her bed, praying, with tears running down his cheeks. It wasn't so much that Llelo found such open pain embarrassing, but rather that he'd intruded on the man's private communion with God. He hovered in the doorway, uncertain, but Taran merely stood, nodding and thanking him for being willing to give him a brief respite. Llelo didn't know if Taran had eaten any of the food he'd been brought over the last two days but thought it unlikely. He was relieved to see him willing to walk away, even for a quarter of an hour.

"I have been touching her lips with water from the holy well," Taran said as he left. "If you could continue while I'm gone, I would be grateful. I can't think of anything else to do. Nor can anyone else. Sister Efa says we just have to *wait*." He bent his head for a moment. "Much longer and I will have nothing to wait for."

"Has she responded to you at all?"

Taran's expression was suddenly transformed to one so full of hope it was almost as painful to see as the tears had been earlier. "Several times she has opened her mouth enough for the water to pass her lips, and then she's swallowed it. Abbess Nest says her body knows what it needs and wants to live. So I keep giving it to her."

Though Llelo knew nothing of healing, that did sound hopeful to him too, and he assured Taran he would continue.

So he sat beside Helen and fed her the holy water, drop by drop. In between drops, he thought about the investigation, about how she had been attacked and why that might have been. He honestly didn't see why the intruders, these fake monks or Frenchmen or whatever they were, had felt they needed to harm her so badly they left her for dead. She'd fought back, yes, but she was a middle-aged woman. She would be no match for virtually any man Llelo knew.

He fed her another few drops of water, all the while repeating perhaps the same prayer Taran had: *please God, let her wake up!*

Helen seemed to be accepting more and more water. Beyond just letting the drops wet her lips or roll out of her mouth and down her cheek, she was actually swallowing, as Taran had said. In between drops, as Llelo's prayers grew more fervent, he found himself on his feet, even pacing around the bed the best he could in such a small space.

But even now, his prayers gave way to his questions, which were manifold: 1) Why had Helen been in the guesthouse at all? 2) Once there, why had she confronted the intruders, or they her? 3) Why had their encounter been so violent? and 4) What had prompted the tearing apart of Cristina's room when there was nothing valuable in it—neither in hers nor in Owain's?

Or was that wrong?

Truly, a large part of any investigation was knowing the right questions to ask.

While he didn't know any of the answers to his questions, he was beginning to craft a story in his own head about how Helen had come to be lying on the bed. It fit all the facts as he knew them, at least about the attack on her.

First off, it was incontrovertible that she'd been stabbed. Were her wounds what the bloody rags on King Owain's bed had been about? Had those men attacked her elsewhere so she retreated to King Owain's room to tend to herself? His mother thought there was too much blood for that, implying instead that she had stabbed one of the men. Regardless, Helen had ended up in Cristina's room in an attempt to escape their clutches.

It hadn't saved her. They'd broken down the door, cut her belly, swung the bed slat at her head, and then fled, leaving her for dead. While the room was small enough that a struggle could explain some of the chaos they'd seen when they'd arrived, it couldn't justify the way Cristina's clothing had become scattered on the floor. Regardless of who had ransacked the room, Helen hadn't given her injuries to herself.

It was the implications of that thought that preoccupied him. His parents were busy seeing to the whole of the investigation, which left Llelo free to focus on just one thing: *why?*

He kept repeating the same thoughts over and over again: Helen had come upon the intruder in Owain's room; she'd left the room to come to Cristina's; the intruder had needed to break the latch and frame to get inside.

Why was he that desperate? Why not just patch himself up, as he had ultimately done, and leave?

Llelo found himself hesitating more and more over the spot where they'd found Helen lying. And the solution, when it ultimately stared him in the face, was that Helen herself had taken something and then hidden it. And it was something the intruders had wanted.

Llelo turned slowly on one heel. Taran had declared that nothing was missing from King Owain's room, but what if he was wrong? Maybe Helen had made sure they didn't find what they were looking for. And what if that something was hidden inside *this* very room. If he was right, that would explain the desperation the intruder exhibited, the violence, and the aura of frustration.

He began at the top of the walls, though as a much smaller person than Llelo, to get up there Helen would have had to stand on a chair. He himself was tall enough to reach the room's ceiling, and he ran his hands around the posts and beams that held up the roof.

Truly, if this was the first place Llelo thought to look, it would have been the intruder's too.

Since that was something Helen would/could/should have known, Llelo was unsurprised to find nothing. Next he did a full circuit of the room with one hand on the wall. These were coated in plaster and distressingly free of holes or blemishes. Had any been in evidence, they would also have been obvious weak points that might have hidden secret spaces within the walls. Even more, because this was an abbey, the walls remained unadorned, so even the queen's room contained no warming tapestries or rugs. The only decoration was the thick blanket on the bed under which Helen lay.

Ignoring the bed, which he wouldn't disturb anyway, and trunks, which had been thoroughly searched by the intruders, Llelo decided any hiding place had to be a natural feature of the room itself. That put him on his hands and knees on the floor. The disdainful half of him told him he was wasting his time, that it was a fruitless errand to search for something that wasn't there. The other half replied that he had nothing better to do between giving sips of water to Helen.

Then, just as he was about to quit, having felt all around the base of the wall for any soft spot or hidden cranny, a piece of floorboard gave way under his hand.

Just at that moment, a voice spoke from above him. "Congratulations, Llelo. I see you found it at last."

35

Day Four

Llelo

Llelo had crawled underneath the table upon which the water jug rested, and he was so surprised at the voice that he jerked upwards and banged the back of his head on the underside of the table. Fortunately, the table was very heavy, and he only jostled the pitcher of holy water on top of it, rather than upending the whole thing.

Pulling out, he sat back on his haunches to gaze in astonishment and joy at the sight of Helen pushing up on one elbow to stare down at him from the bed. "I promise I would have told you where it was if you hadn't found it yourself. I've had a feeling for a while that time is of the essence. My apologies for not speaking sooner."

Llelo scrambled to his feet, his eyes wide as he looked at her. "You remember! You know my name!"

"I didn't at first." She wrinkled her nose. "I've been awake a while."

Llelo's eyes narrowed, feeling a strange kind of suspicion replacing his momentary ebullience. "How long is *a while?*"

"Since yesterday."

As he gaped at her, she made a motion with her hand that she might have meant to be apologetic. "I didn't know who any of you were, where I was, or how I'd arrived here. All I saw was a man weeping and praying by my bedside. I didn't know to trust him—" She moved her head in a slight shake before putting her hand to it and wincing, "—I suppose that suspicious part of me survived even when I didn't know my own name. But watching you root around on the floor brought it all back."

As she finished speaking, she coughed, and Llelo hastened to refill the cup of water and helped her drink from it. This was her first real sustenance in days. He was astounded that she would deprive herself for a whole day rather than let anyone know she was awake.

"You could have died," he couldn't resist saying.

"It wasn't going to come to that. I was sleeping too, much of the time. And Taran." She shook her head again. This time, something he could only describe as hope entered her face. "He loves me."

"He does, as much as I have ever seen anyone love anyone else. Is it true he's waited for you since you were a girl?"

"It's true." Her eyes showed sadness for a moment, before brightening again. "But he doesn't have to wait anymore." She motioned towards where Llelo had been on his hands and knees. "Press again on that floorboard to the right of the table leg."

Llelo immediately did as she instructed. The slat popped up, revealing a scroll of paper tucked into the little cranny beneath.

"As I said, if you hadn't found it yourself, I would have pointed you right."

He supposed he believed her. In truth, while he was glad to have finally found what she'd hidden, he was far more fascinated by the way she'd lain in bed, hour after hour, not letting any of them know she was awake out of a fear that she'd been ... *what?* Captured by an enemy? Clearly so. He didn't know that he would have had the courage, the wherewithal, or the sense to do as she had done.

As he plucked out the scroll, his first thought was that this was an awful lot of fuss for a piece of paper, an idea duly confirmed when he unrolled it to reveal the treaty between King Owain, Earl Ranulf, Prince Henry, and King David that was never ratified in Carlisle. With it spread wide between his hands, he turned to look at Helen. "You almost died for this?" As far as he was concerned, it might as well be a blank piece of paper for all the good it had done Gwynedd.

Having scooted herself up on the bed under her own power, she took her own sip from the cup of water. A moment ago, she had also transferred Taran's last uneaten plate of cheese and bread to her lap and started taking tiny nibbles of both. If Llelo were she, he would have been starving and probably have been face down in the food. "*That* is the most valuable item in King Owain's treasury."

Llelo looked down at the paper, his expression dubious. "How so?"

"How can you not know?" She scoffed. "I will be speaking to Owain on the matter, I assure you. Taran too. I would suggest they burn it. If an idea could be flammable, that would already have gone up in smoke."

Llelo wasn't convinced. "It was never signed."

"You Welsh are so naïve!" Even as she spoke, she waved away the insult before Llelo could take offense. "It doesn't matter that it was never signed; it shows intent!" Then she nodded as understanding entered Llelo's eyes. "Which of your king's enemies would gain the most from having it in their possession?"

"Madog." He didn't even have to think hard. It had to be, though he still wasn't entirely sure why.

"Yes, Madog. We are here because of him, aren't we?" Helen made a *pouf* sound with her lips to show her disgust. Even though she was mocking his ignorance, he was kind of impressed that she could be so certain while half-dead. "If Madog knew that his own allies, my brother among them, had promised all Wales to Owain, what would he do?"

"Burn their alliance to the ground." Of that, Llelo, for all his youth, knew for certain. "Maybe you should have let him have it. He has been allied with Ranulf against us far too many times. It would have driven a wedge between them."

Helen blinked. "I honestly never thought of that. Then again, likely he would blame Owain and come at him with all the more force."

"Without Ranulf, though."

"A spy in the making." She laughed. "I thought as much."

Llelo didn't know about that. He was just seeing the truth like it was a road laid out before him. That was new. Oddly, he felt more like a man in this moment, with Helen mocking him from the bed and all the ways they had failed to understand what was going on in this investigation starkly laid bare before him, than at any time up until now.

Llelo looked back to the space beneath the floorboard. "How did you know where to hide it?"

Helen glanced around the room with an amused look on her face. "I lived here, right here in this room, long before Nest was the abbess. I am a bastard daughter, and my father needed a place to leave me. For a time he wanted me to become a nun, and when I refused, he found me a husband."

"Someone who wasn't Taran."

Her expression softened. "Not Taran. My father forbade me ever to speak his name in his presence."

"Will you tell me how you came to be in the guesthouse that night?"

"Certainly. I followed Jacques."

"Is that the man who attacked you? You *know* him?"

Instead of a snort, she scoffed again. "That was why he attacked me. Or rather, it was because of that and the fact that I snatched the treaty from his hand and ran."

"I'm guessing you stabbed him along the way?"

She had the grace to look a little sheepish. "I bought myself time."

"Why didn't you just run out of the guesthouse?"

"I tried. I wasn't fast enough. I knew this room." She looked around it. "And therefore knew just what to do."

"Your friend from the village, Henri, told us one of King Owain's companions, a man named Iwan, is Madog's spy. Do you know him? Do you think he could have ordered this?" At her blank look, Llelo said Iwan's name the French way, *Jehan*.

Helen's brow furrowed. "Someone told you Jehan was a spy for Madog? No." She made to shake her head but then put her hand to it instead. "That can't be right. I have known him a long time. He was the one who enabled Prince Henry to escape last summer. I use him often as a go-between. Having told him what I knew of Eustace's movements, he passed word to Owain's men, who escorted Henry to Gloucester. I wouldn't have said he's ever met Madog, much less agreed to work for him."

"People are not necessarily who you think they are." Llelo himself had been continually surprised by a whole number of aspects of this investigation. "Henri was very certain. What I don't understand is why you came to the guesthouse when you had already arranged to meet him at the Travelers' Rest near the Answer Stone?"

Helen managed to shake her head for real this time, albeit slowly, because no doubt it hurt. "I truly don't know what you're talking about right now, Llelo. I never made an appointment at the Travelers' Rest—and certainly not with anyone named Henri."

36

Day Four

Dai

Dai breathed in the morning air, glad to be out with Aron on the simple task of walking Henri to the Travelers' Rest, and feeling rested himself far more than yesterday. Mornings like this one always lifted his spirits. He'd seen the sunrise, a rare occurrence in January because it rained so often. The dawn had turned the sky orange and pink, and the brisk wind had sent the clouds slicing across the sky like Danish longships, except through air instead of water.

He was just turning to Henri to make a comment about the weather, which was all he could think of to talk about, when a stranger with an axe burst out of the trees to the left of the road and leapt at Aron. Simultaneously, as the first sounds came out of Dai's mouth, Henri turned on Dai himself, unsheathing his dagger and slashing at Dai's face with a thrust so sudden Dai could avoid only the worst of it. His neck wasn't slashed, as Henri intended, but the blade opened the flesh along his jawline.

Dai staggered back, gaping at the blood even as he raised his forearm to block another blow and knock away Henri's blade. Having lost his dagger in the dust, Henri fled into the trees in the same direction from which the other man had come. It was only then that the pain of the wound hit Dai.

Aron hadn't managed to clear his sword from its sheath either, but he had been able to get in under the guard of the man with the axe in the manner of an experienced skirmisher, moving towards him instead of away. In so doing, he wrenched away the axe and swung it at the other man's belly. The man scrambled back just in time. Like Henri, he acknowledged this particular tide had turned and departed. It looked to Dai that killing them had always been secondary to allowing Henri to escape. Otherwise, they would have combined their strength and finished the job.

Dai would have followed the two men, but Aron was upon him a moment later, clapping the bottom half of Dai's own cloak to Dai's face, while his other hand kept a tight hold on the opposite side of Dai's head.

Then Aron eased Dai down to sit on a squat stone beside the road. "You're going to be all right."

Part of Dai believed him. The other part was grateful not to be standing up anymore.

"I won't lie to you," Aron continued as he squeezed closed the edges of Dai's wound. "The cut is deep. You'll have a scar. But your quick movement saved your life. He was aiming for your throat."

"I didn't see it coming." Dai was definitely feeling woozy now. He wanted to lie down. He would have if Aron hadn't been holding him up.

"Nobody could have seen it coming." Then Aron barked, "Stay with me, man!"

Dai tried to take another reasonable breath, moments from passing out, and had a stray thought that Aron, of all the Dragons, was the only one never to call him "boy" or "son." While he knew that when the others did so they were being affectionate, they still didn't see him as their equal. Well, that was probably deserved, because he wasn't. He knew also his mind was wandering, if not blundering about. He couldn't focus on anything for more than a few breaths. His vision was darkening around the edges, and all he could see of Aron was his eyes. "He was good with a knife."

"Mayhap he was Helen's attacker."

"That seems obvious now." Dai started blinking fast, fighting the light-headedness, though it would have been easier to give in to it. He hadn't realized how much passing out might *hurt*. "But if so, why come to the encampment at all? Why not just run?"

"I don't know. Though, you know me. I can guess."

"Guess, then." Dai was discovering that talking helped keep him conscious.

"Hold on, Dai." Aron picked up Dai's right hand and put it to his jaw. "Press hard."

Dai obeyed, because he had no choice but to obey, holding the hem of his own cloak to his face and feeling the blood seeping through the fabric. Head wounds bled like the devil's own, so just because he was bleeding didn't mean he was dying, but that didn't make this head wound any easier to experience.

Aron had needed two hands to remove his own cloak, tunic, and undershirt, leaving him with nothing against the chill of the morning but bare skin. He then proceeded to tear strips from the hem of his shirt, after which he folded the bulk of what remained into a makeshift pad.

All the while, he explained what he was thinking. "It doesn't seem he got what he came for. Maybe he thought to try again. Maybe he assumed Helen was dead and thought he could insert himself in the investigation as a friend. Your father says it isn't uncommon."

"Abbot Rhys knew him." Or at least, that was what Dai meant to say. To his own ears, his words were slurred.

Aron understood anyway. "He knew him a long time ago. Besides, Henri didn't know Abbot Rhys was here or who he really was until he saw him."

"So is Iwan Madog's spy or isn't he?"

"Again, I'm guessing, but Henri would know that by blaming Iwan, he could buy himself some time. Your mother wasn't going to confront Iwan right away, not at a peace conference between Madog and Owain—"

"Henri thought we wouldn't show him to Iwan either. Of course, if we had, *Iwan* might have recognized *Henri* as Madog's spy." It was like the world had suddenly grown brighter and was starting to make perfect sense, if only Dai could stay conscious long enough to articulate it.

In quick movements, Aron moved Dai's hand, clapped the new makeshift bandage on his face, and then tied it to his head with the strips from his shirt. Then he put back on his overtunic and cloak, shrugging his shoulders at the sudden warmth. "I have the tools in my purse to sew you up but you wouldn't thank me for the job I'd done in the long run, not when we have an abbey full of healers half a mile away."

Dai could barely speak, since his jaw was now tied shut, but he moved his lips enough to say, "Thank you."

"Let's get you home." Aron lifted Dai to his feet.

"You should leave me. You need to follow Henri!"

"We will." Aron's tone was grim and assured. "But not until you're safe."

"They counted on that. They are using your honor against you."

"Better to play the fool for them than to lose you."

Once upright, Dai found he could walk, though he kept his arm around Aron's shoulders while Aron's arm clutched his waist as they hustled as quickly as they could along the road. Every step jarred Dai's face, so he kept his free hand to his jaw, using gentle pressure to hold everything in place the best he could. The wound was still seeping blood, and the half-mile back to the monastery, much of which was uphill, was the longest walk of his life.

By the time they reached the infirmary, Dai was near to passing out again, and Aron's own face was as white as the shirt he'd wrapped around Dai's head had once been.

"Help him!" Aron called into the quiet of the infirmary, having propped Dai in the doorway. "We'll get him, Dai." Then he was gone.

Dai didn't have a great deal of hope for the search, not with Henri having such a head start, not without dogs, which they hadn't brought.

On his own volition, he took some steps towards one of the beds, which to his rapidly narrowing vision looked like an island of serenity in a cold and painful world. Before he reached one, someone caught him, whispering soothing words like he was an infant with colic. Next thing he knew, or maybe was aware of, if he'd actually passed out and hadn't known it, he had a host of people clustered around him. This included his grandmother, who fretted about behind Brother Adam as he cleaned the wound, slathered it with salve, and sewed Dai's skin together with a fine hand.

Llelo's tone was dry as he looked on. "The way everyone is fussing, you would think nobody has ever had their jaw slashed open before."

Gwen didn't even dignify the comment with a glare at Llelo, instead kissing Dai's forehead, which was the only part of his face that didn't hurt. "We've had three pieces of good news today: Helen's awake, we have a plan now, and you're going to live."

37

Day Four

Gwen

"We know Cadwaladr met someone at the mill. He's secretly working with Madog." Gareth spoke in a harsh whisper, deliberately loud enough for anyone within of the guesthouse to hear, though ostensibly he was merely talking heatedly to his own wife in the corridor outside their room. "I *must* tell the king of the danger before Cadwaladr betrays all Gwynedd *again*!"

"Not until morning." Gwen's voice was equally whispering and equally loud. "You know how the king gets. While he will not take it well, no matter when you tell him, it's Susanna's birthday. You cannot ruin the moment for all of them with accusations against Cadwaladr!"

With a motion of his head, Gareth suggested it was time for them to move towards the common room, though not before he said, in a lower tone but still one that could penetrate the wooden door of their room, "You are right. I will wait until the morning. But no longer than that! Come. We don't want to wake the children."

Gwen certainly didn't want to wake Tangwen and Taran either, and she and Gareth had actually had a quick semi-argument before settling on their current plan as to whether or not it was worth waking their son in particular in order to successfully convey their message to Marged, who was in their room with their children until such a time as Gareth and Gwen came to bed. In the end, they'd decided to say what needed to be said quickly and in a manner Marged wouldn't view as suspicious.

Which was important because the entire conversation was a ruse. They *wanted* Marged to overhear. Thus Gwen had allowed herself to be persuaded, and sure enough, a moment later, before they'd even reached the central table, a wail came up from behind them.

Gareth shot her a look of apology. Gwen shrugged; she'd known their loud voices would wake Taran and was at the door as Marged was opening it to stick out her head.

"I'll wait out here for you." Marged's expression showed resignation. Gwen had been trying all day not to imply anything was amiss or that she didn't trust her. She didn't, of course, and their entire strategy was based on the notion that Marged *was* untrustworthy.

"There's no need," Gwen said, continuing the plan they'd worked out. "I'll stay here for the rest of the night."

"Really? Are you sure?" The hope in Marged's voice was hard to hear, given what they were essentially tricking her into doing.

"Of course. You should go enjoy yourself." Gwen cocked an ear. "I think I can hear Prince Hywel all the way from here. He's singing for his aunt. No sense in both of us missing all the fun."

"Don't you have—" she paused and swallowed, "—more work to do tonight?"

"No." Gwen yawned elaborately. "I can't keep my eyes open a moment longer."

Gareth came up behind Gwen and gestured for Marged to move out of the doorway so he could enter their bedroom. "We're both turning in." He yawned too. "We've not had enough sleep the last couple of nights, that's for certain."

Marged bent her head respectfully. "I wish you pleasant dreams, my lord." She turned away, and Gareth closed the door behind them.

Gwen went immediately to where Taran was sitting up in bed. He was no longer wailing, now that he had what he wanted—namely, his mother. She settled herself next to him and looked at Gareth, who had sat in a nearby chair to pull off his boots. "Do you think this will—"

He didn't let her finish. "Yes."

Gwen settled down, pillowing her head on her arm. They had discussed this mad plan with Hywel and then roped in Abbot Rhys as well, just so he wouldn't unintentionally ruin what they were doing. The conversation had been held around Dai's bedside, with Gwen holding her son's hand.

The consensus among the conspirators was that once Marged learned they were moments away from accusing Cadwaladr of treason, she would tell Geraint all about it. He would then immediately tell Cadwaladr. They hoped the treacherous prince would then become so fearful of the repercussions that he would flee to England in the night, as he'd done in the past. He might even take Geraint with him. By this point, the possibility of Cadwaladr insinuating himself into any of the available foreign courts and using what he knew of Gwynedd against them later was better than having to endure his schemes for one more day.

Most likely, he would ally himself openly with Ranulf and/or Madog, as he'd also done in the past. Once he betrayed Gwynedd again, there would be no coming back for him. Every person in the room had been more than willing to let that happen and damn the consequences. It no longer mattered to Hywel that manipulating Cadwaladr into running wasn't his decision to make. Before Rhun's death, they'd left him where he was, free to pursue his every whim and scheme, thinking it was better to have him where they could see him.

They'd been wrong. Because they had not acted, Rhun had died.

In truth, though they had enough information to accuse a few people of wrongdoing, Cadwaladr wasn't one of them. All they knew about him still was that he'd gone to the mill, which wasn't a crime, no matter how much they wanted it to be. It would be futile to take that bit of information to the king.

Instead, they'd decided they were out of time, and Hywel was no longer willing to watch and wait, even if he'd counseled them many times to do so. Cadwaladr was well aware of how much Gareth hated him, knew he would do anything to ruin him, and also knew that in a contest between Gareth's word and his own in front of the king, he might lose.

If Cadwaladr truly was guilty of something, they were simply giving him a push. Besides, any of those foreign courts (belonging to Ranulf, Maud, Stephen, or even Madog) had their own concerns, plans, and intrigues. Each magnate might choose to march on Gwynedd, but Cadwaladr's standing wasn't so high with any of them that his defection would require it. It might act as a tipping point, but Hywel believed now that Madog was coming anyway—and not to the peace conference. They would next see him across a field of battle. Whether Cadwaladr was or was not at his side at this point was immaterial.

Even with all that, the commitment to the endeavor they'd so far made was minimal. All Gwen and Gareth had done was speak about what they knew at a place Marged could overhear. If Marged did not tell Geraint what she'd heard, then there was no harm done. If she did and Cadwaladr fled ... well, they could at least give up the charade that Madog would be arriving soon.

Otherwise, without some kind of change, they would have to go to the king with what they knew: Henri/Jacques had attacked Helen; someone else had attacked Marc. The trail to apprehend either had gone cold. These people were as the Dragon Cadoc had once been, spies and assassins, trained to leave the scenes of their crimes to serve their masters somewhere else. Abbot Rhys himself had lived that way for many years. And since none involved were native to Tegeingl, when they left, they would be gone for good.

Gareth had even resigned himself to not getting his man, for the greater good. Their only consolation, which admittedly wasn't much of one, was that nobody had died (yet), so it wasn't quite the black mark on his record it would have been otherwise.

Gwen reached out a hand to her husband. "Leave tomorrow for tomorrow. We have to give this plan a chance, and that means staying right here, even if every instinct has you wanting to head down to the pavilion to keep watch."

Gareth let out a heavy breath. "I know."

And then, to Gwen's utter relief, because she knew how much he needed it, he lay down beside her. Hardly three breaths later, he was sound asleep.

38

Day Five

Dai

Dai had been kept overnight in the infirmary, with Llelo sleeping in the adjacent bed. Like the rest of their co-conspirators, they were intentionally making themselves scarce so Cadwaladr could do whatever he was going to do, out from under the gaze of any of the principal investigators. That included the Dragons. The night before, Prince Hywel had let it be known in the pavilion that their search for the men who'd attacked Dai and Aron had failed (which it had), but that they'd found indications the men had taken the road to Denbigh (which, as far as they knew, they had not). The word had thus gone out that Hywel had sent his men to continue the search in that direction.

In actuality, the Dragons hadn't gone that far, just out of sight of the encampment, in order to leave the field clear for Cadwaladr to flee Holywell in any other direction without hindrance.

For Dai's part, he'd had a miserable night, having refused all but an initial dose of poppy juice, since he hated the way it made him feel once it wore off even more than the pain itself. But without it, his jaw hurt more than any hurt he'd ever taken. Finally, as dawn broke, he swung his feet to the floor and sat on the edge of the bed, staring blankly at the wall and willing himself to get up before his brother woke. Llelo would try to stop him from leaving. While Dai had been awake most of the night, Llelo had slept straight through. Dai knew that because he'd spent the night listening to his brother breathe.

Dai's face hurt, no question, but what he didn't understand was why every other muscle in his body hurt too. He felt as if he'd been run over by stampeding horses. For that reason, he couldn't hold back the groan as he pushed to his feet, at which point Llelo opened his eyes and was upright a heartbeat later. "What are you doing?"

"Walking out of here."

The look Llelo gave him was dubious but, to his credit, he didn't argue, just put his arm around Dai's waist and walked with him to the door. By now, Sister Efa had noticed the commotion and come over. She took one look at Dai and Llelo and began wagging her finger back and forth in front of Dai's face. "You should be in bed."

"I'm hungry. And I have to use the latrine."

"It's going to hurt to eat."

"So then I'll drink.'

She glowered first at him and then turned her gaze on Llelo. "He may have thin porridge and milk. Mead will do him no good today, not after the poppy."

"Understood." Llelo bobbed a nod.

Her mouth working, perhaps holding back a host of other things she wanted to say but had the wisdom not to, Sister Efa stepped aside. "He sleeps here tonight as well."

"Yes, Sister," Llelo said, "I will see to it."

Dai opted to let his brother continue to speak for him because the little bit he'd said so far had hurt enormously. In truth, he didn't know how he was going to eat anything at all.

But then Sister Efa stopped them again. "Wait." She went to the cup from which Dai had been drinking last night, removed the reed straw, and gave it to him. "I admit you need something in your stomach. If you drink mead, don't drink much."

Dai wrinkled his nose, though that hurt more than it should have too. "Yes, Sister. Thank you."

They set off towards the encampment, Dai holding the straw down at his side like it was a dagger.

"I'm glad Henri missed," Llelo said.

Dai tried not to laugh, but he couldn't help himself. He had never given much thought as to how crucial movement of one's jaw was to one's very existence.

Llelo kept talking. "You're going to invite attention and comment, which you aren't to worry about. You and Aron were set upon while attempting to apprehend Henri, who was behind the attack on Marc. They fled, but we are to express confidence that, with all Wales on alert, they'll stand out like a sore thumb." He shot Dai an amused look. "Or a bloody jaw."

Dai managed a snort and the words, "And Cadwaladr?"

"If anything happened overnight, we'll find out soon—"

A roar came up from the pavilion just ahead of them, sounding much like it had two nights ago when Susanna had arrived. Thinking Madog might finally be here, meaning all their plotting was for nothing, they hurried forward—

—to find they hadn't been wrong at all, and that Cadwaladr was squarely in the midst of yet another of his stratagems.

In person.

He hadn't run.

(More's the pity.)

Instead, Cadwaladr stood in the center of a cleared space between tables, brandishing a document in the air above his head. King Owain stood a pace away, as did Prince Hywel, though his legs were spread as if bracing himself against the buffeting of a high wind.

"This man and his companions have been spying on us for Madog!" Cadwaladr's voice was as confident as ever. "They attacked Marc, our king's servant, and left him for dead!"

At that point Geraint brought forward Henri, who was bound and gagged, and forced him to kneel in the grass at Cadwaladr's feet. His companion came next. They didn't yet know his name, but Dai recognized him as the same man who had attacked Aron.

Gareth settled near Dai and Llelo, his arms folded across his chest. "Our wayward prince can be clever sometimes, I'll give him that."

"Too clever by half." Gwen had come up behind her sons, tsking under her breath at what she saw. "Henri will tell a very different story."

"Will he?" Gareth said. "He's gagged for a reason. My guess? He won't be given a chance."

Rather than have the two men confess what they'd done, the only story the people in the pavilion heard was Cadwaladr's version of events, related with triumph, not to say glee: "Three nights ago, I saw that man—" he meant Henri, "—sneaking about outside the pavilion. I followed him to the mill, where he met with that man—" He pointed to Aron's attacker. "They passed this note between them, confirming Madog's treachery. He intends to betray this alliance. War is upon us!"

Llelo spoke in an even lower tone, right in Dai's ear. "Do we actually have to thank *Cadwaladr* for bringing these men in?"

Heaven forbid.

Dai wasn't going to answer, in part because his face hurt, but also because he was listening hard to the tale of intrigue pouring forth from Cadwaladr, who waved the paper above his head again before handing it to Owain. The king passed it to Hywel without reading it.

Cadwaladr kept speaking, now addressing King Owain directly instead of the crowd. "Madog set these men the task of murdering you, brother. He isn't coming. He was never coming. Even now he is marching towards us with an army—" he cut himself off abruptly, letting the silence build. It was clear he had more to say, and his audience held its collective breath to hear it, "—isn't that right, Susanna? You knew about this, didn't you? Were you to wield the knife yourself if these men failed?"

Dai's jaw would have been in the grass if it hadn't been tied shut. For the last fifty years, Susanna had done nothing but defend Cadwaladr, and he had just hung her on the line to dry, like she meant nothing to him. That was what he did, of course. There was nobody he wouldn't betray if it served his interests and better ensured his own survival.

Owain swung around to look at his sister, who had been standing behind him on the dais. She could have made any number of responses, but the one she chose was unexpected nonetheless. Lifting the hem of her skirt with one hand, she gracefully stepped off the dais and moved towards her brothers. The circle around them parted like the Red Sea, allowing her to walk right up to Cadwaladr—and slap him hard across the face. "Of course I knew about it, you imbecile. But as usual, you know only half the story. And it was the wrong half. I came here to save his life."

In that moment, the sun came out from behind a cloud, lighting not only the world around but filling the pavilion itself with a golden glow. Susanna couldn't have managed that encounter better if she'd planned it. She was an angel, coming to rescue her brothers. Nobody could deny this truth.

Then a laugh boomed out from even farther behind Dai, causing him to nearly jump out of his boots.

"This is a banner day, isn't it! Good for you, my queen!" In great high spirits, Godfrid the Dane, Prince of Dublin, strode into their midst, along with a diverse collection of followers. These included a dozen Danes, the rest of the Dragons, who'd ostensibly been sent to hunt down Dai's attackers, and several of Owain's own men.

"Good thing I brought my own army—and yours besides! Where should we point their spears today, Owain Gwynedd?"

39

Day Five
Gareth

"So we will have no secrets among us, I stand before you today with the news that King Madog of Powys has allied with Earl Ranulf of Chester and is marching against us even now! We came in peace, but we are men of Gwynedd. We are always ready to defend our way of life!" King Owain raised his hands above his head, his voice booming out for all to hear. Cadwaladr stood at his right hand and Hywel on his left, with Godfrid looming just behind. Gareth kept his eyes on Cadwaladr and couldn't help thinking he was preening.

The field before them was filled with men. Many of them were from the encampment, but most were part of the force King Owain had been forbidden to martial and had done so anyway. They had been encamped a few miles to the west, off the road to St. Asaph. Ever since Madog had taken back Mold Castle in a surprise move last year, the men of Gwynedd had been itching for a fight, but instead

Owain had given them a long, quiet winter. That was about to change.

Action was something with which every man in the encampment felt comfortable. Action allowed one to expend one's energies and frustrations in a fruitful direction. Certainly the few of them who knew what had really gone on the last few days would have been happy to attack Cadwaladr instead. But for now, Susanna had done a fair job for them. She knew the truth about him, that was plain. She hadn't betrayed him in the sense that he had attempted with her, but with Madog's plans exposed, she had been free to tell what she knew.

Even Taran and Helen had ventured down from the guesthouse for the first time to hear what she had to say, though not until Henri and his companion had been led away. Helen herself appeared to know Susanna well enough to clasp her hand as they greeted each other. It occurred to Gareth as he looked at them that she may have spied for Susanna too. She could even have chosen to coordinate her return to Wales with the onset of the peace conference because Susanna had asked her to. As always, Helen's love for Taran, while genuine, took second place to duty.

Whether Gareth was right in his suspicions wasn't a question he was ever going to voice, much less ask of her newly betrothed, who couldn't keep the smile off his face, no matter how perilous the coming battle.

Owain continued, repeating the words Susanna had used when she'd told him what she knew. "Even now, Madog's army is marching up the old Roman road along the Dee. We will take the high ground just past Hen Blas. And we will stop them."

The place to make their stand had been the subject of a heated discussion—one that hadn't been contentious so much as urgent. Owain was worried about the community of monks who had taken over the former Welsh *llys* of Hen Blas. These had been established by Madog back in 1132, when he'd controlled this area completely. They couldn't be given any warning that Owain's army was coming. To that end, Owain and his battle leaders had decided to march the men along Wat's Dyke, an old barrier in this part of Tegeingl, built by the Saxons to keep the Welsh out of England, though a less substantial barrier than Offa's Dyke to the west. Nonetheless, it followed the high ground and using it would give Owain a good view of the road and the Dee. He was also reveling in the not-so-secret pleasure of turning a former weapon against the Welsh back on the *Saesneg*.

"Much like Cadwaladr did to us, eh?" Cadoc said as an aside to Gareth. "He takes the evidence we had against him and turns it on us."

"Not on *us*, really," Evan said when Gareth didn't immediately answer. "On Madog. You could even say he has done us a favor. We have the men responsible for the attack on Helen in our custody. That is no small thing."

"How is it that you are always so hopeful?" Aron said.

"Because I'm married to the best woman in the world." He was speaking of his wife, Angharad, who wasn't here. He spoke of her often, and clearly missed her, but nobody was sorry she and his newborn son were well out of this war. "You should try it."

Aron cleared his throat. "After the battle. I promise."

Cadoc grunted. "I'm concerned that we still don't know who he really met at that mill. From the tracks Llelo followed, it was not either of these men."

"I fear that villain is long gone," Gareth said.

"It's almost too bad Madog won't trust Cadwaladr again after today," Cadoc added.

"I'm quite sure Madog never entirely trusted Cadwaladr in the first place. What might change going forward is that he may decide not to use him for a while, especially with the force we're bringing to bear against him." Gareth paused. "It may even be that Cadwaladr has been considering this option for some time."

"I too would have seriously reconsidered my choices the moment I learned King Owain had ignored the prohibition against bringing an army east with him," Aron said.

Evan was still being forgiving. "Even without our subterfuge, Cadwaladr could have lifted his head to sniff which way the wind was blowing and decided for once to do the right thing."

"For Cadwaladr, the right thing is always what is best for him. The fact that it coincides with our interests in this moment is purely coincidental." Gareth couldn't even muster a laugh. "The best I will believe of him is that he decided his moment of rebellion hadn't yet come."

"He could have snuck Henri into the encampment and let him murder the king," Evan said. "That option was always available to him. He chose another path."

"Again, you are looking on the bright side." Cadoc shoved his shoulder. "Don't upset my equilibrium!"

"He did also have the choice to warn off Madog," Evan continued, ignoring the other Dragon. "Maybe we really do have to be grateful to him."

Gareth shuddered at the thought.

They were standing well out of range of anyone hearing them and, truth be told, Gareth was glad to see everyone else in high spirits. He found the plan they'd come up with an intriguing one in that they were going to begin their march now, in the middle of the day, and attack Madog's force with the sun behind them as it set. Cadwaladr's betrayal of Madog was so complete that he'd even told them where the Powysian army planned to camp: with those selfsame monks at Hen Blas, fewer than three miles from Holywell. Their intent had been to march at first light tomorrow and attack Holywell with the dawn.

That is, if Cadwaladr wasn't lying to them again and walking them into a trap.

Owain's scouts had confirmed much of the information, however. That meant, right now, Madog's army was marching along the old Roman road from Chester. In a few hours Madog's soldiers would be watching the light fade, thinking ahead to an early rest at the monastery and preparing themselves for their victory tomorrow.

Madog's plan had been a good one. If King Owain hadn't brought his army—and, even more, if Cadwaladr hadn't revealed Madog's treachery—it might have worked.

40

Day Five

Gwen

The men were gone.

Her men, marching away along the Dyke and her heart with them.

She had already spent several hours on her knees in the church. As the sun began to sink behind the hills to the west, she thought she could hear shouts of battle, though her logical self knew three miles was too far for that sound to carry.

Gwen didn't know much about battle plans of attack or defense. She hadn't even gone to the field to listen to the king's speech, preferring to stay with her children and hear afterwards from Gareth how it had gone. And how things were supposed to go. She needed them to win, of course. She needed them to survive. But for her, it was all about the aftermath.

Nobody cared about the investigation anymore, not even particularly Gareth. It had begun with the attack on Helen, and from her own mouth, they knew who had attacked her, why they'd done so, and who had sent them, with the impetus for the entire endeavor laid at Madog's feet. Gwen would have thought, with Cadwaladr at court, she would be used to being lied to by now. But the breadth and depth of Henri's lies, in that everything he'd told her was a complete fabrication, was still a struggle for her to get her head around.

And that was even being a spy herself, though admittedly never to the extent of pretending to be someone other than who she was, Gwen ferch Meilyr. She had never before thought about the distinction between spying for Hywel and actually *being* a spy. She had never thought of herself as a gullible woman either by any means. But she had *believed* Henri.

Cadwaladr had lied too, extensively. And even if his lies had led to the capture of Henri and his companion and revealed the existence of Madog's army, they were still lies. Thus, Gwen remained unsatisfied. She wanted the truth, no less than her husband always did. What's more, she knew where she might find it: in the prison tent in the center of the encampment where Henri was being held.

With the army gone, only the women, children, and a handful of guards remained, but Hywel had personally ensured that two incorruptible men were in charge of Henri's security, namely Aron and Dai, paired together again. Aron was still blaming himself for Dai's injury, so this was, in a sense, a penance for him. Dai had initially insisted on marching with the army, but he'd been convinced to stay home, since he wasn't going to be allowed to fight anyway and someone needed not only to guard Henri but to defend the encampment in case Madog and Ranulf's forces thought to sneak around them.

Owain hoped to surprise Madog's army, but in so doing, he'd left the encampment vulnerable. Even if Henri himself was contained, the borders between Powys and Gwynedd were porous. Who was to say that every man now fighting for Gwynedd was loyal, and someone hadn't warned Madog they were coming?

Dai had brought a chair into the tent, which he gave up to his mother as she entered. His expression was querying, but Gwen didn't immediately explain what she was doing. Instead, she carried the chair closer to where Henri and his companion were tied to a pole holding up the center of the tent. Then she set the chair down and sat herself in it. Folding her hands primly in her lap, she asked, "What don't I know?"

"What *do* you know?" Henri snorted derisively, in exactly the manner Gwen had expected. And hoped for. She had asked the question with those words specifically to elicit that superior response. Truly, she was pleased she'd read her man right.

She allowed herself a small smile. "I know you were looking for, and found, an unratified treaty between King Owain, Prince Henry, Earl Ranulf, and King David of Scotland."

Henri's face stilled.

"What I don't know is if your friend here—"

"He isn't my friend."

Gwen didn't allow her expression to show her jolt of glee at Henri's need to correct her. Instead, she played into it. "Etienne, then."

Henri tsked. "Close. Emile."

Emile visibly rolled his eyes and kicked out with one leg at Henri. "Imbecile!"

Gwen tried not to blink at the third use of this particular French word in this investigation, especially given the little amount of French being spoken at Holywell. Brother Iolo had overheard one of the so-called monks say it. In the pavilion that morning, Queen Susanna herself had insulted Cadwaladr with it. And now again. Of course, it was now clear that Emile had been one of those *so-called monks*. Perhaps it was a favorite word.

Gwen went to stand in front of him.

From behind her, Dai exclaimed, "Mam, no!"

She waved a hand at her son. "He is no threat. Not anymore."

Dai subsided, but both he and Aron approached closer. Meanwhile, Henri glowered, and Emile merely shifted his shoulders against the post. She guessed he was the only one among them who didn't understand Welsh.

Emile's hands were tied behind his back and then tethered to a post, so she had to lean forward in order to push up first one sleeve and then the other. His left arm was marked by parallel scratches.

Helen's doing.

Gwen smiled to have one small mystery solved. Then she switched to French for Emile's benefit. "You attacked my son and ran. Why didn't you keep running?"

"Don't tell her." Henri spoke out of the corner of his mouth.

Gwen didn't even try to keep the smirk off her face as she poked Henri in the right hip.

He recoiled with a spasm of pain that left him gasping.

"War wound indeed. Should I call a healer to tend it?"

"It isn't that deep. I've been taking care of it."

Emile let out a puff of air. "Why are you here? We have nothing to gain from talking. They are going to hang us regardless."

Gwen looked him in the eye. She wasn't yet sure which of the two men was the weaker link, so she was trying to split her attention between them. "Maybe you don't have to hang." She threw out the thought like a fisherman with a line, not expecting much to come from it.

Emile's expression flashed to one of hope, however, as if instead he was a drowning man to whom she'd tossed a rope.

Then the look was gone. "So you say. Why would you offer us that?"

"Because I don't believe a word Cadwaladr said in that pavilion. He didn't capture you; you came to him."

But Emile's expression had closed like a door shut in Gwen's face. His and Henri's mistake had clearly been with that fateful meeting. Gwen still didn't know how that had come about. Geraint might know, and perhaps he would tell Marged. Gwen still hadn't decided what to do with the couple. She was loath to lose her nanny, but would anyway if Geraint and Marged married. Cian, her son, could stay with them if he wished. Gwen had never considered all the ways loyalty could be fluid, since hers was absolute. She would try not to make that mistake again.

Sighing for the prisoners' benefit, she returned to her chair. "Perhaps I should start with telling you what I know. If you're going to hang anyway, *I* have nothing to lose. Otherwise, you'll take your secrets to the grave." Gwen motioned airily with one hand. "The pair of you came to Holywell as spies for Madog. Lady Helen, who was traveling here as well, recognized you and knew instantly you were up to no good. She followed you into the guesthouse where she found you in King Owain's room, the treaty in your hand. She took the treaty from you and fled to the queen's room. You broke down the door and attacked her. However, she'd already hidden the document where you couldn't find it. You tried to force the truth out of her and, in the struggle, she was rendered unconscious. You ransacked the room in your search, and left her for dead after finding nothing. Henri's real name, of course, is Jacques."

That shocked Henri. He had tried to keep his expression noncommittal throughout her recital, and was realizing only now that Helen was alive and had related all of this to them. Gwen told herself not to be so pleased she'd surprised him. If they'd done nothing else well in this investigation, at least they'd kept the attack on Helen a secret. "Helen got you good, both of you. Why *did* you take the bed slat from the room? My son wanted to know."

Henri glowered and didn't answer. Gwen told herself not to be too proud of herself. The point was to get them to talk, not lord over them with her excellent guesses.

So she continued. "Almost at the exact same moment these events were taking place, Cadwaladr went to the mill to find the note he was waving about this morning. He claimed he'd intercepted it from you, but it had actually been intended for him. Are you really going to let him get away with such a lie?"

When neither man replied, Gwen went on as if they'd admitted everything she'd said was true. "Furthermore, unbeknownst to the two of you at the time, a third person attacked Marc, the king's servant, in the field next to the pavilion. Then he fled. You are responsible for the events in the guesthouse, but Cadwaladr either knows nothing of them or has chosen not to state them publicly. Why not share the blame while there's blame to be shared? Who is this third spy?"

Henri's gaze remained deliberately blank. "I have no idea what you're talking about."

Aron scoffed from behind Gwen. "Of course there's another spy. You could not be in two places at once. Are you saying Cadwaladr really did come upon you and Emile at the mill and that *you* felled Marc with a slung stone?"

They'd continued speaking in French for Emile's benefit, and his eyes were the first to narrow. "We did not."

"Don't talk to them, Emile!" Henri said.

"Why not?" Emile said. "You're the one who told her my name! If it saves my neck from being stretched, I will say what needs to be said. I don't take orders from you."

"You can't trust them."

"And we *can* trust Cadwaladr? He's the reason we're here! *And* the reason we are about to be hanged!"

"If you say one more word to her, I will kill you myself." Henri's voice was as cold as any man's Gwen had ever heard.

She tried not to let it affect her. "Who is the third person?" She paused. "The boy. We found his footprints."

"Tell us." Dai had retreated to leaning against a post. He was definitely looking pinched. His face had to be hurting and really he should be in bed, but since he'd refused to be coddled, as he'd said, he was here.

Henri's eyes went briefly to him and then focused back on Gwen. "We will not talk."

"What has Madog done to earn such loyalty?" Aron asked.

Henri switched his gaze to the Dragon and said simply, "He pays us."

Gwen was embarrassed at how profoundly his comment shocked her. She should have been more worldly than that. "Emile?"

The other man simply looked mutinous.

"So you're saying that note really was meant for the two of you? I am the one who's lying? Why are you protecting the very man who put you in this position in the first place?"

"I'm not protecting *him!*" Henri spat on the ground. "Cadwaladr's no better than a snake!"

"We agree on that, at least." Gwen leaned forward in an attempt to imply they were allies. "You could not have been anywhere near the mill because you were in the guesthouse with Helen." She drew from her belt the dagger he'd left in the dust after slashing Dai. She'd been carrying it around since Gareth marched away. It had been thoroughly cleaned. It also bore an inset stone the same color as the ring on Emile's left hand. She wondered suddenly if they were actually brothers. They did look a bit alike, with similar coloring, chins, and noses. It would make sense if they were, too. She knew as well as anyone that family could be trusted when others couldn't.

Then again, King Owain had the entirely opposite experience.

"You did not meet there. You did not pass on any message there. The prince was there because the message was intended for *him*."

Henri raised one shoulder in a shrug. "Then you know everything already. You don't need us."

"And yet, I can't know who that third person is until you talk."

For better or for worse, Gwen had revealed to them how much she wanted an answer.

Henri knew it too and leaned more comfortably against the post to which he was tied. He had leverage now—a leverage Gwen had deliberately given him, though she didn't mean for him to realize it. She wanted him confident. That was the entire point of laying out what she knew.

The tent was quiet for a long count of ten. Within the silence, a hammering sound could be heard in the distance.

"They're building the gallows," Aron said. "Whatever the outcome of the battle, you have hours at most to live. If nobody comes back alive from the fight, Dai and I are charged with carrying out your sentence."

This wasn't true. Gwen didn't know what the hammering was about, but nobody was building gallows. That was a Norman tradition. The Welsh view was simpler. The nearest tree would do.

Emile seemed to fold in on himself. "What do we get if we tell you?"

Gwen was quick to answer. "As I said earlier, I can ensure neither of you hangs for your role in these events."

"Though even if we win the battle," Aron said, "you can be sure if you haven't told the truth, Cadwaladr will ensure your deaths. He wants your mouths permanently closed, as the two of you are the only ones who can gainsay him." He made a motion with his head. "You two and this third person. Perhaps when we find him he will be more forthcoming."

Henri didn't seem impressed by the threat, though he did lean into Emile in order to hold a whispered conversation in French.

Gwen let them talk. They weren't going anywhere, and Cadwaladr really would hang them if someone didn't intervene. In her head, she was already crafting an argument about preserving them to use against Madog later. King Owain would accept the reasoning, particularly since it had never been the Welsh habit to hang people as punishment anyway, never mind that neither of these men were Welsh.

The two spies separated. "What guarantee can you give us?" Henri asked.

Gwen coughed a laugh. He had shown himself capable of lying with every breath. She herself had no expectation that the next thing out of his mouth wasn't going to be a lie as well. So her impulse was to say *none*. But then she turned to Aron with another thought. "Get Abbot Rhys for me, will you?"

She would have sent her son, but he didn't need to be walking anywhere, even if only a matter of yards.

Aron understood the imperative. "Right away."

Gwen waited patiently, happy to give the two men who faced her more time to think. Likely, anything they told her could not be used immediately regardless. Cadwaladr's word was always worthless, but today he was in favor. Even if King Owain believed what these men said, he wouldn't act on it. Gwen wasn't intending to put him in that position, not yet.

But if she couldn't accuse Cadwaladr today, she needed another witness, an impartial one, to bring forth later who could testify that he had heard these men's confessions too. Dai and Aron were trusted or they wouldn't be Dragons, but Cadwaladr would be able to shout from the rooftops that their word was false because of their personal loyalty to Gwen.

He couldn't say the same about Abbot Rhys.

When Rhys arrived, he took in the scene with a single glance and said, for the second time in as many days, "Tell me what you need."

"I need you to listen. You may ask any question that occurs." Then Gwen returned her gaze once again to Henri and Emile. "Abbot Rhys is Welsh, but he speaks fluent French and for many years was in the court of Empress Maud. You knew him then, Henri. Do you trust his word?"

Henri turned his gaze on Rhys, and the two men gazed at each other through several heartbeats before Henri nodded. "We will tell you what we know."

They knew the outline already. Gwen had already related much of it. Henri did additionally admit that he was, indeed, tasked with murdering the king if he could. For that alone, he deserved a hanging, except, to Gwen's mind, the neck that should be stretched was Madog's for ordering it. The world was arranged such that the majority of men served the few whose throne perched on top of the heap, and when one's lord pointed in a certain direction, one went. Or one became Gareth. Or Rhys.

Henri hadn't that fortitude. Madog had told him to find the treaty and murder King Owain in advance of the arrival of Madog's army, and that's what Henri agreed to do, with the help of Emile.

"The document Cadwaladr was waving about told him when the attack would come. He claimed he had taken it from the two of you, but that isn't true," Rhys said. "The note was meant for him. *Who left it?*"

Gwen endeavored not to grin at the way Rhys had gone to the same salient point that had preoccupied the rest of them. "That would be this third person we keep going on about. Who is he?"

"That's where you went wrong from the start. In fact, *she* was right there in the pavilion when Cadwaladr brought us in. You have been blind to her for years." Henri shook his head in a manner that was dramatically pitying. "King Madog won't thank me for telling you, but if it spares me a hanging I will. She serves Queen Cristina as her maid. She's probably already warned Madog your army is coming."

41

Day Five
Gareth

Gareth and Llelo were going to stand together because Gareth wouldn't countenance anything else. It would be far worse to have his son off in another area of the battle where anything could happen to him. Gareth had briefly contemplated positioning the two of them amongst Godfrid's men, but then he decided it would be better to stick with what was familiar. That meant he was crouched amongst the trees between Evan and Prince Hywel, with Llelo just behind, watching Madog's men come on.

With Aron remaining behind in the encampment, it was left to Cadoc to provide the wry comments. "Doesn't he know we have arrows?"

Gareth chose to answer straightforwardly. "The men of Gwynedd aren't known for their archery like those of Gwent. Most have spears, not arrows."

"Spears can be thrown." Iago hefted his.

"And knives." With Steffan, it was all about the knives, and he was bristling with blades of every length. He had never been one to use a bow, but was ready for hand-to-hand combat when it came to it.

"Besides, he doesn't know we're here," Hywel said.

Or so it seemed. Or so they hoped.

Gareth held a bow in his hand and wore a quiver on his back. He hadn't been practicing as much since he'd become steward to Hywel, who carried a bow as well. Cadoc was the expert, of course, and they would be following his lead today, as they always did when it came to archery.

Madog and Ranulf's joint force of nearly a thousand men marched below them on the old Roman road. The sun hadn't yet set, but it was sinking. Over the last hundred yards, the marchers had picked up their pace. They smelled home, just as Cadwaladr had promised. It would have been aggravating that he was right if it wasn't also a relief.

Armies could move in the dark and often did for strategic reasons, but nobody ever liked it. If they weren't led by men who knew the area well, they had to light torches, which could be seen at a distance. This army had moved during the day for the same reason Owain had moved his this afternoon: the element of surprise.

They'd been aided today by sunshine and a much colder wind. The trails they'd followed had even frozen over in places, allowing for much faster movement along them. Owain's army had marched all of three miles anyway, an unusual situation in Gareth's experience. Gwynedd had always been protected by its mountains, and it had been a long time since Gareth had fought in a battle that required so little preparation. Then again, rarely had Owain been so surprised.

This, in fact, was the source of one of Madog's many grievances against Gwynedd: that Powys took the brunt of any attack from England and always had. Owain could have countered that Gwynedd protected Powys from incursions from Ireland, but it had been many years since the last Irish raiding party had ravaged Gwynedd's shores, and seven years since Cadwaladr had hired Godfrid and his fellow Danes to murder the King of Deheubarth and later invade Anglesey. King Owain had made friends in Ireland, both Danish and native Irish. It was in that same spirit he'd come to Holywell.

From behind Gareth, Llelo said, "How do we know when it's time—"

He broke off as Madog's force was cut through by a sudden volley of arrows.

By the time Llelo mumbled, "I see," Gareth was standing and loosing his own arrows. They'd been told to loose at will, their party being one of several spread out along the hillside above the road. Even if Madog's army had known they were here, and it was that danger, rather than the setting sun that had been the reason for their quickening march, they were still hopelessly outmaneuvered. The Roman road was the only good one to Hen Blas, not to mention the fastest. They had believed speed to be more important than stealth and thought they'd had it on their side.

The first waves of arrows sent the army below them into chaos. Men shouted and horses reared. They tried to get into a defensive formation, but the arrows kept coming, followed by thrown spears and javelins. All they could do was cower behind their shields. They'd lost half their number, most wounded rather than killed, before they'd even had a chance to fight back.

This was standard Welsh warfare, which Madog should have known. His army was combined with Englishmen, however. While many may well have been veterans of battles between the forces of Stephen and Maud, in which their lords had participated, that didn't mean they were prepared to be cut down by a hail of arrows. The nobility called this Welsh way of battle unchivalrous, not to say of the devil.

King Owain called it *winning*.

Then the Danish bellow pierced the air, coming from the south. And though Godfrid had brought a matter of two dozen men with him, their battle cries were blood-curdling as they leaped into the fray with gusto.

An onslaught of actual men was something Madog's men were trained to face, and those closest to the Danish attack ignored the arrows in order to reorient their position. They knew anyway that once the fighting moved to hand-to-hand, the men of Gwynedd could no longer shoot at them, out of fear of hitting their own men.

A few select archers would continue to pick off targets, Cadoc among them. The rest put aside their bows and descended the hill to the battle zone.

42

Day Five
Gwen

"Stay with them! I'll find the queen." Gwen threw out a hand at Aron and Dai as she left the tent, her heart pounding out of her chest. She lifted the hem of her skirts and ran to where she thought the queen might be, knowing she was too late because, even now, the men of Gwynedd should be meeting Madog's in battle.

And walking into a trap.

She might have cursed herself for being so blind. If she had been smart, she would have followed up on what Sioned had told her about Cadell. At the very least, she should have pursued the name with her husband because, now that she was pressed on the matter, she remembered that Cadell was the man who spent the night in the mill the day they'd arrived at Holywell. While she didn't yet know for certain he was the same person, and everyone else had been fooled by Sioned too, the consequences of not being aware of her treachery could not be higher.

The lies and more lies Gwen had been told during this investigation reared up to strike her in the face. Henri's were one thing, since Rhys had identified him as a spy as soon as he saw him, though with no knowledge he'd sold his services to Madog. But Sioned had been lying to all of them for *years*. Her betrayal struck to the very core of Gwynedd's court. Gwen felt she should have known there had to be an explanation for Sioned's ability to put up with Cristina. Her devotion to Madog had to be considerable.

Gwen had heard of battles where an army was lured out of hiding by an easy victory, only to be flanked and destroyed. King Owain planned to ambush Madog, but if Sioned had warned him about what was coming, King Madog could easily turn the battle against him.

Against Gareth, and Llelo, and Hywel, and Godfrid. Against the men Gwen loved.

Cristina's tent was empty, as was Susanna's. And while a few people occupied the pavilion, Sioned was not among them. It came to her that the maid herself had fled, confirming Gwen's worst fears, and she burst through the entrance to Taran's tent, without first asking permission of the guard outside, in hopes she could at least confess her suspicions to him, since he hadn't ridden into battle with the king.

Only to pull up short at the sight of Cristina, Susanna, and Sioned settled around the bed, upon which Helen lay huddled. She was still very gray and had the blankets pulled up to her chin. Gwen's anger flared. *How* dare *Sioned pretend to care about her? About any of them!*

Anger was better than fear.

Susanna turned, a smile on her lips. "You look as if you've seen a ghost, my dear. Can I offer you a cup of wine?"

Gwen had been ready to shout her accusations, but Susanna's manner was so serene that she gaped instead, the half-formed words on her lips. The Queen of Powys had always treated Gwen well, but this was a touch too solicitous, given the events of the day.

"Don't look so worried, Gwen," Queen Cristina said. "Owain will win the battle."

"Not if she warned him we were coming!" Gwen found her voice and pointed a finger at Sioned.

And then, as the other women continued to smile at her, not so much with happiness but, in the case of all four of them, with something that looked no more or less than satisfaction, Gwen understood she had entirely misread the situation. As had Emile and Henri. And likely, King Madog himself.

Gwen let out a puff of disgust, all emotion draining through her body like water after the plug has been pulled from a tub. She said to Susanna, "I came here to warn you of Sioned's treason, but now I see she has been working for you all along. Madog thinks Sioned is his but she's yours, isn't she?"

"And mine," Cristina said, never one to be overlooked. "For many years now."

The anger was back, though somewhat tempered with relief. "It was she who left the note for Cadwaladr at the mill." Gwen took an urgent step forward. "She almost killed Marc!"

"That event was regrettable," Susanna said. "Sometimes in war there are casualties."

"Like with Gwalchmai?" Gwen asked, with real tart in her voice, surprising herself with the pain of that old wound.

Susanna had the grace to pause for a heartbeat. "Just so."

That continued to be all the apology Gwen—or Gwalchmai—was ever going to get. Giving up, knowing any hope for more was futile, Gwen gestured to encompass both Sioned and Cristina. "That night in the guesthouse, did you know Sioned had just half-killed Marc?" She held her ground despite the women's glares. Maybe she wouldn't have been so forceful if she hadn't been so resentful of all the lies. Had there been repercussions and ricochets from *her* reporting to Hywel all these years? She hadn't slung a stone at someone's head, but there were more ways to harm a person, not to say ruin their life, than a physical attack.

Cristina's mouth turned into a thin line. "No. She had not yet told me. Only that she had accomplished her mission." The queen might have sent a hint of a glare in Sioned's direction.

"So King Owain knew already that Cadwaladr was in communication with Madog?"

"Of course," Cristina said. "That has never stopped."

"Did he know what was in the note? All that about the timing of the attack? Did you *know* Madog's army was coming?"

Sioned deflated, which made Gwen feel a little better. "We didn't know about any of it. He doesn't tell me everything, or even most things. He has been king a long time and has learned never to allow any single man to know the whole of his plans. Not Cadwaladr. Not Henri. Not me." She paused. "Maybe not even Ranulf."

Cristina explained further on Sioned's behalf. "The note was sealed. We couldn't risk breaking it. She is not that kind of messenger."

"I get passed messages and pass them on to Cadwaladr."

"Who was it that gave you this one?"

"Henri."

Gwen felt a bit better to know her distrust of Henri wasn't misplaced. "Where did you get the key to the mill?"

Sioned swallowed. "From the Cadell I told you about."

"Who, I assume, will *not* be coming home with us?"

"No." Her chin wrinkled in what Gwen hoped was sign of regret.

Gwen thought a moment. "Why were you so upset when you found Helen in your room? That part never rang true to me."

"I told you the truth about that, except for Cadell's role."

"For me, it was the shock. All that blood." Cristina shivered.

Gwen found herself disbelieving—of both of them. "You must have recognized Helen."

"I had never met her before. We spoke to each other for the first time today." Cristina shot Helen a grateful look. "Not that I hadn't wondered at how good Owain's information always was."

Sioned looked at the two queens. "With your permission, I would like to tell her the rest, my ladies."

Susanna looked a bit dismayed, but nonetheless gestured for Sioned to continue.

"I was mistress to Madog, long ago. I gave him a son, who died. I was younger then, of course, and, in truth, younger than my years. The king was—" she paused, her eyes going upwards for a moment as she searched for the word, "—uncharitable towards me. I'd had it in my head that somehow I would be given status within his court. But my son didn't live, and Queen Susanna cared for me instead."

Susanna nodded. "Having learned my own husband's nature long ago, I arranged a suitable marriage, but when her husband died—"

"—Susanna gave Sioned to me," Cristina concluded.

"That still doesn't explain what happened in the guesthouse." Gwen knew she was behaving disrespectfully, shockingly so, and yet they hadn't slapped her down for it.

"As I said, I did feel guilty for not being in the guesthouse. I knew immediately the attack had to have been perpetrated by Madog's men. I had done his bidding, but I had slung a stone at Marc to protect myself—"

"—to protect *us*," Cristina amended.

"And Cadwaladr," Susanna said.

For a moment, Sioned looked fierce. "Prince Cadwaladr can fend for himself. He betrays whomever he wishes at his own whim." When Susanna's lips formed what might have been a protest, the maid then added, "My apologies, my lady, but we all know it's true. He sold you out this morning!"

Susanna's lips were pressed together in a thin line, but she didn't argue, even though she looked as if she wanted to.

With a worried glance at the queen, Sioned hurried on. "I came into the field to find Marc standing alone. I assume now he was waiting for Cerys, but when he turned to face me, it felt as if he'd been waiting for *me*! His back was to the lights from the pavilion, but they were in my face. I couldn't see who he was, but I was sure he recognized me. I couldn't let him say my name. I had no choice but to silence him." Her voice trembled, but she carried on. "So when later I saw this stranger on the floor, it was as if the stone that I'd slung at Marc had ricocheted all the way to the guesthouse and killed her too. I thought she was dead—" She broke off one more time, her hand to her mouth and tears forming in the corners of her eyes.

Gwen couldn't tell at this point if Sioned's tears were genuine. She had been spying for at least seven years now, serving in Owain's court and passing information Cristina gave her on to Madog. She could be able to summon up any emotion, any lie, when it suited her. And yet, if she was that good a mummer, they could all be grateful she was on their side.

Helen, who up until now had been looking on without speaking, seemed to pull herself together, and when she spoke, her voice was stronger than it should have been for someone with her injuries. "We do have a problem now, however. Henri and Emile gave Sioned up to Gwen. That means Gareth will know too, and then Prince Hywel, as soon as they return from battle. Sioned can no longer serve as she has done. She must go to Powys with you, my queen."

"I disagree." Cristina had a stubborn look in her eye. "Those men's necks will be stretched before the truth can get back to Madog."

Gwen wanted to insist *you can't hang them!* But she knew too that she needed to rein in her temper before these queens or they would stop listening to her. They *had* been listening. She wanted them to keep doing so. "I told Henri and Emile I would protect them if they told me the truth. I would hate to have lied to them, even if unknowingly. Besides, it is my thinking they are more valuable to you alive than dead. I'm sure there is some way they can be of use without that fact getting back to Madog."

"I don't see how. If Sioned stays here, they can't go back to Powys," Helen said flatly. "It's either her or them."

"I agree. All of Gwynedd saw Cadwaladr bring them in," Cristina said. "That can't be swept out with the rushes."

Cristina appeared to want to say more, but Susanna stayed her with a flick of her fingers, looking to Gwen instead. "You think we are too cavalier at meting out death? You would stand judgment on us?"

"My lady, I have served Gwynedd all my life. I am loyal to her and to Owain and Hywel. But I respectfully submit that some lines should not be crossed, even with loyalty."

"Like husband, like wife." Susanna nodded. "I see you are finally coming into your own power." She turned to look at the other women, and it was as if they spoke to each other in some secret language, communicated through glances only—glances Gwen couldn't begin to read.

"So then what about me?" Sioned said, as if in reply to this unspoken conversation that had been going on amongst them.

"Sioned *must* stay with me," Cristina said. "We have no one to take her place. She has been invaluable in helping us see into Madog's mind. If our goal is to manage him and Owain—"

"And Cadwaladr," Susanna said, for only the second time in Gwen's experience openly denigrated her youngest brother. The first time had been when she'd slapped him that morning.

Gwen found herself thunderstruck at what these women, these queens, were conveying to her: they had no real power over their husbands, but they would use every speck of available influence, both above board and below, to do what they believed must be done.

"Just so," Cristina said. "To limit the loss of life, to maintain the status quo, we need her."

Susanna turned to Gwen. "You say we cannot do what we deem necessary. What do you propose we do instead with Henri and Emile?"

"There are other ways to silence a man besides killing him. They know their lives are on the line, and neither wants to die. The easiest plan would be to send them both to Ireland with Prince Godfrid." And then Gwen allowed herself a shrug, which was a motion she might never have made in the queens' presence before this moment. "Or, not to contradict you, Helen, but we *can* send them back to Madog, to serve him as before. They will simply attest they never talked. Madog will believe them. Henri and Emile would not want to be known as men who betrayed their master."

"They knew about Sioned before." Susanna nodded slowly, in a manner Gwen interpreted as appreciative. "They'll know about her after. It will appear she remains undetected and loyal to Madog."

"When Madog loses, won't he blame me for not warning him?" Sioned asked.

"You had no chance to know the battle plan, and certainly didn't have time to send word before it was implemented. You and I will simply say we didn't know. We can lay everything at Cadwaladr's doorstep." This was an amazing conclusion coming from Susanna.

Nobody contradicted her. Certainly, Gwen would never betray this pact. None of the women appeared to have any concerns about the way Susanna had just hung her youngest brother on the line with her husband.

"So they pretend they escaped?" Cristina tapped a finger to her lips.

Susanna shrugged, and if a shrug could be queenly, Susanna's was. "Henri and Emile must back us up. Cadwaladr himself will never learn they talked, not from any of us."

"With the army gone, there will be nobody to gainsay us," Helen added. "But we have to turn them first, and we have very little time in which to do it."

"We don't need time," Gwen said. "Henri and Emile's loyalties lie with the one who pays them. All you have to do is pay them more than Madog does. If I were you, I'd make it a great deal more."

43

Day Five
Gareth

Llelo had never fought in an out-and-out battle with two opposing forces like this. Gwynedd hadn't really been part of any war at all since the one in 1136 against the Normans in Ceredigion, which they'd won. Surprise attacks on castles, sieges, and ambushes allowed the greatest chance of success. If it meant keeping his son alive, Gareth cared not at all that his Norman opponents called that kind of warfare cowardly.

But Madog and Ranulf had fielded upwards of a thousand men. Spread out along the old Roman road as they were, they presented a formidable force, one that had to be taken down quickly else the loss of life would be severe. King Owain wanted to govern Tegeingl. Killing half the fighting men of Powys was not the best way to go about it. They all had kin there. Perhaps many were kin to Owain himself. At the very least, they were kin by marriage to Queen Susanna. It wasn't their fault they had been born in the wrong place and become vassals of a coward who hadn't even bothered to come himself.

"That's Llywelyn in the center, Madog's heir." Hywel and Gareth descended the hill side by side, swords at the ready. "If we capture him, the battle is over."

"Capture?" Gareth wasn't opposed to the idea. He just wanted to make sure he knew his lord's mind correctly.

"He is my cousin, and I promised his mother I would save him if I could. He is not responsible for this war."

Cadoc remained on the hill above them, picking his targets like the assassin he was. Gareth preferred to see him as their guardian angel, watching over their endeavors. On the whole, he would have much preferred being mounted, since there was protection in being raised above one's opponents, swinging his sword at their heads. But the terrain here hadn't allowed for it.

With a prayer of hope and forgiveness for all that might prevent him from reaching heaven were that to be his fate today, Gareth stormed onto the road amongst his companions. Llelo was still behind him, which Gareth hoped would be a safer place from which to fight. But as Gareth met the blade of his first opponent, he took too many steps forward that Llelo didn't match, and they separated. All he could do was keep himself glued to Prince Hywel's side and hope his son's training would keep him alive amidst the rest of the Dragons, who'd also entered the fray.

And then his entire world narrowed to what he could see through the narrow field of vision supplied by his helmet, and the sweat streaming into his eyes. He had no time to clear them, as one hand held his sword and the other his shield. Always up ahead was the white plume on Llywelyn's helmet, reminding Gareth of the last time he'd fought on a road like this, when Prince Rhun had died.

Thanks to the targeted arrows raining down from above, the efforts of Prince Godfrid's men to the southeast, and King Owain who led his men down the road from the northwest, Gareth could tell they were winning, whatever that meant in this context. They hadn't won, however, and through the shouts and screams and grunts of effort, he fought on. He kept being diverted from the direction he really wanted to go by one assailant after another. At one point, he went down on one knee under the onslaught of a particularly large member of Llywelyn's guard, saved only by a precisely timed arrow on Cadoc's part.

It was Steffan who reached the Powysian prince first, buttressed as always by Iago. Both men had heard their prince's orders too, and as Llywelyn confronted the larger Dragon, Steffan got in behind him, grabbed him around the shoulders, and put a knife to his throat. "Tell them to hold!"

Gareth then lost track of them because he had to counter another lengthy attack from a red-bearded man. At last he got him on his back, prepared to drive his sword through his belly.

At which point Llywelyn's call finally came. "Hold! Hold, I say!"

Gareth took a single heartbeat to thank God for his own survival, and then he swung around, his eyes searching first for Llelo. He found him on his knees, but still alive, his head leaning exhaustedly into the cross of his sword. And then there was Prince Hywel, standing tall before his cousin, whose life he had insisted on saving.

Gareth stepped over the body of a man with an arrow protruding from his chest, sickened by the entire day, angry beyond measure that Madog had chosen this course, and relieved it was over. He'd killed again, tarnished his soul again, but also told himself that he followed this path so others wouldn't have to.

Like Madog's men, he went where his lord pointed, and his lord had lived to fight another day.

44

Day Six

Gwen

Dawn had come and gone, and still Gwen lay on her side, watching her children and husband sleep, relishing what felt like a stolen moment together. They were back in their wagon, the entire guesthouse having been given over to the wounded from both Gwynedd and Powys. The Hen Blas monks had done their part too, taking in a fair share, but their monastery was smaller than Holywell, with fewer hands to help.

Gareth opened his eyes and looked at her.

Gwen looked back at him with all the love in her heart. "I never want to see you march off to battle again."

She'd told him the previous night that they might be having another child. He'd taken the news with joy … and trepidation. Not only with a third child would they be outnumbered, but after the events of yesterday, life appeared increasingly fleeting. There was a cost to serving kings and princes. When a father paid it, so did his child.

"We are marching today to Mold."

"I know."

"The scouts report it has a skeleton garrison. Madog is gone, if he was ever there. It won't be much of a siege."

Gwen rapped her knuckles on the wood of the bed. "Don't say such things. You won't know the truth of it until you get there."

"I trust Aron's word, and he was among those who saw it."

Gwen found herself easing a bit more into the mattress. Tangwen had her own pallet on the floor between the beds, and baby Taran was sprawled close to Gwen, his arms and legs akimbo, sleeping as only a child could sleep, like he hadn't a care in the world.

Gwen wanted to keep him that way forever and knew it was impossible. "Do we have enough men?"

"For a siege? Yes. Even more, we have the archers." He looked at her with a painfully gentle expression. "I am going for that reason and no other. We'll burn the castle to the ground rather than let Madog keep it."

"What about Susanna?"

The men had started trickling into Holywell with the wounded within an hour of sunset. From that moment on, Gwen had been busy beside Saran, succoring the wounded, and hadn't had even a moment to inquire if Susanna had stayed in her encampment or left to join her husband wherever he had retreated. Or was hiding. "She will ride to Hen Blas, to visit their men there, and then on to Dinas Bran. She is carrying word from King Owain that Llywelyn lives and is well. Even with this betrayal, Owain is not planning to lay siege to all of Powys, even if he knows he could win the whole kingdom."

"Is that restraint? Or simple practicality?"

"He wants to rule Tegeingl. He would have Madog bow to him. But to take Powys by force? That is not his way. We have too many other enemies for Welshmen to be killing Welshmen."

"He may be the only one who thinks so."

Gareth grunted his agreement. "But the fact that he thinks so is why he is the preeminent ruler of Wales. He didn't need that treaty signed to know it."

"And Cadwaladr?" Gwen found herself looking sideways at her husband. She hated to even ask the question, but it had been on the tip of her tongue, and she couldn't stop herself.

"He remains in favor. How could he not?" Gareth shook his head. "I would never have thought I'd have call to say this, but to know that both Cristina and Susanna are monitoring Cadwaladr too leaves me almost shaking with relief. We aren't alone in this anymore."

"Just as long as we remember Susanna doesn't work for us. She's not even really on our side. She is playing her own game."

"As is Cristina, though her spying is more committed to Gwynedd directly. Susanna just wants to keep the peace." He spoke almost musingly. "One day that might mean betraying us."

"But not today," Gwen said softly, "not for either of them."

Gareth reached out a hand to Gwen, careful not to disturb the sleeping children between them. "Not today."

45

Chester Castle

Day Ten

Ranulf

anulf looked at Madog over the rim of his cup. "I have thought of a way to turn the tide against Owain." They were back in his receiving room in Chester, before a fire and drinking wine again.

"Have you? Why should I care?" Madog scoffed. "We lost half our army. Owain was even aided by those damnable Danes. I *told* you they weren't to be relied upon. And now my son sits at Owain's table, hostage to my good behavior. I have widows and orphans to care for now, all because I trusted you! You said it was a good plan!"

"It was a good plan."

Ranulf had ridden the fifteen miles home the moment a messenger brought he news the battle had gone badly, without waiting for Madog to tell him so. He hadn't wanted to still be at Mold when Owain decided to take it back again. Which he had by the evening after the battle, in what might have been the shortest siege in the history of warfare. Losing the castle was better than having him burn it to the ground, which would have meant that, when Ranulf took it back, as he was confident he eventually would do, he'd have to rebuild. It seemed pointless to waste resources that way. Owain was going to use Mold as an outpost of Gwynedd, not as a base from which to attack Chester. Or even Powys, which Madog would realize as soon as he calmed down.

"What happened was regrettable—"

"Regrettable!" Madog's face was redder than Ranulf had ever seen it, and that was saying something. "Owain *knew* we were coming. He was ready for us! Cadwaladr betrayed us; betrayed *me!*"

That did seem to be the situation, from what Ranulf had been able to piece together from the survivors of the carnage on the old Roman road, as well as from what Madog's spies had later reported after their escape from the Gwynedd encampment. Ranulf was quite certain there was more to the story, but more than anything he thought Madog should be grateful he hadn't been out there leading his men himself. His son lived. It was a gift, under the circumstances.

"So you're ready to lie down in front of Owain and expose your belly?"

Madog clenched his hands into fists. If a man could have caught fire, his hair would have been in flames. "No."

"Then maybe you should listen to me."

Madog's chin jutted out, but he didn't say *why should I?* nor repeat his accusation that the attack had been Ranulf's plan. Instead, he barked, "What is it? Just tell me since you clearly want to."

"Perhaps the men of the south could be put to good use."

"The men of the south?" Madog's tone was nothing if not mocking.

"Yes, the men of the south." Ranulf, in turn, was all patience.

"How?" At last, and perhaps despite himself, Madog's voice held real interest. He wanted to win. Even more, he wanted Owain dead, and he'd reached a point where he would do anything to accomplish that goal. Ranulf could have told him selling his soul might actually be required.

"You might consider an emissary to Cadell of Deheubarth."

Madog instantly deflated. "Cadell is in Gwynedd's pocket. His mother was Owain's sister."

"Your daughter is married to Owain's son," Ranulf said in mild rebuke. "*You* are married to Owain's sister. What difference is that making to you? Besides, Gwenllian was only Cadell's stepmother."

Madog had been pacing, as was his wont, but now he came to a sudden stop, really listening for the first time since he'd stormed into Chester with the news Owain had his son. "Tell me what you're thinking!"

"Gwynedd's price for avenging Gwenllian's death was Ceredigion." Now that he had Madog's attention, Ranulf was enjoying the dramatic telling of his idea. "Cadell is not the appeaser you think he is, I assure you. He has been watching the goings-on in Gwynedd for some time with great interest. Ever since they took Ceredigion from his father, and murdered his brother, he has simply been waiting for his moment to take back what is rightfully his."

"And you think that time is now?"

"You might suggest as much, in light of our own issues. Owain cannot be in two places at once. He cannot fight two wars at the same time."

Madog's eyebrows were in his hairline. "Owain cares as much about Ceredigion as he does about Tegeingl. Maybe more. It's Cristina who wants to keep Tegeingl."

"So he will send Hywel south, split his force, and make his position precarious instead of strong, as it is now."

"That is a thought." Madog's voice might have been admiring.

Ranulf was feeling better too, having voiced aloud something he'd been thinking about for some time. This had always appeared too farfetched a plan, but now that it was in the open, it was beginning to look more viable. And once again he was going to be able to enlist a Welsh lord to do most—if not all—of the work for him. "And then Cadell will owe you."

"We won't tell Cadwaladr anything about it."

Ranulf gave his co-conspirator a rare smile. "We will wait for him to come to us, which he will. And you will take him back when he does."

"I will not—"

"You will, and so will Cadell."

"That will never happen. He murdered Anarawd!"

Ranulf found it astounding Madog could be so naïve. "Cadwaladr hired those Danes with Cadell's blessing. All this time, did you really think murdering the King of Deheubarth was Cadwaladr's own idea?"

As soon as he spoke in that tone, Ranulf knew it had been a mistake to do so, because Madog expression turned mutinous again.

He hurried to make amends. "Unlike Cadwaladr, you will rise above the past because you have your eye on that larger goal we've talked about."

"Gwynedd." In Madog's world, no other word carried as much weight.

As the King of Powys began to pace again, Ranulf could see he was imagining the possibilities. He wanted to rule Gwynedd, but he had not yet figured out that Ranulf himself shared that ambition. For both, the avenue to the throne went straight through Cadwaladr. If a weakening of Gwynedd could be accomplished with little sacrifice from Ranulf, it was worth temporarily increasing the power of Deheubarth. It also justified a continued alliance with Madog. He had proven himself useful in the past, and might well do so again in the future. One never knew how the winds would shift.

When they did, Ranulf, as always, would be ready to shift with them.

Historical Note

The root of Prince Cadwaladr's resentments appear to have resided in the fact that he was the youngest of three sons, and thus shut out of the main inheritance of the crown of Gwynedd. When Cadwallon, who was the eldest of King Gruffydd's sons, was killed in battle in 1132, Owain became heir to the throne of Gwynedd. In the same way, when Owain's eldest son, Rhun, died, Hywel, the second son, took his place as the *edling* (*The Lost Brother*). In Wales, unlike in England, it mattered not at all that Owain was a legitimate son and Hywel illegitimate. All sons were equally eligible for inheritance.

That broke down, of course, when it came time to select who should sit on the actual throne. It could be occupied by only one person at a time, unless the kingdom itself was divided among multiple sons, as also happened many times in Welsh history. King Owain, in his attempt to name only one son as his heir, viewed primogeniture as one piece of inheritance law the Normans got right.

Earlier, Owain had tried to head off conflict with his brother by giving Cadwaladr suzerainty over pieces of Gwynedd, Aberffraw and Meirionnydd among them, as well as Ceredigion after they conquered it in 1136. Cadwaladr's leadership skills had, in all cases, proved inadequate to the task, which made the accident of birth that had put him third a gift from God rather than the injustice Cadwaladr thought it was.

Similarly, King Owain was determined not to mar his own legacy with conflict among his sons after his death. To that end, he tried to give each something to inherit, passing out lands as a test of their abilities while he was still alive.

For example, Hywel, as the *edling,* was given Ceredigion—once Owain removed it from Cadwaladr's grip after the assassination he'd orchestrated of the King of Deheubarth (*The Good Knight).* Iorwerth, although a younger son, was Owain's eldest legitimate son. Once he was of age and married (*The Prince's Man*), he was given charge of the area around Dolwyddelan, taking over an ancient seat of the Kings of Gwynedd. Another son, Cynan, oversaw Denbigh (*The Lost Brother*).

Of all of King Owain's adult sons, only Madoc declared himself uninterested in that kind of authority and instead took up with his Danish relations in Ireland to be trained as a sea captain. He was determined to explore the vast world far to the west, which his Viking relations had found. But that is another story.

History records Owain Gwynedd referring to himself as *Waliarum princeps,* meaning *principle leader of Wales,* in a letter written in 1165 to the French king. Since Roman times, the title *princeps* had been understood to mean *first or principle leader,* not the son of a king as it does today

(https://www.etymonline.com/search?q=prince).

This transformation in meaning developed after the conquest of Wales and the subjugation of its rulers by the English. But again, that's another story!

Gwenffrewi is one of only two Welsh saints who remain in the official Catholic calendar, the other being St. David (in Welsh: Dewi Sant). The well at Holywell dedicated to her has been a place of pilgrimage since the sixth century. The story goes, as officially documented in the 12th century, that she had a suitor who was enraged at her rejection of him to the point that he decapitated her. A healing spring flowed from the spot upon which her head fell, and then St. Beuno, her uncle, who had established a church nearby, restored her head to her body.

After this miracle, Beuno turned to her suitor, Caradog, described as leaning on his sword and unrepentant, and called up to the heavens. Caradog was struck down on the spot. According to the story, Beuno then seated himself upon a stone, which now stands in the outer well pool at Gwenffrewi's Well, and promised that "whosoever on that spot should thrice ask for a benefit from God in the name of Gwenffrewi would obtain the grace he asked if it was for the good of his soul."

As a woman myself, it's a little disheartening that the saint aspect of this story is actually all the doing of Gwenffrewi's uncle, Beuno, who was known for raising seven different people from the dead and the establishment of eleven churches.

However, Gwenffrewi herself did go on to have an auspicious career in the church. She lived at her holy well for a time before becoming abbess of the convent of Gwytherin, a position her aunt had filled. As was the case with many Welsh religious houses of the era, the position was likely hereditary.

Two small pieces of an oak reliquary from the 8th century were discovered in 1991 and identified based on earlier drawings as belonging to Gwenffrewi's reliquary, which probably contained an article of clothing or another object associated with her, rather than her bones. According to one scholar, the existence of this reliquary provides "good evidence for her having been recognized as a saint very soon after her death" and may even be "the earliest surviving testimony to the formal cult of any Welsh saint" (Bord, Janet. 1994. "St Winefride's Well, Holywell, Clwyd", *Folklore*: 105: 1-2).

It is after her death that Gwenffrewi becomes Winifred and enters the records as an English saint, when her bones were transferred from Gwytherin to Shrewsbury at the behest of the monks at the Abbey of St. Peter and St. Paul. This story is memorialized in the Brother Cadfael novels, by Ellis Peters, which I highly recommend. To top off this English appropriation of Welsh sanctity, an abbot from the same abbey in Shrewsbury later appropriated the bones of her uncle, St. Beuno, and built a shrine for him at St. Peter and St. Paul as well.

Back in Holywell, for centuries after Gwenffrewi's miraculous resurrection, the well was overseen by Welsh monastics, who cared for the site and catered to the pilgrims who made the journey to the well every year. Five hundred years later, having taken the cantref, known as Tegeingl, from the control of Gwynedd, King Madog of Powys brought in an order of Benedictine monks, housing them nearby in a former *llys* of the Kings of Gwynedd, known as Hen Blas.

By 1147, these Hen Blas monks had joined the Cistercian order, under the patronage of Earl Ranulf of Chester. He was often at odds with Owain Gwynedd and, over the next three years, control of this region of Wales went back and forth between these different lords—Owain, Madog, and Ranulf—multiple times.

Matters came to a head in 1150 with the battle described in *The Honorable Traitor*, known to history as the First Battle of Ewloe, between the forces of Owain Gwynedd on the one hand and King Madog of Powys and Earl Ranulf of Chester on the other. As depicted in this book, Owain won that battle and maintained control of Tegeingl for the next few years.

He did eventually lose control of the area, however, which had the effect on Gwenffrewi's well that Abbess Nest so feared. After 1157, with the Earl of Chester ruling the cantref, the Hen Blas monks were moved to the current location of Basingwerk Abbey on the Dee Estuary, and the Welsh were forced to cede control of the holy well and its associated church of St. Beuno to the Normans.

I have invented the double monastery run by Abbess Nest, who is not a true historical figure. Despite the fact that double monasteries had been condemned by Rome at the second Council of Nicaea in 787, they continued to thrive for generations afterwards in Celtic lands, particularly Wales and Ireland. In the 12th century, in fact, double monasteries experienced a revival, returning to favor in certain circles. No evidence of Welsh monastics at Holywell remains, though pilgrims can visit Gwenffrewi's healing well to this day.

About the Author

With over a million books sold to date, Sarah Woodbury is the author of more than forty novels, all set in medieval Wales. Although an anthropologist by training, and then a full-time homeschooling mom for twenty years, she began writing fiction when the stories in her head overflowed and demanded that she let them out. While her ancestry is Welsh, she only visited Wales for the first time at university. She has been in love with the country, language, and people ever since. She even convinced her husband to give all four of their children Welsh names.
She makes her home in Oregon.

Thank you for continuing this journey into the Middle Ages with me! Please don't worry that this is the last *Gareth & Gwen Medieval Mystery*. There will be more! If you'd like to know as soon as the preorder for the next book is available, feel free to subscribe to my newsletter at
www.sarahwoodbury.com